*Nick —
Hope you
enjoy!
Connie Lacy*

ALBEDO EFFECT

P9-CCW-518

The Shade Ring Trilogy Book 2

Connie Lacy

August 2016

~ ~ ~

Atlanta, GA

Copyright © 2016 by Connie Lacy
Cover design by James at GoOnWrite.com

All rights reserved. No part of this publication may be reproduced,
distributed or transmitted in any form or by any means, including
photocopying, recording, or other electronic or mechanical methods,
without prior written permission of the author, except for brief quotations
in book reviews.

This is a work of fiction. All names, characters, businesses, places, events
and incidents are either the product of the author's imagination or used in
a fictitious manner. Any resemblance to actual people, living or dead, or
actual events, is purely coincidental.

ISBN-13: 978-1537114668

ISBN-10: 1537114662

Contact the author
Email: connielacy@connielacy.com
Website: www.ConnieLacy.com

For the scientists

~~~

Also by Connie Lacy

The Shade Ring, Book 1 of The Shade Ring Trilogy
The Time Telephone
VisionSight: a Novel

Chapter 1

When raindrops began to fall, it was like a much-needed cleansing. Neave imagined the showers purifying the landscape as rivulets of water raced through bone-dry arroyos and hot mist rose from city streets, creating an open-air steam bath. She hoped it might flush unwanted contaminants from her psyche.

With all she'd been through, the rain was like a comforting balm. And who wouldn't welcome a deluge as the mercury reached 120 degrees, heat ripples shimmering above Atlanta's glass, steel and concrete.

By the time she and Will finished giving their statements to police, relief turned to apprehension as the source of the rain grew in intensity. Pascual had mushroomed into a mega hurricane and changed course as it barreled through the Gulf of Mexico. It was now tracking to the northwest, heading directly for the Galloway home on what was left of the Florida panhandle. They were both frantic about his family's safety, forcing them to divert their attention from recent events. She had no choice but to put her faith in the legal system to bring her father to justice. While it wouldn't bring his victims back to life, at least he would pay for his crimes.

She longed for more time to rest and recover, and, yes, for intimacy as well. She had envisioned the two of them in the charming upstairs guest room at his family's home – a place that seemed idyllic when they visited only a few weeks ago. But that was before her father's lust for power caused innocent – and not so innocent – people to die, and before Neave went through hell to stop him from perpetrating a hoax on the nation he was sworn to serve. Now the Galloway home was in danger of being washed away and she could see the anxiety etched in Will's face.

They picked up two fully-charged rental trucks, Neave and Will in one, with Rosa following in the other. Will insisted on disengaging the autonomous mode, arguing the trucks would drive too slowly. And while she understood they were racing against the clock, he was driving too fast for road conditions and she was afraid they'd end up in a ditch before they ever reached the coast. Still, she refused to nag him to slow down. How could she, knowing what was at stake?

Of course, she also knew that unlike a lot of people who were afraid to drive because they did it so seldom, he actually enjoyed it, being something of a throwbacker.

"We should've left sooner," he grumbled, as the windshield wipers slapped back and forth like a finger-wagging teacher annoyed with their tardiness.

"We didn't know how bad it was."

Pascual was the first category six storm of the 2117 hurricane season in the Gulf. And when the heavy rains arrived in Atlanta, everyone knew why, although forecasters initially thought the storm was aiming for Louisiana.

Hurricanes had become more common as oceans heated up. They were also more violent, with warmer water revving the storms' energy levels. Even less powerful hurricanes generated more rainfall and bigger storm surges. Which is why insurance was impossible to get. That, coupled with a fifteen foot rise in sea level, had triggered a mass exodus from the coast.

Ironically, Pascual was providing thick cloud cover over

more than a million square miles, temporarily increasing Earth's albedo effect – reflecting more of the sun's rays back into space and bringing the temperature below the hundred degree mark for a change. It was one small silver lining that Neave appreciated, although she knew there would be a steep price to pay for the respite.

Still, she knew Will was right – they should've been paying closer attention.

"Can you call my mom and see how many trucks they've got?" he said. "We'll need a fleet if we're gonna save the damn warehouse inventory."

"Are those antiques really worth it?"

"I tried talking her into leaving that stuff behind and just hightailing it out of there but she wouldn't listen."

She clicked on Angela's number.

"Neave, honey, is everything all right?" Angela blurted, huffing like she was running a race.

"Yes, we're on our way with two trucks. Will wants to know how many you've rounded up."

"Well, Charlie arrived this morning with one he rented in Tallahassee. Jaz and Toni both struck out. But we've got our own truck too, and it's fully charged and ready to roll. So with the two you're bringing, we'll have four. We've already started loading furniture in Charlie's truck. Careful, Gib!" There was a crashing sound like someone had dropped something and Angela groaned softly. "We'll take what we can. That's all we can do. Now, I've gotta get busy. Drive safely and look out for my Rosa, okay?"

"Definitely," Neave said and tucked her iCom back in her pocket. She started to speak but Will cut her off.

"I heard," he said. "I swear, if I weren't a rational human being, I'd suspect your father was somehow causing the hurricane to wreck our house, just to punish me."

"But you *are* a rational human being," she replied, studying his profile.

His long chiseled nose looked like something off a Greek statue. But right now his brows were low and furrowed, as though he were heading into battle, and there was no hint of a smile lurking at the corners of his handsome mouth. He hated her father nearly as much as she did, and suspected his ulterior motives long before her eyes were opened to the truth. While they both knew it was ridiculous to suggest that Robert Alvarez could somehow seek retribution by manipulating the weather, she understood where Will was coming from.

God, she didn't want to think about her father right now. About how he used people, hurt people.

Her hand found its way to his shoulder. He glanced her way in reply, nodding his head slightly, but kept his focus on the wet road stretching out ahead of them.

She switched to the other truck to take over driving and give Rosa a rest when they made a quick stop three hours out of Atlanta. The wind picked up in south Georgia and the rain came down in sheets. But the farther they went, the less traffic there was on the freeway, and what traffic they encountered, was heading in the opposite direction. Which was good and bad – good because their side of the highway was empty, and bad because they were driving right into a killer storm.

Within a few minutes she heard Rosa mumbling to herself in Spanish. She wasn't sure what she was saying but she didn't sound happy.

"You excited about seeing Angela again?" Neave asked, hoping to ease the stress a bit.

"Claro que si. But I'm also nervous."

Neave gripped the steering wheel tightly as the wind buffeted the truck, concentrating on keeping pace with Will's truck up ahead.

"I'm a lot older now," Rosa continued, "and we've led very different lives."

"I think the years will fall away when you see each other."

In reality, Neave wasn't sure about anything but she hoped pretending to be confident might help them both. While Rosa was her father's cousin, she'd also been their housekeeper. And, as she was growing up, it was Rosa who provided the only warmth in their cold, dysfunctional family. She cared a great deal for Rosa and found it romantic when she and Angela re-connected after so many years of forced separation. It made her angry all over again thinking about how her own father threatened to hurt Angela if Rosa didn't give her up all those years ago. Cruelty came natural to him. But now that he was behind bars, they were finally free to reunite.

Neither of them was really in the mood to talk so she asked Rosa to find a weather update they could listen to. The report from the National Hurricane Center said Pascual's sustained winds were now approaching 200 miles an hour with the storm gaining speed as it plowed toward the coast. Damn, she thought, the Galloway home might as well have a target painted on its gabled roof. All their precautions – building the house ten feet off the ground on concrete pilings and setting it a couple hundred feet from the beach – would mean nothing for a category six storm. She wished the family would just get the hell out of there as fast as possible but they were intent on saving as much as they could. So here they were, playing chicken with a mega hurricane.

By the time they reached the state line the wind had intensified so much, she worried the "Welcome to Florida" sign might fly off its braces and smack the truck in greeting. That's where the cracked asphalt began. Florida was a basket case – no revenue for the solar roadway panels now in use on interstates in most other states. And it struck Neave that it was kind of like going back in time to when freeways just absorbed heat and crumbled, rather than reflecting heat and generating electricity.

When they finally turned onto the beach road she was alarmed to find it partly submerged. The tide ignored the small dunes, spilling around them to form deep puddles on the pavement. She peeked at the ocean with a feeling of déjà vu, just for a second reliving her nightmarish flight to Savannah in the heli-scooter to save Will from the tsunami. While there was no tsunami this time, the surf was rough, with menacing grey swells and whitecaps as far as the eye could see.

"Dios mio," said Rosa.

Turning left into the long driveway, their path was blocked by a large branch. She put the truck in park and jumped out to help Will drag the limb out of the way. The wind whipped her hair into knots and she was drenched by the time she slid behind the wheel again.

They parked in front of the house, which looked very different from the last time she was here. Dark green shutters covered the windows, creating a cold, unwelcoming facade. Rosa stared wide-eyed for a moment before making a dash through the pouring rain, a large umbrella over her head. The wind promptly turned the umbrella inside out and all three of them were soaked by the time they reached the door. Rosa's short, dark hair was plastered to her head, her yellow top clung to her body. She dropped the ruined umbrella as they stepped into the living room and the wind slammed the door behind them.

A high-pitched squeal greeted them as little Isabel tore into the room, her black pigtails bouncing, her arms outstretched.

"Will! Will!" she cried, running headlong into her big brother's arms.

He picked her up and hugged her tight.

"Eww, you're wet!" she cried.

He set her down and she immediately turned to Neave.

"You're wet and icky too," she said. "And your hair is drippy. It doesn't look very reddish right now. It looks like seaweed. I'll hug you when you dry off, okay?"

"Sure thing," Neave laughed.

"Are you Aunt Rosa?"

"Why, yes I am," Rosa said, straightening her short frame, trying to look as tall as she possibly could.

"I'm Isabel and I'm six years old. Mama told me you were coming."

"Rosa!"

Angela stood in the kitchen doorway, a tender smile on her round face, a blue bandana covering her short salt and pepper Afro, streaks of dirt on her freckled cheeks. It was the first time Neave had seen her without a colorful caftan or pretty skirt. She was clad in jeans and a shirt – and not as plump as Neave remembered her.

"Angela," Rosa whispered, instinctively pushing her sopping hair out of her face and smoothing her top.

The two closed the distance between them and wrapped their arms around each other and hugged for a long moment, prompting Isabel to smile and wag her head back and forth at Neave and Will.

"I think they're happy to see each other," she said.

7

Which elicited chuckles from the two women as they pried themselves apart.

"Now you're soaked too," Rosa sputtered, wiping tears from her eyes and pointing at Angela's blue shirt.

They were gazing, teary-eyed, at each other when there was a loud thud on the roof, causing everyone to jump. It was like the angry wind was reminding them there was no time to lose.

"Probably another branch," Will said. "Unfortunately, Mama, you two lovebirds are gonna have to postpone your romantic reunion until we're safely back in Atlanta."

"Work now, romance later. That's what I always say," Angela said, grinning as she took Rosa's hand.

"We'll have to double-time it to load the trucks and hit the road before suppertime," Will added. "Pascual is a violent son of a bitch and we want to vacate the premises before he takes possession."

"Watch your mouth," Angela said, eyes wide, nodding at Isabel.

"Right," he agreed.

Angela led Rosa into the kitchen with Isabel skipping along behind them. Neave touched Will's his arm to get his attention.

"The storm…" she said.

"I know."

"Someone could get hurt. It's already dangerous out there."

"That's why we need to get moving."

"Will…"

His worried eyes were more steel grey now than sky blue. She kissed him, making sure he heard the unspoken 'I love you.'

"We'll leave by four-thirty," he said. "That'll give us time to get out of harm's way."

"That's just two hours from now."

"Which means time is of the essence. Let's do it."

Chapter 2

"Mama, why can't we just ride out the storm in the safe room like we did last time?" Gib said.

"Gib, honey, like I said before, this is not a category four, or even a category five," Angela replied. "This is a cat six and we're smack dab in the bullseye. The storm surge is gonna be a whopper."

"And the wind will be way more powerful," Charlie added. "Our luck finally ran out, plain and simple. I think we knew it would happen eventually."

"Rosa," Angela said, "these are my other sons, Gib and Charlie. Gib's fifteen. Charlie's twenty-one."

Neave had prepared Rosa for how diverse Angela's kids were since they were all clones she'd adopted. And she'd explained how Angela named them after her favorite authors. But she watched as Rosa eyed each one – Isabel, the inquisitive six-year-old Asian-Latina with shiny black pigtails and a sunny smile, named after Isabel Allende; Charlie, tall, handsome, half black, half white – named after Charles Dickens; and Gib, who looked like a Middle Eastern prince, cloned from a man with Egyptian and Iranian ancestors – named after author Naguib Mahfouz. And there was Will – tall, blue eyes, shaggy brown hair – a clone of the man Neave grew up mistakenly believing was her grandfather. Will's name was William Shakespeare Galloway and he was known for quoting the bard when the notion struck. Obviously, Rosa knew about Will. She was the one who delivered him to

Angela to save him when he was a toddler – the last time the two women saw each other.

Rosa opened her mouth to say something just as a striking young black woman rushed into the kitchen from the hallway.

"I hate to be rude, Mama, but can we save the socializing for later?"

"That's my daughter, Toni," Angela explained, "who usually has better manners."

Which surprised Neave who thought it was Jaz. She was tall, dark-skinned and had the same large, almond eyes. Or nearly the same. Toni was the only Galloway Neave hadn't met.

"You're Rosa," Toni said, then turned to Neave. "And you're Neave Alvarez, I presume."

But she didn't get a chance to reply.

"Mama!" Isabel cried. "Can I take my doll bed?"

"Lordamercy," Angela said, shaking her head slightly as if to organize her thoughts. "Everybody, listen up! I know we're in a big rush right now and we're all sad about leaving our home, but I want to introduce you to Rosa, the love of my life. Besides you kids, of course."

She kissed Rosa on the cheek. It was hard to tell how everyone felt about the new addition to the family with Pascual breathing down their necks.

"Welcome to the family," said Will, giving her a reassuring nod.

There was a brief pause and then it was back to the emergency at hand.

"Mama," Charlie said, "We pulled another truck up to the back steps. What do you want us to load first?

"Kitchen stuff. Make sure my oven..."

"Already working on it," Gib called out, his head inside

Angela's antique yellow oven.

"Mama! Can I take my doll bed?" Isabel repeated, raising her voice to be heard.

"Yes, yes," Angela replied, waving her hand in dismissal.

Neave watched as Angela glanced around her beloved kitchen, and for a fleeting instant, thought her future mother-in-law was about to cry. But she pulled herself together and turned to Rosa.

"Maybe you can help Isabel carry her things to the truck," she suggested.

"Yes, yes," Rosa replied, moving immediately to Isabel's side. "Where's your bedroom, chiquita?"

Just then the back door flew open and Jaz filled the doorway. She looked like a tall ninja preparing for guerilla warfare in a black, hooded rainsuit, water dripping onto the floor around her black boots.

"Chop chop, people!" she barked. Her husky voice was more intense than Toni's even though they were cloned from the same rich Nigerian woman who rejected them both. The "twins" were named after authors Jazmin Lopez and Toni Morrison. "Time's a wastin'!"

Right on cue, Will helped Gib hoist the yellow oven onto a hand truck and Gib hauled it straight toward Jaz, who hopped out of the way so he could roll it down the ramp and into the truck.

Toni and Gib hauled stuff out the back door while Charlie and Jaz loaded another truck through the front door. Angela was the general, telling everyone what to take. She'd put tags on furniture and other items to help speed the process but it was a madhouse. And within minutes the floor and rugs were covered with muddy footprints. No one said a word about it, though, knowing the house was about to be dismantled by a seemingly enraged Mother Nature.

Will backed the Galloway's big truck up to the warehouse and he and Neave hauled antiques up the ramp as fast as they could go, the wind howling around them. This was where they kept many of their valuable finds, marketing them to museums and antiques dealers. Neave had never even thought about what people left behind when they abandoned coastal homes until Will explained that when the family's demolition company moved in to do teardowns, they got to keep whatever was inside the buildings.

She was headed out the warehouse door carrying a lamp wrapped in plastic when a gust of wind took her by surprise. She paused before stepping onto the loading ramp, catching sight of Gib dashing toward them from the house just as something flew through the air, striking him on the head. He went down in the mud. Neave cried out as she hurried toward him and Will jumped down from the back of the truck. Blood oozed from a gash above his ear.

"I'm okay," he mumbled, trying to stand.

"Let's get you inside," Will said, pulling his little brother to his feet. He was a lanky teenager, already as tall as Will.

She looked down as they helped him into the warehouse and noticed a blade from a wind turbine on the ground.

"Will!" she said, gesturing at the piece of metal. "That could've killed him. Next thing you know, the solar panels will turn into missiles."

She could see frustration and anger flash in his eyes. Once they were inside, he pulled out his iCom.

"Shit!"

"What?"

"We've lost communications." He closed his eyes for a moment. "Neave, can you run to the house and spread the

13

word – we're pulling out in fifteen minutes, even if it means leaving stuff behind. Tell 'em you and I'll take the big truck. Make sure everyone's assigned a truck and they understand there's no way we can use driverless mode. Not with roads washing out and stuff flying through the air. I'll get the first aid kit and take care of Gib."

She hurried out the door, her wet hair whipping her face in the wind.

"Hold your arms over your head!" he yelled after her. "And don't tell Mama about Gib!"

The inside of the house looked like a dust devil had swept through the rooms, with piles of belongings scattered everywhere and bare spots where furniture used to be. Everyone was moving fast. Urgent voices added to the cacophony as wind and rain thrashed the house like a kickboxer intent on a knockout.

"Mama! Mama!"

Isabel darted through the kitchen, a box in her arms, Rosa two steps behind her.

"There's no more room!" Jaz announced, poking her head through the front door.

Neave spotted Angela in the ruined living room as Isabel reached her.

"Mama, we have to take my seashell collection!"

She looked on the verge of tears, holding the box out in front of her.

"Jaz, is there room for one more little box?" Angela cried, taking it from Isabel and rushing to the door.

"That's it! No more!" Jaz snapped, accepting the box and rushing down the ramp to the truck.

"Angela," Neave said. "Will says we've gotta pull out in fifteen minutes."

"Why didn't he message me?" she said, looking at her iCom, then groaning when she realized they had no signal.

"All right, everybody," Angela called, "finish up what you're in the middle of and then get some food and water for the trip so we can get going!"

"Will and I are taking the big truck," Neave said. "Does everyone know which truck they're in?"

Angela rushed to the front door just as Jaz returned.

"Jaz, you and Charlie take this one," she said. "Rosa and I will drive the one at the back door with my oven in it. Toni and Gib can have the yellow truck we loaded this morning."

Neave hurried back through the kitchen, pausing only long enough to grab a jug of water and some snacks. As she stuffed the items in a bag, she heard Isabel's voice again.

"Mama, can I ride with Will and Neave?"

"I'd rather you rode with me," Angela said. "Does anybody know if we packed the antique doll my grandmother left me? My Patty Jo doll from the 1940s? She was in a box on my dresser!"

Neave scooted out the back door, down the steps, past the truck with Angela's precious kitchen stuff, and across the yard to the warehouse, squinting to keep the raindrops out of her eyes. Will and Gib were loading an odd-shaped chair wrapped in plastic when she returned. Suddenly she heard a loud ripping noise behind her and turned just in time to see a piece of siding fly through the air. After loading a couple more small pieces of furniture onto the moving van, Gib darted back to the house, a lampshade on his head.

They piled into the cab of the big truck and Will cranked the engine, then honked the horn three times. He pulled slowly around to the front of the house and honked twice more, watching Jaz and Charlie climb into the white truck while Toni and Gib settled into the cab of the yellow truck, also parked out front. Will sounded the horn again, waiting for his mother, Rosa and Isabel to join them. The fourth truck finally appeared from behind the house, bouncing along the washed out driveway. Will rolled down his window and called out to his brother at the top of his lungs so he could be heard over the roaring wind.

"Charlie, you take the lead! I'll bring up the rear. Let's go!"

Charlie nodded and honked his horn as he drove under the flailing branches of the live oaks lining the driveway, towing the family van behind him. Angela's truck followed, then Toni and Gib's truck, towing the other family car. Will pulled behind them, completing their ragtag convoy.

Neave was thankful to finally be on the road but unnerved every time a big gust of wind broadsided Toni's truck in front of them and the vehicle it was towing, causing them to wobble. The rain was coming down so hard the windshield wipers couldn't keep up, forcing them to drive at a snail's pace.

Will mumbled something.

"What?" she said.

"I'm just glad Mama taught us how to drive. It's a dying art."

Her iCom buzzed and she pulled it from her pocket, glad their communications had been restored. She was surprised when she looked at the screen.

"Mother, what's up?"

"I'm concerned, dear. Where are you?"

"We're heading inland. Don't worry."

"I don't know if you've seen the latest storm report but winds are strengthening again. They say sustained winds now exceed 210 miles an hour."

"We're making tracks fast as we can."

She hoped to reassure her mother without lying. But just then a powerful crosswind slammed the big truck, causing it to swerve before Will could compensate to keep it on the road.

"Mother, I'll call you when we're back in Atlanta. I've gotta go now." And she hung up.

"Dammit," Will muttered.

"What?"

"We shouldn't have wasted time loading all that stuff."

She bit her tongue, remembering watching video in her climatology classes of the orderly departure from coastal areas back when they were densely populated. Forecasters would lay out the timeline for a hurricane and government officials would issue an evacuation order. Freeways would be transformed into one-way exit routes heading inland. But all of that preparation was undertaken before the weather turned violent. Those who tempted fate would hunker down in their safe rooms and hope for the best. The Galloways had waited much too long.

The highway heading north to the interstate was an obstacle course with fallen branches and other debris. They passed a rain-swollen creek that flowed through a culvert under the pavement and Neave wondered how long before that dip in the road would be impassable. They both heaved a sigh of relief when they reached the freeway, although it was scary how abandoned it looked. They'd been driving nearly an hour as the weather worsened when Neave's iCom buzzed again. This time it was Jaz.

"Need for you to let Isabel call Mama," she said.

"What?"

"Have Isabel call Mama!" she shouted as though they had a bad connection.

"Isabel?"

"Mama regrets not making Isabel ride with her and Rosa."

Will took the iCom from Neave's hand.

"Jaz, what's going on?"

"Just... let... Isabel... call... Mama! To tell her she's okay!"

Neave clearly heard her words but they didn't compute. She thought for a second Jaz had accidentally clicked on the wrong iCom code. But then she had a sick feeling in her stomach.

"Isabel's not in our truck," Will said, like Jaz was an idiot.

"What do you mean she's not in your truck?"

"She's supposed to be riding with your mother," Neave whispered. "I heard your mom say so."

"I'm hanging up," Will said, handing the iCom back to Neave. "Call Toni. She must have her."

But Toni didn't have her. No one did.

Chapter 3

The drive back to the Galloway home made the first leg of their journey seem like walking on a treadmill bike on a pleasant winter morning. Will battled to keep the unwieldy moving van on the road as the wind rocked it from side to side. Branches and sticks careened through the air, slapping the windshield and crashing into the side of the truck. And there were moments when she felt like they were under water, with rain so heavy they had to slow to a crawl as the wipers were completely overwhelmed.

There was also the terrifying mental image of little Isabel all alone, at the mercy of the ferocious storm, no one to protect her. Guilt weighed heavily and she knew she wasn't the only one filled with self-recrimination.

Angela insisted she and Rosa should've been the ones to go back. Neave overheard Will's conversation with his mom and she could hear Angela crying as he argued that he was younger and stronger than she was, and strength might be needed. He promised his mother over and over he would find his little sister and keep her safe.

"Damn!" he yelled, stepping hard on the brake as a large scrap of metal sailed across the highway directly in front of them, tumbling end over end, before wrapping itself around a tree. He took a weary gulp of air and let it out, gradually accelerating again.

When they turned onto the beach road, parts of it were washed away. Will cussed under his breath as he inched along the left side of what remained of the pavement. Each time a wave rushed around the small dunes, the road disappeared entirely.

Bouncing up the long driveway, they could see several more pieces of siding had been ripped from the house, revealing grey cinder block walls underneath. With rain falling in horizontal squalls and the trees thrashing wildly, he pulled up to the front steps and they charged inside, holding pieces of cardboard over their heads to protect themselves from flying debris.

They called Isabel's name repeatedly, splitting up to search the house – Neave taking the upstairs while Will checked the first floor. When they returned to the living room breathless and empty handed, he closed his eyes tight in exasperation.

"God, I hope she didn't leave the house and try to follow us," he said, punching the wall with his fist.

"Where would you hide if you were six years old?"

He thought for a moment.

"The safe room."

He dashed through the kitchen to the hallway that led to the family office and what looked like a closet door. Inside was a narrow stairwell that descended into semi-darkness. She followed him, holding the handrail. At the bottom was a steel door.

"Isabel!" he cried, trying the handle and finding it locked. He pounded on the door. "Isabel! It's me, Will! Are you in there?" He beat on the door again.

Then the lock clicked and the door creaked slightly.

"Will?"

Isabel's little voice sounded muffled behind the heavy gauge steel and thick concrete. He pushed gently until the door opened a crack.

"Step out of the way, honey," he said.

And then she was in his arms, clinging to his neck, her baby doll dangling from one hand. He held her close and kissed her cheek.

"Are you all right?" he whispered.

"Yes."

"Well, you're a smart girl to hide in the safe room."

"Gib showed it to me yesterday."

"Gib's a good big brother."

"So are you," she said.

"Not as good as Gib."

"But you came back for me."

"You want me to call your mom?" Neave asked.

"Yeah," he said, carrying Isabel up the stairs.

Neave made a quick call to Angela.

"We've got her. She's okay."

"Thank God," Angela cried, her voice raw with emotion.

Then the connection dropped. They'd lost communications again.

She sat beside Isabel on the small bench seat tucked behind the front seat. They both jumped when something smacked into the truck as they pulled away. Neave could feel the big vehicle swaying. Time was running out.

"Seussilla was happy to see me when I went back to get her," Isabel said, looking up at Neave.

She remembered how Isabel had named her after Dr. Seuss when she found the baby doll in the warehouse.

"Just like you and Will came back to get me."

"Where was she?" Neave asked, brushing the little girl's wet bangs out of her eyes.

"On the window seat. That's where I laid her so she could watch me and Aunt Rosa pack my stuff."

"Ah."

"And when Mama asked if her grandma's dolly was packed, I remembered my baby doll. But I couldn't remember where I put her. So I looked and looked and then the horns beeped. And when I found her she was hungry so I had to find her bottle."

"I see."

Neave wrapped her arm around Isabel as she cradled Seussilla protectively in her lap.

"Will, are you all right?" Neave said.

"I'll be fine once we're all safe and sound in Atlanta."

"It's not your fault, you know."

He didn't reply.

Progress was agonizingly slow and there were times when she worried they might actually be blown off the road. But it wasn't the wind that derailed them.

"Shit!"

Will's voice was a deep, angry growl.

Deep muddy water poured across the pavement. They were in it before he could slow down. It was the rain-swollen creek she'd noticed earlier, now escaping its banks. The guardrail collapsed as the huge puddle expanded and deepened, turning into a swirling, muck-filled pond. Then they felt the truck vibrate.

"The road's giving way," he cried.

A tree teetered and fell in slow motion, landing on the cab, crumpling the roof over Will's head. Neave screamed as he went limp and flopped forward.

"Will!"

Isabel was crying as Neave struggled to unbuckle and maneuver herself into the front. It felt like the truck was losing traction. She looked to her right as small trees and bushes disappeared as though they were being sucked into a whirlpool. She knew she didn't have much time and clambered into the back again, unbuckling Isabel's seat belt, lifting her to the front of the cab. She jumped down into thigh-deep water and carried her to the pavement, fighting the turgid stream as floating sticks and debris scratched her legs.

"Run up the hill, sweetie, and wait for me there!"

She raced back to the moving van, opening the driver side door. The rising water swirled around her legs, making it hard to keep her balance. Her hands were shaking and it took three tries to unbuckle Will's seatbelt. She braced herself and pulled him off the seat. He landed on top of her and they fell together into the water, which cushioned the fall. As she tugged him away from the truck, it started sliding backwards into deeper water. She wrapped her arms around him, clasping her hands together on his chest and dragged with all her might as more chunks of pavement broke off, the soil washing away underneath. She hauled him bit by bit, grunting as she strained every muscle in her body until she escaped the water. Fearing even more of the road would crumble, she continued tugging him up the incline. At last, deciding it was safe, she collapsed on the wet pavement beside him, gasping for breath.

"Isabel?" she called, looking all around. "Isabel!"

Then she heard a sucking sound as the water whirled faster and the truck began to rise. That's when she heard the little girl's voice calling her name. It was coming from the truck.

"Good God!" Neave cried.

She charged toward the truck as the road split open behind it, the water rushing through, draining the huge puddle from the roadway. The fissure suddenly transformed into a gaping maw and the big truck slid into the breach just as she grabbed the door handle. She lifted herself inside the cab and tugged with all her might, finally closing the door as the water lifted the vehicle from the pavement.

Isabel was in the back seat clinging to her baby doll and wailing at the top of her lungs. The truck shuddered and rolled in the water like a small boat on storm-tossed seas. Neave held out her arms, beckoning her, then held her close as she calculated their chances.

If they did nothing, they'd probably drown when the truck turned over and trapped them underwater. If they scrambled out the window into the fast-flowing current, the odds wouldn't be any better. They needed something to hold on to. That's when the truck slammed into a tree, flinging them against the door, which popped open. The vehicle was momentarily stuck but she knew it would break free in a matter of seconds and continue on its way.

"Hold on tight to my neck," she said, making a split second decision.

Then she leaned out the open door, reaching for a tree branch.

"Whatever you do, don't let go!" Neave shouted.

As Isabel's grasp tightened, Neave seized the branch and pulled herself out of the cab. The strength of the current was fierce and she knew if she lost her hold or the limb gave way, they'd be done for. She couldn't let fear paralyze her. Then she reached for another branch and moved further away from the truck. When it broke free, she didn't want to be too close, fearing they'd be swept along with it. Her arms were already tiring when she reached for the third branch and missed. Isabel squealed as Neave dangled from her left hand, water up to her waist. Then Isabel lost her hold on her baby doll and the current snatched it away.

"Seussilla!" she bawled, releasing Neave's neck with one hand, instinctively reaching out in a futile effort to retrieve her doll.

But she couldn't hold on with just one hand – the current was too strong. Neave struggled to right herself, realizing the turbulent water was about to sweep Isabel downstream. The little girl's hand slipped and she dropped several inches. The fast-flowing water was prying her away. Neave's left arm felt like it might break as she dangled from the branch, but she used her right arm to reach down and latch onto Isabel.

"Climb up!" Neave cried. "Pretend I'm a tree!"

She had to get more of Isabel's body out of the water or they'd both be dragged under, but the little girl was frozen with fear.

"Isabel! Climb up!"

Terror in her eyes, Isabel tried to pull herself closer as Neave strained to hold onto her. The truck slipped further into the water, threatening to break free and slam into them.

"Come on!" Neave cried, straining with all her might to sound encouraging without coming across as panicked.

Isabel gradually pulled herself closer. Then she reached for a twig with her right hand but it snapped, and she squealed as she slipped back into the water.

"You can do it," Neave said.

Isabel managed to draw herself close again, fastening her hands on Neave's waistband. Then she wrapped her legs around Neave's legs and bit by bit, shinnied up her body. Finally, her arms encircled Neave's neck.

She clung to the tree with one arm and Isabel with the other, frozen in place for a moment, wishing a Good

Samaritan would come to their rescue. But she knew they couldn't just cling to a spindly tree and wait for help. No one was on the way. No one, that is, except Pascual. And he'd already made it perfectly clear he would show no mercy.

"You've gotta be strong," she said, as much for herself as for Isabel. "Don't let go. Hold on tight."

She reached once more for the third branch just as the big truck shifted again, sliding a few feet downstream. She let go with her left hand, pulling them through the water. When both hands were firmly planted, she scoped out her next target – a large pine tree that had fallen over the water, its roots exposed in the wet soil of the stream bank. They would use the horizontal trunk as a bridge.

She felt a limb beneath her feet and used it to steady herself as she guided them to the next branch, which she hoped would be close enough so they could reach the fallen pine.

That's when the moving van dislodged. She watched as water filled the cab while the back of the truck swung around in the stream until it was sideways in the current. Then it bobbed in the fast-flowing water and flipped over, the back end clipping the bank on the other side. The current carried it along with all the other debris for a moment until it struck another stand of trees, leaving only the wheels and belly of the truck above the water line.

Isabel whimpered but Neave gently shushed her. Then she crossed to the next branch, and the next.

"Okay, you see that sideways tree there?"

The little girl turned her head to look.

"We're gonna use it as a bridge to get back on solid ground," Neave explained. "I need for you to hold on tight to my neck. Don't let go, okay?"

Isabel nodded.

"Here we go."

She slid lower along the branch until the water reached her chest. Isabel let out a shriek.

"Just hold on," Neave said.

Then she used her hands to slide further along the branch, causing it to dip just below the surface of the water. Isabel's grip on her neck tightened, making it hard for Neave to breathe. She tried to slow her pounding heart. She'd have to push off and make what amounted to a short, but risky glide from her current perch to the trunk of the fallen pine. There was no other choice, but it was a struggle to control her nerves. She knew if she lost Will's baby sister, she'd never be able to look him or Angela in the eye again. She also knew she'd never, ever forgive herself.

Thinking of Will made tears well up. God, she didn't even know if he was still alive! She'd been forced to leave him lying on the pavement in the pounding rain to rescue Isabel. She knew if she lost him, she would never recover. He was the love of her life, the man who made her feel whole, the only man who ever accelerated her electrons.

But she also knew she couldn't afford to stall out.

"Wrap your legs around my waist."

Isabel did as she was told. Then Neave turned toward the shore, hoping to protect her small body when they collided with the tree, and pushed off. She reached out with her left hand for a small stub of a branch sticking out from the trunk. But the current was stronger than she anticipated and the left side of her body struck the tree instead, knocking the breath out of her for a second. She scrabbled around with both hands trying to find something to hold onto before they went under. Her left hand finally caught a small limb protruding from the underside of the trunk and she threw her right hand over the top, sandwiching Isabel between her and the big pine.

"Isabel, I need for you to hoist yourself up onto the tree."

Which only made the little girl cling to her more tightly.

"You've gotta be a big girl and do as I say. It's the only way."

It was a strain for them both but Isabel finally managed to haul herself onto the pine tree, her arms and legs wrapped around it, her cheek against the rough bark. Then Neave did the same. They both lay hugging the tree, exhausted.

"We're gonna scoot across until we reach the bank. Understand?"

There was no reply.

"You hear me?" Neave called to Isabel behind her.

"I'm scared," Isabel blubbered, and promptly tuned up to cry.

"I'm scared too. But we have to hurry. You can cry later, I promise. Just keep hugging the tree and pretend you're an inchworm."

She could feel the sticky pine sap on her hands and face as she moved forward.

"Keep up with me!" she called out.

Little by little, they wriggled across the trunk, like a mother worm leading a baby worm to safety. The water beneath them was rushing by so fast, it made her dizzy to look down, so she focused on the shore, except to turn and check on Isabel behind her. They were about two thirds of the way when the tree suddenly dropped so that the underbelly of the trunk was now in the water. They both stopped moving and clung tightly for a moment.

"Let's go!" Neave called.

When they got close to the uprooted base of the tree, she relied on instinct to figure out the next step.

"Now I want you to crawl on top of me, kind of like a baby

monkey clings to the mama monkey's back. But you have to do it very, very slowly."

Isabel followed instructions and when she had her arms around Neave's neck, Neave inched forward until she reached the protruding roots. That's when the tree suddenly sank further into the water. There was no time to waste, she decided, clutching Isabel's leg with her left hand and pulling them forward with her right hand, swinging onto the upstream side of the roots and muscling her way through the muddy root ball like a mama monkey scurrying to save her baby from the jaws of a predator – in this case a terrifying flash flood. When she reached the soggy creek bank, it was hard to get traction, the soil was so waterlogged. She groped for handholds, dragging them several feet from the edge of the rising stream.

She wanted desperately to lie there in the mud and rest but they had to get back to Will. She didn't even know if he was alive.

Chapter 4

She pulled Isabel to her feet and held her hand. They slogged through the mud, holding their arms over their heads as a shield against flying debris, squinting against the relentless barrage of stinging raindrops.

Now that she had time to think, she remembered from her Climatology courses that the majority of hurricane fatalities were caused by water, not wind. And while storm surges killed a good many people when they used to live along the coast, most drownings were the result of inland flash floods caused by heavy rain – just like the one she and Isabel had escaped by half a hair's breadth. She blamed herself for not being more alert. She should've been sitting up front with Will watching out for flooding and other obstacles.

The burning question now, though: was Will all right? Which made her forget the aches and exhaustion, because she knew if she lost him, the searing pain in her heart would be unbearable. This, she knew from experience. And her mind wandered back to the dark days when she thought he'd been killed by his clone "twin," hired for the job by Nat Patel, her father's right-hand man. But she really didn't want to go there.

It seemed like an eternity before they finally reached the highway. They found him right where she left him on the wet pavement, water puddling in his eyes and ears, his hair plastered against his skull, his skin pale. He looked so much like a corpse, it made her shiver.

"Is he dead?" Isabel whispered.

"He just bumped his head. He'll wake up soon," Neave replied, although, in truth, she was far from certain and had to fight back tears as she knelt beside him. There was a gash above his left eye and a large knot that was turning purple on his hairline. She had no clue how serious that contusion might be.

"Will?" she said, but the wind swallowed her voice.

His eyes fluttered and he reached up with one hand to shield his face from the unrelenting rain.

"He moved!" Isabel whispered.

"Will, can you hear me?" Neave said, touching his shoulder as she tried to maintain her composure.

He moaned in reply, removed his hand from his face and gradually opened his eyes, looking disoriented.

"I think you suffered a concussion when the tree hit the truck."

"Tree?"

She leaned down and kissed his wet cheek.

"And you bumped your head," Isabel added.

He blinked.

"How do you feel?" Neave said.

He closed his eyes.

"Can you walk?"

He grunted, slowly pulling himself to a sitting position, studying the washed out road.

"Where's the truck?" he asked.

"It floated down the river," Isabel replied.

He looked at his little sister and then at Neave, lines creasing his face.

Isabel suddenly cried out in pain as a branch bounced off her back and tumbled past them. Although drownings may have killed more people during hurricanes, if you stayed out in the open when two hundred mile an hour winds arrived, your chances of survival were slim to none.

"Can you walk?" Neave asked again, more urgency in her voice.

As wearying as it was to contemplate, her next challenge was to find shelter. The light was fading fast, which would very quickly make it impossible to see, just as Pascual made landfall.

She helped him to his feet and wrapped her arm around his waist to steady him. They plodded up the hill, bracing themselves against the unforgiving wind. A large branch scudded by close on their left and she reminded Isabel to cover her head with her arms.

When they finally topped the hill, they were blasted by a powerful crosscurrent, knocking Isabel off her feet. She yelped in pain, landing on all fours on the rough pavement. Neave pulled her upright as the wind whipped her wet hair. Isabel whimpered and wrapped her arms around Neave's waist.

"We have to keep moving," Neave said, though she knew Will needed to rest.

She wrapped her arm around his waist again to steady him and held Isabel's hand, then scanned both sides of the road for anything they could use for shelter. If she'd been desperate before, she was unnerved when she spotted an old road sign impaled in the trunk of a large tree. But just beyond it, she saw what appeared to be a small building. Frantic for protection, she guided them in that direction. As they got closer, she could see several of them, whatever they were. When, at last, they reached a narrow road with a short, curved brick wall on either side, she recognized what she was looking at: an abandoned housing development. The tiny concrete buildings were safe rooms, but the homes they were intended for were never built – victims of the rise in sea level that inundated the southern part of the state along with the entire Florida coastline. She wanted to cry tears of joy but she was too dehydrated and didn't have the energy.

The wind shoved them from behind, causing her to stumble. They bypassed the first structure because it had no door. But the second one did. Will and Isabel collapsed on the floor. Neave stood in the open doorway holding her shoe outside, filling it with rain, and each of them took a drink. She struggled mightily to close the door, fighting against the tempest, finally pulling it tight, and joined them on the hard concrete. Will lay on one side and Isabel on the other, sniffling in the darkness.

"Let's get some sleep," she said, stroking Isabel's sopping hair, trying to calm her. "It'll be all right."

"But Seussilla is gone. I left her in the truck and went back to get her and then..." but tears overcame her.

Neave almost reassured her that she could get another doll, but it seemed the wrong thing to say. So she hugged her close with one arm, reaching for Will with the other. She hoped he would be okay in the morning. But she was filled with apprehension and dread as the wind raged outside their mini sanctuary. Who knew whether it might come apart at the seams. They lay on their backs, their drenched clothing creating puddles beneath them, too tired to care. And then, amazingly, she fell asleep.

She was startled awake by loud crashes intertwined with Will's voice.

"I can't see!" he cried.

She sensed he was sitting up and reached over to touch his arm.

"It's okay. It's the hurricane. But we're in a safe room made of concrete."

"Turn on the light!"

"We don't have a light but we're protected from the storm."

She sat up and scooted closer, wrapping her arms around him.

"Neave?" Isabel cried.

"I'm right here, sweetie." And she extended her arm until she felt Isabel's body.

"I think I might throw up," Will mumbled.

Then something whacked into the structure with great force, causing it to vibrate. She imagined a tree ramming the shelter or maybe a big piece of metal.

It was at that moment that he turned away and retched. The smell quickly overwhelmed the tiny enclosure. When he was done, she rubbed his back softly, but he pushed her hand away and refused to lie down.

She stretched out next to Isabel, listening to the violence of the hurricane for a long time as the little safe room was tested to the limit. She didn't want to dwell on what might happen if the concrete walls couldn't withstand the storm's punishment. Eventually, Will curled up and dozed off, in spite of the howling wind lashing the small hut. She and Isabel did too.

When she awoke again it was eerily quiet. The smell of stale vomit reminded her of the long, unpleasant night. When she opened the door, light flooded the room and Will covered his eyes. Isabel joined her in the doorway looking like a Dickensian ragamuffin – muddy face, filthy, ragged clothing so dirty, you couldn't tell its original color.

The hideous landscape made Neave tremble at their

narrow escape. It looked like the aftermath of an atomic bomb, the ground blanketed with fallen trees, branches and trash. She couldn't see a single tree still standing. The power of the storm was mind-boggling. She was shocked the safe room withstood the wind's savagery.

It was also stiflingly hot. And her first thought was that they needed water. The second: how long it would take for someone to rescue them.

They found a spot near the road to sit in the shade of an uprooted live oak tree. Shards of glass protruded from the trunk, making it appear they'd wandered into a combat zone. She scoured the area for any kind of container, finally spotting an empty biofoam bottle. She left Will and Isabel in the shade and walked the mile or so back to where the road collapsed and carefully rinsed and filled the bottle from the swollen stream. By the time she made it back to their resting spot, she felt like she might pass out from the heat, estimating a temperature of at least 115 degrees along with high humidity. They rationed the water, each of them taking small sips throughout the day. Will mostly slept while she and Isabel kept an ear out for a vehicle. Isabel talked whenever the mood struck, including when her sadness welled up about losing her doll.

"Did you ever have a baby doll, Neave?"

"I didn't have a baby doll but I had a teenage doll and a rag doll that Rosa sewed for me."

"Rosa can sew?"

"Rosa can do just about anything."

"Well, I loved my baby doll a lot."

"I know you did."

"She was my friend."

Isabel looked down at the ground where she was sitting

cross-legged.

"I've never had a real friend," she continued. "Did you have friends?"

"I had one very good friend. But I didn't have any sisters and brothers like you have."

Isabel appeared to give it some thought before turning her attention to breaking small twigs and piling them into a mound in front of her.

When evening arrived, Neave contemplated another exhausting walk to the stream for more water. She also wondered where they should spend the night – a distressing thought. The little safe room would be a sweltering hellhole tonight. She leaned forward, resting her head on her knees for a moment. Thankfully, that's when she heard a noise in the distance. She stood up, waving her arms above her head. It was Charlie and Jaz in the family's small van.

Charlie picked Isabel up in his arms and hugged her as he looked over her shoulder at Neave and Will, obviously assessing their condition. Which wasn't good. Neave knew they looked like characters out of Les Miserables.

"The truck?" Jaz asked.

"It floated down the river," Isabel replied.

Which was all they needed to know right now. Wisely, neither of them asked any more questions. Jaz distributed water bottles. And once they were in the van, Charlie passed out whole wheat peanut butter and jelly sandwiches, bananas and boxes of raisins as Jaz cranked the engine to begin the long drive back to Atlanta. They couldn't call Angela because communications were still out.

The trip took a lot longer than usual because the roads in south Georgia resembled a Civil War battlefield after the Union Army moved through. Instead of body parts, tree parts and other detritus littered the driving lanes, left there by the mega hurricane rather than a superior fighting force. They stopped repeatedly to remove branches or drive around fallen trees or uprooted road signs. Isabel gave Jaz and Charlie her version of their perilous escape, which boiled down to her failed rescue of Seussilla, how the baby doll and the truck were both swept away, and how Will got bonked on the head by a tree. She obviously had no clue she'd nearly gotten all three of them killed. And no one pointed that out to her. She was only six years old, after all.

Though they were a stinking, muddy mess, Neave finally relaxed now that they were out of danger and drifted off to sleep. She didn't know how long she'd slept when the buzzing of her iCom awoke her. She was stunned to see who the message was from.

"Cariño, I wanted you to know I'm in China. The US agreed to extradite me. I'm sure you'll be relieved to know there won't be a trial and you won't have to testify against your own father. I also wanted you to know that although I'm far away, I'm still keeping tabs on you. And I will not tolerate my daughter marrying a clone."

Then the message promptly disappeared.

Chapter 5

She couldn't believe prosecutors let her father off scot free when there was strong evidence he was behind the murders of her cousin Lena and Dr. Terrance Osley, his one-time rival for climate secretary. But more importantly for the US government, the whole shade ring plan had been a scheme to make her father rich, with precious little regard for any real impact on rising seas. He intentionally lied to the White House and world leaders about his involvement with the Chinese companies guaranteed to get the contracts for the giant project. And everyone knew it! She was hugely disappointed and frustrated. Here she was thinking he was locked up and awaiting trial, that he was no longer a threat to anyone. She pounded the arm rest, waking Will who was seated beside her in the back of the van.

He yawned and rubbed his eyes, looking at her for a clue to what was going on. She shook her head angrily.

"What?" he said.

"My father's in China."

His eyebrows knotted up as he processed the news.

"Why?"

"They extradited him."

"Yeah, it's been all over the news," Jaz said. "Supposedly, China will try him first for financial fraud. But everyone knows that's a crock o'shit. Amazing, even now, your father still has political clout."

Jaz continued to hold her parents against her, which pissed

Neave off. She had half a mind to blame Jaz for whoever her parent was. But she didn't know who Jaz was cloned from. She only knew that whoever it was, rejected both Jaz and Toni as not being perfect enough to raise as her child, abandoning the two of them like they were outmoded electronics that should be recycled or ground up and dumped in a landfill. She bit her tongue instead, realizing everyone was dead tired, herself included. They'd been driving all night. It was just after 6:00 a.m. and the sun wasn't up yet.

"I just got a message from him," Neave explained.

"Saying?" Will asked.

"That he's got spies watching us and..."

"And what?"

"That..." she began, not sure she really wanted to tell him. "That... he's not going to tolerate his daughter..."

"Marrying a clone," he blurted, shaking his head angrily. "Your father is a piece of work. And what the hell are our illustrious leaders doing letting him go to China?"

She stuffed her iCom back in her pocket, wondering why she suddenly felt guilty.

"Of course, it's not your fault," he added, taking her hand in his, giving it a little squeeze.

"I need to go pee pee," Isabel announced.

"Can you wait five minutes?" Charlie said. "We're almost there."

Isabel nodded.

Neave assumed they were going to a hotel but they turned off the freeway into her old neighborhood.

"Where we going?" she asked.

"Your mom said we could use her house as long as we need it," Jaz said, turning onto Maple Avenue. "She moved into a condo."

39

Neave studied her childhood home as they pulled into the driveway. It looked a lot like the other unpretentious houses on Maple Avenue – adobe exterior, screened porch, a giant saguaro cactus out front. But it was not at all what it seemed, with most of the rooms underground.

"I'm not staying here," she said.

"She's letting us live here rent-free," Charlie explained. "And right now the income stream is a bit tight."

"I'll call a cab."

"We'll get a hotel room," Will said, "but let's go inside for a few minutes. I need to talk with my mom."

She didn't want to set one foot in that house. Too many unpleasant associations. She'd never be able to go into her old bedroom again, not after what Nat did to her. A part of her was glad he was dead. Nat Patel was her father's deranged assistant, a seemingly bright doctoral student who had an obsessive fixation with Neave. She cringed recalling how he drugged and raped her in her own bed. She took a deep breath before mounting the front steps.

The smell of Rosa's breakfast enchiladas greeted them as they walked through the door. Isabel rushed into Angela's waiting arms in the dining room. There were tears of relief as Angela hugged her youngest child and kissed her.

"Are you okay, honey?" she cooed.

"Uh-huh," Isabel said. "Will and Neave came back to get me. But the truck floated down the river. And so did Seussilla." She buried her face in her mother's shoulder.

"Will, are you okay?" Angela said, reaching out to him. "When Charlie texted me, he told me about your nasty bump to the head."

"I'm fine."

"I'm so sorry," Angela said, her voice catching in her

throat. "I was focused on my business instead of my family. Please forgive me."

"Mama," Toni said, "we were all focused on the business. We were all rushing around like monkeys searching for food in the desert."

"But now everyone's safe," Charlie added.

"No thanks to me," Angela said.

Then Isabel piped up.

"I think it was my fault," she said. "Because I forgot my baby doll two times."

There were tears in her big brown eyes and Angela squeezed her tight.

"Oh, honey, if there's anyone who's not to blame, it's you. And I'm sorry about your baby doll. Truly I am. But I'm so relieved everyone is safe and sound. I love you all very much."

Isabel wrapped her arms around her mother's neck.

"Let's eat," Rosa said.

Neave and Will headed for different bathrooms, quickly scrubbing their faces and washing their hands. Otherwise, they still looked and smelled like the homeless people who spent the hot daytime hours sleeping under the freeway on the edge of the city.

The table was weighed down with enchiladas filled with eggs, black beans, veggies and cheese, a big bowl of grits, sliced tomatoes, orange juice and coffee. Everyone found a perch and filled their plates as they chatted.

"How come we lived at the beach, Mama?" Isabel said.

"Yeah," Gib said. "I was wondering about that too. I mean, if it was, you know, a dangerous place."

"Well," Angela started, leaning back in her chair, her eyes unfocused, "I always loved the beach. Loved the images in old movies of the sand glinting in the sunshine as the waves rolled in. And, after Will and Charlie arrived, I wanted to protect them from the harsh realities of being a clone. I couldn't stand the thought of them being hurt. So I used part of the money my parents left me to build a house close to the shore, far from the maddening crowd, as it were." She chuckled at her little joke. "I also figured the Florida panhandle was a good spot to launch a demolition and antiques business. I'd been doing some buying and selling of antiques for a while and knew one of the best ways to find old stuff was to do teardowns of submerged cities. So I used the rest of my money, along with a loan, to buy a demolition company."

She clasped her hands together and pursed her lips for a moment before continuing.

"I created my own little universe there, populating it with my darling children, keeping them away from the unkindness of others, trying to shore them up with strong self-esteem and surround them with beauty. And my family and our business thrived beyond my wildest dreams."

No one said a word as she gave each of them a loving smile.

"It was an awesome place to grow up," said Charlie. "And you are the best mother in the world."

Toni jumped up to give her mother a hug and all of her brothers and sisters followed suit.

"You really are the best mama in the world," Isabel said, kissing Angela on the cheek.

"Now let's eat before this yummy food gets cold," Angela said, dabbing her eyes.

So the eating and chatting resumed.

"I wonder if any of that stuff in the truck might be salvageable," Toni said. "I'm sure we could find it."

"Yeah, there were some valuable items in there," said Charlie.

"No kidding," she said. "I was planning to pitch some of them on my sales trip next week to Oklahoma City." She turned to Will then. "You did load that mahogany telephone table, didn't you?"

"God, I hope so," said Jaz. "Straight out of the 1940s. Didn't they used to call it a gossip chair?"

"I actually wanted to keep it," Will said. "It was like a symbol of a simpler time when people really talked to each other. I kept hoping we'd find an antique telephone to go with it."

"What's a telephone?" Isabel asked, breaking the spell.

"An old-fashioned, primitive iCom," Gib explained. "Except it didn't have a computer in it. I've read all about them and seen pictures and video. I'll show you after you take a shower." And he pinched his nose with his fingers, silently mouthing "P.U."

She stuck out her tongue at him.

"Well, I'll bet we could get a pretty penny for that chair," Jaz said.

"I think it's time to dump the antiques and demolition business," Will said, triggering immediate looks of disbelief around the table. "Our insurance company won't cover any more coastal projects because of the tsunami losses. Now the hurricane has, no doubt, flattened the warehouse. We've lost our big truck. And, by the way, anything in that truck is ruined beyond even the most expert restoration, including that old telephone chair. I think we should focus on the energy business. Besides the profit potential, we all know there's a huge need for more green energy. I mean, we talk the talk, but we need to walk the walk. 'Talkers are no good doers: be assured we come to use our hands and not our tongues.' Richard the third."

"We definitely need to quote Shakespeare right now," said

Jaz, rolling her eyes.

"We're making pretty good money selling antiques," Toni argued. "I like doing both. You know, diversification?"

"We could make a lot more if we focus on solar and wind energy," Will said. "And I'm thinking we could expand into hydro power as well."

"You going to the doctor tomorrow about your concussion?" Jaz asked.

"Very funny," he replied.

"I'm serious."

"Yeah, well, I've been thinking about shifting over to energy for a while," he said. "It's just that with our losses from the hurricane, now's the perfect time to make the transition. No doubt, our house is a pile of sticks and the warehouse is history, along with all the stuff inside. And the hotter it gets, the more big mutha hurricanes there'll be and the more dangerous it'll be for demolition. And there's also the matter of ingress and egress. Those roads and bridges aren't properly maintained or mapped. Why would the government spend money paving roads and rebuilding bridges when no one goes to the coast anymore and they're just gonna get clobbered over and over again by storms? I just saw a report as we were coming into town that another stretch of Interstate 10 has washed away."

"I thought you were concerned about coming out of the closet," Jaz said. "And if you expand the damn energy business, well, you might as well stand in the Atlanta JetTube station and shout: look at me – I'm a clone!"

"Well..." Will started.

"You gonna wear a scrolling t-shirt that says clone for hire?"

"Jaz!" Will thundered.

"Children, please," Angela cried.

"How many times have I heard you say you didn't want to tempt fate by announcing to John Q. Public that you're a clone?" Jaz said, practically yelling.

"Times are changing!" he roared back.

"I don't know about that," Toni argued.

"Yeah, just because Neave's mother came out of the closet doesn't mean the world is gonna welcome you with open arms," Jaz said.

It was the first time Neave had seen any friction in the Galloway family and she was taken aback.

"I have to admit I'd miss running the antiques business," Angela said from the other end of the table where she sat with Isabel on her lap. "Don't you think there's still a market?"

"Mama," Will said, "most of our inventory came from coastal teardowns. And if the insurance company won't cover that anymore, that's a problem. The loss of the XT deconstructor at Savannah cost us big bucks."

"Well, whose fault was that?" Jaz spat. "You weren't exactly operating on all cylinders in Savannah. I still don't understand why you were working solo."

"I..." Will started.

"That goes against every safety rule we..." she said, her voice even more husky than usual.

"I know, I know!" he barked.

"And after that bonk on the head, I'm not too sure you're operating on all cylinders right now," she shot back.

"Children, children!" Angela intervened. "Enough."

"Well, if we're careful and don't take those kinds of risks, I think the business will be fine," Toni insisted.

Gib chimed in then.

"I really like the antiques business," he said. "I've been

training with Toni and she even said I could go on that sales trip with her."

"Don't worry, Gib," Toni said. "We're still going. We just need to check the inventory at the Savannah warehouse to see what we've got to offer the museums."

Gib looked nervously around the room.

"I understand we've been doing this a long time," Will said, trying for a calmer tone. "But we all agree clean energy is what'll slow the warming. We've made a good start on our solar/wind business. If we add hydro to the mix, we could do installations almost anywhere. I'm sick to death of tiptoeing around, doing jobs no one else wants, flying under the radar because I'm a clone. I'm just as good as anyone else!" His voice rose again and he slapped the table for good measure, startling everyone. "And..." he continued more quietly, "we can bring in good money with energy installations and make a real contribution at the same time. So I've started putting out some feelers to find investors."

There was a hush. Apparently, no one wanted to speak first. Finally, his mother filled the uncomfortable silence.

"I certainly understand your frustration," she said. "But you're wrong, Will. You're not as good as everyone else. You're way, way better than the vast majority of people I've known in my entire life. In fact, I'm not surprised you want to make the world a better place because you're just that kind of person. So let's cogitate on it and talk about it again when everyone's rested."

"Good idea," said Charlie, who liked nothing better than de-escalation.

Toni and Jaz exchanged knowing looks, making it obvious they'd talk more later in private.

"We fixed Neave's old bedroom for the two of you,"

Angela said, trying to change the subject.

"We're going to a hotel," Will replied. "But it has nothing to do with the family business, believe me. Neave just doesn't feel comfortable sleeping here."

Angela nodded, obviously embarrassed it hadn't occurred to her.

When they'd eaten their fill, Neave and Will said their goodbyes and stepped onto the front porch to wait for their hub car. Rosa joined them, looking truly distressed.

"It was my fault. Angela asked me to help Isabel bring her things to the truck. I was supposed to be looking out for her. But I let her down. I let you all down, risking your lives. Lo siento mucho. I'm so sorry."

"Rosa, it's not your fault," Neave said, giving her a hug.

"I think maybe we're all to blame," Will said. "But it's water under the bridge. Literally. And we all survived, thanks to Neave."

He held her gaze for a moment as the driverless car pulled up.

"I still don't know how you did it," he said.

~~~

Their grimy appearance, along with their hard-earned stench, caused a good many raised eyebrows at the hotel. The desk clerk assured them discretely that they'd find the water pressure and the shower to their liking. And they did. What a relief, finally washing off all the mud and crud, along with layers of stale sweat.

After sleeping on concrete in the middle of a mega hurricane, then catching some z's on the long, cramped drive back to civilization, lying on a real bed was like resting on a fluffy cloud. Nestled side by side, they used Neave's iCom to order delivery of a few items. Neither of them had anything to wear. She also made an appointment for him with their family doctor, despite his protests that he didn't need to go.

Then she snuggled up in her striped hotel pajamas and kissed his cheek, finding his two-day stubble surprisingly sexy.

"I think your family will come around on the energy company," she whispered.

"If they don't, that's okay. They can run the demolition business. I'm done."

"I think it's exciting. Consider me your first hire."

He pulled her close and kissed her, running his fingers through her hair.

"Glad you've got your auburn back," he said, draping a strand along her cheek. "The reddish locks look nice beside your greenish eyes. 'Shall I compare thee to a summer's day?'"

"From a Shakespeare sonnet, right?"

"Indeed."

She was distracted by a thrumming in her ears.

"I looked like a dirty wet mop," she said, glad she was wearing PJ's so he couldn't tell exactly how aroused she was.

"A comely dirty wet mop." He kissed her again. "I wish I could make love to my first hire – and former dirty wet mop – but I think my head might explode."

Obviously, the pajamas weren't providing enough camouflage. She forced herself to tamp down the desire oozing from her pores and kissed him on the nose.

"I love you," she said. "Now close your eyes."

"They're closed," he replied softly, sliding one hand under her shirt and tenderly cupping her breast.

"God, I wish..." he whispered, but never finished his sentence.

She watched as he drifted off, the lone dimple on his right

cheek giving a charming asymmetry to his dreamy face. She had to resist the urge to kiss him and let her fingers wander through his inviting forest of chest hair. He needed rest.

Relief washed over her that they were safe and they were together. Surely, good times were just around the corner.

But her father's extradition was disturbing. And so was his message. She waited until Will's breathing slowed and gently disentangled herself from his embrace. She went into the bathroom, turned on the light and clicked her iCom. There were dozens of articles. She read the three most reliable ones. She also read a couple of columns by political analysts. Their take was that releasing him to Chinese custody was a gesture of goodwill by the president to keep China in the geo-engineering fold. Which meant the US government still wanted to take action to reduce runaway global warming, even if it wasn't the solar shade ring Dr. Alvarez had so brazenly championed. If it hadn't been for Neave busting into the shade ring treaty signing, he might've succeeded in pushing the scheme whose true purpose was to make him a rich man.

The columnists also pointed out that China had a big stake in fossil fuels, much of it marketed to poor countries. So, naturally, China would support the shade ring to delay transitioning to clean energy. The longer that transition took, the more money to be made from coal especially.

As for her father, Neave wanted to know if he were put on trial in China and received a sentence there, whether he would ever be returned to the US to face charges. After all, there was the rather significant matter of justice for two murders. It made her blood boil to think he might not have to answer for those crimes.

And it bothered her that he'd been able to text her. What

did it mean if he had access to an iCom? She was more than a little troubled by his threat, saying she shouldn't marry Will, implying he had spies keeping an eye on her. Was that possible? Or had he become delusional?

She decided to visit Yong Li to get his take. He knew something about the Chinese government.

Chapter 6

Dr. Okonjo said to take it easy for a couple of weeks although some problems might persist. That's all Will would share about his examination by the doctor. So Neave looked up the symptoms for concussions, which ranged from headaches to irritability to sensitivity to light and noise. And those were just some of the milder ones. The medical websites said not to make major decisions right after suffering a concussion.

"Can't you at least take one measly day off?" she said. "The doctor said you need rest."

They were having gazpacho soup and bagels at Coffy's Café, trying to keep cool and rehydrate.

"Too much to do," he said, shaking his head.

"Nothing has to be done today."

She reached across the table to hold his hand. But he was distracted, antsy.

"We can't afford a hotel for long," he said.

The way he rubbed his eyes reminded her of some of her college classmates who worked all night and took classes by day, bolstering themselves with infusions of caffeine.

"My mother says we can stay at her condo for a while, till we can find a place of our own. She's got two bedrooms. So that's taken care of."

He made a small snorting noise.

"I know you're not used to being in business for yourself," he said, "but we have to have an income stream. And that means we've gotta hustle, whether it's demolition and antiques or the energy company."

"Just one day."

"Gotta get moving. And I want my family to know I'm serious."

"I think you made that pretty clear yesterday."

"Tell you what," he said, "we'll go back to the hotel, I'll make a few calls, we'll work on a to-do list, maybe you can make some calls too. No heavy lifting, no rushing around. Deal?"

She leaned across the table and kissed him, holding his freshly shaven cheeks in her hands.

But he was on his iCom all afternoon, contacting potential clients, investigating loans for Galloway Energy, checking on a small hydro power company he was considering buying. It was certainly not her idea of taking it easy. She arranged for them to move into her mother's place, which would give them some breathing room till they had time – and money – to find an apartment. But when he finally finished with his calls and messages, he announced he was flying out the next day on a business trip.

"You're kidding."

"Got a hot prospect for an installation in Guatemala."

"Guatemala?"

"Solar power. Maybe hydro power too."

"I'll go with you."

"Not this time. Too dicey. And I'll bet you haven't had your shots. You can start working on our to-do list."

"But..."

"I won't be gone long, just a couple of days. You can get us moved in to your mom's place and make some of those calls. We really need to get rolling on that."

When they crawled into bed that night, he curled up behind her, kissing her neck and caressing her. But his touch was like a light breeze wafting over her skin and he was asleep in minutes. No discussion about his trip. He wouldn't even let her accompany him to the airport the next day.

She checked them out of the hotel and took a hub car to her mother's new condo. Dr. Sullivan wasn't home. As usual, she was working long hours. So Neave carried their things to the guest room, which felt more like a motel room than the one she'd just left, with bare white walls and pale blue curtains. That only took a few minutes, and feeling dreadfully lonesome, she rented a scooter and headed over to see the Galloways.

"Neave!" Isabel cried when she strolled into the kitchen. "I got to sleep in your bedroom last night. Me and Jaz and Toni. Toni said it was like a slumber party! We watched Niagara Falls on that big view wall and pretended we were American Indians from hundreds of years ago."

"That sounds like fun."

"And Mama gave me her Patty Jo doll that her grandma gave her!"

She held the doll up for Neave to see.

"She's not a baby doll," Isabel explained. "She's a little girl doll. Mama says she was the first black doll to have lots of clothes and hair you could fix."

"She's beautiful," Neave said, admiring the doll's cute red and white checked shorts outfit.

"But Toni and Gib are leaving today on the JetTube," Isabel continued. "And Jaz and Charlie are leaving too, so it'll just be me and Patty Jo tonight."

And she skipped out of the room holding her new doll in her arms.

"I thought the sales trip was next week," Neave said to Angela, who was sitting at the kitchen table having coffee with Rosa.

"Toni wanted to get a move on," Angela said. "And it's true, we do need the income. I guess if there's one thing I've managed to instill in all my children, it's a strong work ethic."

"Did Will tell you he was flying out today on a sales trip to Guatemala?"

"What?"

"Jesus," said Jaz, striding into the kitchen in jeans and a white sun shirt. "It's like he's got something to prove! That he's even more industrious than the rest of us! And, by the way, what did the doc say about his concussion?"

Neave felt trapped, not wanting to reveal anything Will wouldn't want her to.

"I'm sure the doctor didn't say go on a friggin' sales trip to Central America," Jaz said, pouring herself a cup of coffee. "Probably something more like 'rest, don't exert yourself, don't make any important decisions, don't operate heavy machinery.'"

"You want me to fix you some food to take with you?" Rosa said to Jaz – her way of trying to defuse the tension.

"We'll just take some snacks."

Neave wondered if it was just her imagination or if Jaz was being intentionally aloof with Rosa.

"Jaz and Charlie rented a heli-scooter so they can fly down to see what's left of the house," Rosa explained.

Neave nodded, wishing she could sit down at the table and talk privately with Rosa like she used to. But now Rosa had her long-lost sweetheart to share her life with. Ironic, they were setting up housekeeping in the Sullivan/Alvarez home – the same house Rosa had lived in all these years against her will. The same unhappy home Neave had grown up in.

"I've gotta go," Neave said, a little too suddenly. "We're moving in with Mother for a while."

"Your mother's been so generous," said Angela. "She has no idea how much I appreciate it."

"All this time I didn't know the house belonged to Molly," Rosa commented, shrugging her shoulders. "I had no idea Roberto's name wasn't on the deed."

Neave's next stop was the university. She wished she had her cooling cloak but it was still in her storage unit with the rest of the stuff from her apartment. She was wrapped instead in a sheen of sweat that was starting to soak through her teal capris and white top. When she arrived at Yong Li's new office in the Climatology building, the door was locked with no schedule posted on the door or online. Classes didn't start for another week. She clicked on his code but he didn't answer.

Returning to the scooter lot, her eyes were drawn to the rotating skyscrapers that dominated the Atlanta skyline. In the bright sunshine, they splintered and refracted the sun's rays like giant blazing candles, so hot, they would surely burn up the city. She messaged Will, hoping he would reply. But her iCom was silent.

She donned the helmet, pulled her sun visor down and was about to wheel out of the parking lot when her iCom buzzed. She yanked it from her pocket but it wasn't Will. Instead, it was another message from her father.

"Dearest Neave, don't underestimate me. You must stop consorting with the Galloway family."

Then the message disappeared.

She was livid.

She popped the helmet off and called Barry King, the president's press secretary who she'd met at a White House dinner that summer. Maybe she could use her charms on him to find out why her father was allowed to leave the country. After all, Mr. King seemed rather taken with her when they sat next to each other that night. Naturally, he didn't answer so she left a brief voice message, trying to sound as friendly as possible.

At loose ends, she returned to her mother's condo, had a banana and a cucumber cooler as she dived into the research she and Will had discussed – evaluating possible clients, looking up contact information. But as the afternoon wore on, she was getting more and more frustrated at being ignored. Finally, there was a call from Barry King.

"Miss Alvarez, so good to hear from you. May I call you Neave?"

"Mr. King..."

"Please call me Barry."

"Barry, I appreciate your returning my call. I know you're busy. But I've been getting messages from my father."

"Oh?"

"I know about his extradition, but I thought the idea was for him to face charges there first and then be brought back to the US to face charges here."

"That's right."

"Well, I wondered if you could explain why he has access to an iCom which he's using to send me threatening messages."

"Threatening messages?"

"Yes. Messages that disappear as soon as I read them, not surprisingly. He's trying to intimidate me about my relationship with Will Galloway."

"The clone?"

She almost said yes, but caught herself.

"My fiancé."

"Funny, during the state dinner I thought you and Mr. Patel were a couple. And that wasn't so long ago."

"Nat and I were never a couple."

"Right, right. I did hear about your statement to police after his death… him holding you captive and…"

"Mr. King…"

"Barry."

"Barry… my question is this: is my father going to face charges in Beijing?"

"That's what I understood to be the case when he was released."

"And he'll be returned to the US to stand trial here?"

"I believe so."

She had the distinct impression he was bullshitting her and it was a struggle to maintain her polite tone.

"Is it normal for a prisoner to have an iCom in China?"

"I really have no idea."

"Well, it seems like the US government would want to keep tabs on a man who committed the kind of fraud my father did. Not to mention his involvement in the deaths of Lena Ruiz and Terrance Osley."

"I agree. And I'll make sure your concerns are passed along to the powers that be."

"Could you also let the president and secretary of state know their former climate secretary is now sending threatening messages to his daughter?"

"Absolutely. But I don't believe for a minute he's in a position to make good on any threats."

"I hope you're right. But I would appreciate it if you would pass his new iCom code along to the FBI, or whoever would monitor his calls."

She transmitted the code and thanked him for his help.

"Always a pleasure to talk with you," he said. "In fact, I would enjoy talking with you again. Over dinner, maybe. Would love to see you if you're in New Washington. Might help my political image, being seen with a half-clone. I'd definitely make room in my schedule for your lovely green eyes."

It was like he hadn't heard her say she and Will were engaged. She didn't feel any safer after hanging up. It was as though she'd been talking to Rosa's vacuum bot. Although if she'd been wasting her breath on the vacuum, she wouldn't feel an overwhelming urge to take a shower. And what was with that half-clone comment! She decided he was an idiot. An idiot she couldn't afford to alienate.

She checked her iCom to make sure she hadn't missed a call or message from Will, beginning to feel some sympathy for the people who complained that she never answered her iCom or returned messages.

~~~

When Will still hadn't called her back the next morning, she buzzed Angela.

"Quite frankly, I haven't heard from any of my children except for Isabel who's right here in the house, running around like she's in Colorado at Disney World. I'm sure we'll hear from him soon. Isabel! Get down from there! Come on over if you want to. We could use some help unpacking."

She clicked on Yong Li's code. She wanted to tell him about her father's messages. But he didn't answer. She tossed the rest of her unfinished breakfast in the compost chute, exasperated, and headed back to campus, hoping to track him down. His office was still locked and her level of vexation was growing by the minute. She called Kwan. Thankfully, he an-

swered. Twenty minutes later they met at the university cantina, Kwan showing up in black spandex shorts and a tight red
tank, the better to put his buffness on display, she was sure.

"So where's Li?"

"I love it when you're all fuzzy and friendly like that," he
said, giving her a hug.

"You're right. Sorry. I'm just a little pissed."

"About?"

"About… well… everything."

"Damn!"

She chose a yogurt while he loaded his tray with synthetic
chicken, mac n' cheese and vegetables.

"Is that all you're eating?" he said as they slid into a booth.

She gave him a mind-your-own-business look.

"So where is he?" she asked.

"Hell if I know. He's been, like, brutally busy – meetings
and stuff. He told me he wouldn't need me till next week. Your
best chance might be to come to class."

"He hasn't even returned my calls."

"Like I said, he's busy."

"I've had it up to here with 'busy,'" she said, irritably tapping her chin. "And, besides, he's only been on the job a few
days. How can he be so swamped?"

"Calm down, calm down, and tell me why you're
practically foaming at the mouth. Surely, it's not because you
can't reach Li."

"Well, let's see, my father's been extradited to China and
who knows whether he'll ever be brought to justice; somehow
he's sending me nasty messages; Will's family home was
washed away by the hurricane; then he rushed off to Central
America on a business trip and wouldn't let me go with him,
and he hasn't called me once; we're staying with my mother

because we don't have a place of our own; Will's involved in a family feud over which business to focus on; and no one will answer my calls or messages."

"Except me."

She scrunched her nose and screwed up her mouth to look as sheepish as possible.

"Okay, you're a good friend to sit here and listen while I whine, bitch and moan."

He laughed loudly and took another bite of macaroni.

~~~

"Rosa?" she said, heading for the kitchen, hoping they could have a few minutes alone.

She didn't really want to help unpack but how could she say no to Angela.

"Mi chica bonita," Rosa replied from her perch on a step stool.

She was moving some of the old kitchen stuff to the top cabinets to make room for Angela's dishes. Neave was struck by Rosa's appearance. She wasn't sure what it was exactly – more color in her cheeks, the way she carried herself – but she definitely looked younger than she used to. She didn't look like a woman in her fifties, that's for sure.

"I don't suppose Angela's heard from Will?"

"I don't think so. But don't worry, he'll call you soon. I'm sure he's just..."

"Very busy, I know," Neave replied, plopping down at the kitchen table.

Rosa chuckled.

"Well, don't feel bad. We haven't heard from Toni and Gib or Jaz and Charlie either. I think communications are still out along the Gulf coast and I guess Toni's too busy showing Gib the ropes."

"I finally got a call from one of my children!" Angela announced from the doorway.

"Bueno," Rosa replied, a warm smile lighting up her face.

"Oh, hi, Neave," Angela said. "Your significant other just called to say he thinks he's gonna close the deal soon and might even make another sales call while he's there."

Neave immediately checked her iCom to see if she'd missed a call, but found nothing.

"Is he going to call me?"

"I assumed he'd already spoken with you," Angela said, cocking her head uncertainly. "I'm sure he'll contact you soon." And she looked to Rosa for support.

"Si, your iCom will be buzzing any minute now," Rosa assured her.

"I think it's buzzing right now," Neave lied, jumping up and heading for the door. "See ya later."

~~~

Once she boarded her plane she sent a brief message to her mother. "I'm flying to Guatemala to help Will on his sales trip. I'll be in touch. Love, Neave." She decided not to message Angela or Rosa. Or Will.

Chapter 7

After years of not caring who called or messaged her, Neave had been desperate for her iCom to buzz the last twenty-four hours. But now she was tired of stressing over being ignored. So she turned it off.

She didn't know what was up with Will, but she was going to find out. How had they gone from being so happy together after getting back from Washington to him giving her the ice cold shoulder? She kept reminding herself he'd been through a lot – losing his family home and nearly losing his little sister. Not to mention his disturbing fight to the death with Curt Maddux, his clone twin. That may have had more of an impact than she realized. Which piled yet another layer of guilt on her shoulders over how he'd suffered because of her. It was her father who employed Nat Patel to do his dirty work. And it was Nat who hired Curt to kill Will and Lena. He succeeded with Lena but not with Will.

And while it stuck in her craw that Jaz might be right about something, she wondered if the concussion could be causing his strange behavior. Maybe his sudden focus on the energy business was impulsive. She had to admit she'd never heard him talk about making such a big course change. He'd mentioned wanting to expand solar and wind installations, but he'd never said anything about ditching the antiques and demolition business.

The big question, though – the question gnawing at her so she couldn't sleep or eat – had she done something wrong?

Was he having second thoughts about her?

One thing was certain: she wasn't going to sit around Atlanta working on their to-do list, waiting to see if everything would just magically be all right. She didn't give a damn that he'd told her not to come.

When she landed at La Aurora International Airport she hailed a taxi for the trip into Guatemala City. Hub cars weren't as reliable in many places because of poor mapping for autonomous vehicles. And she preferred to surprise him, not for fun, but because she didn't want to tip him off she was coming, afraid he might avoid her entirely.

The cabbie said he was familiar with El Hotel Moderno. He said it was close to Central Square. She touched up her hair and lip gloss as they pulled onto the highway, taking time to notice four stunning volcanoes in the distance, a bank of clouds hugging the tallest one. While it was a beautiful vista, it made her nervous being so close. Two of them had been erupting for decades and she sure as hell didn't want to be nearby when they blew their stacks again.

There were lots of other cabs, hub cars, buses and scooters on the road, but they moved at a pretty good clip until they got into the historic district, where traffic came to a standstill.

"Is it always like this?" she asked.

"No."

He clicked on his iCom and mumbled to himself.

"What is it?" she asked.

"Una protesta," he said. "I losing money."

Traffic had come to a complete halt and he joined in as some drivers honked their horns in frustration.

"Is there a way around it?" she asked.

"Estamos atrapados."

"We're stuck?"

"Si."

And he banged his hand on the steering wheel.

"How far is the hotel?" she said.

"Six, seven blocks."

"I'll hoof it," she said, transferring the cab fare from her account.

The sidewalk was teeming with people, everyone heading in the same direction. She made progress on foot until a block later, when she was boxed in by the growing throng. She was literally shoulder to shoulder with angry men and women speaking Spanish so rapidly, she had no hope of understanding a word. There was a moment when her feet actually came off the ground as the crowd surged forward with people yelling and shoving each other. She was hot and sweaty, and anxious about not being in control. She pulled her hair into a knot on top of her head, which helped a bit, then checked her iCom, looking for an alternative route. When she finally made it to the next corner, she turned right and escaped down a side street, then turned left onto a narrow avenue that ran parallel to the main drag. Although she was able to walk quickly, she realized there were fewer businesses on this street and they seemed to attract a less desirable clientele.

She was on high alert as she hurried several blocks, slapping at insects buzzing her ears. At last, she reached the cross street she was looking for and turned left. Several groups of young people were ahead of her, holding signs, obviously preparing to join the demonstration. When they arrived at the city square, progress stopped once again. She could read the signs now, most in Spanish but many also in English, and realized the protest was about the shade ring.

"Excuse me, do you speak English?" she asked a young

woman in front of her wearing mini jeans and a halter top.

"Yes."

"Why are you protesting?"

"We… angry with America for… break promise."

"What promise?"

"Presidente Cohen promise shade ring… but break promise."

"Why do you want a shade ring?"

The girl grew impatient.

"Necesitamos aire más frío," she said, shaking her head like Neave was an idiot. "Hace mucho calor."

Neave struggled to catch her meaning.

"She say it too fucking hot and we need shade ring," a young man said. "You Americano?"

"Yes."

"You tell your presidente what we say!"

Then they joined others chanting something in Spanish that she didn't understand. For all of her doubts about her father's shade ring plan and his secret motivations, it seemed ironic that she had run into a pro-shade ring demonstration. If people here in Guatemala supported the plan, she guessed people elsewhere were hoping for some relief from the sun as well. They obviously didn't care that the former climate secretary was pushing the technology as a means of self-aggrandizement, not to slow global warming.

It took another half hour to squeeze through the back of the crowd ringing the square before she finally reached the hotel. Despite its name, El Hotel Moderno was neither modern nor luxurious. But she was relieved when she stepped into the lobby that at least it was air conditioned, because right now, she too needed some of that frio air.

A guy behind the front desk eyed her as she looked around

to get her bearings.

"May I help you?" he asked, correctly deducing she was American.

She stepped forward, wondering what tipped him off. Was it her sleeveless summer top and capris? Her auburn hair? Or was it just her clueless expression?

"Yes, I'm here to see Will Galloway. Can you tell me if he's in?"

"So sorry," he said, nodding politely, "we can't give out that kind of information."

His English was flawless, although there was a slight Spanish accent. His name badge said Carlos Ubico.

"I've just arrived to join him on a sales trip. I'm his *prometida*," she said, hoping to ingratiate herself by using a little Spanish.

"Congratulations. But even if you are his fiancée, we cannot give out guest information. Why don't you call him?"

"I'm trying to surprise him," she said, a pleading tone in her voice. "He doesn't know I'm here."

"Very sorry."

And he turned toward a computer holoscreen, clearly dismissing her.

"Please, Señor Ubico," she began, not knowing what would come out of her mouth, but certain she had to get to Will. "I'm..." and then her voice cracked and tears welled up. She wasn't play-acting, wasn't pretending, wasn't trying to be manipulative. She was just overwhelmed with desperation. "I've got to see him tonight. It's important."

"I can't break company policy," he said, refusing to turn around.

She closed her eyes, suddenly feeling very fatigued. She had no idea whether he was in his room at this very moment or whether he was out and about. If he wasn't here, she had no way of knowing when he would return. She sat down on a small couch in the lobby and clicked Will's code. He didn't answer and she chose not to leave a voice message. Instead, she sent a brief e-message: "I've arrived at your hotel. I need to see you."

She sat for a moment waiting for a reply. She pictured herself outside his hotel room, knocking and waiting for him to answer. She thought back to the night he'd opened another hotel room door wrapped only in a towel, making her believe he had a woman in his room. She shook her head, trying to dislodge the memory. But there was a tiny part of her that wondered whether there might actually be another woman this time. No, couldn't be.

Avoiding the disapproving eyes of Señor Ubico, she entered the hotel's rustic restaurant, just off the lobby. A pretty woman wearing a blue printed Mayan skirt with a long braid down her back led Neave to a small table in the rear of the dining room and she was soon eating chilis rellenos and fried plantains. She washed it down with red wine, which transported her back to the first time she ate with Will. It was that unpleasant research expedition to Charleston. He cooked spaghetti and she got very tipsy on the Chianti he kept filling her glass with. That was the night they danced the waltz and she fell in love. Just thinking about how he looked at her that night made her sigh.

She took another drink, then reached up and undid the bun on her head, letting her hair down, smoothing it with her fingers. She nibbled at her food while having three glasses of wine. Finally, she paid the bill and was lifting her glass for one last sip when she spied a tall, handsome man with tousled brown hair, walking toward her. It was Will.

He was dressed in black slacks and a black, long-sleeved, button-up shirt. Very unlike him. He moved like he was walking through chest-deep water, each step in slow motion. She stood up, giving him a tentative smile. He didn't return it. Instead, he squinted as though trying to recall her name. His eyes were bloodshot and angry.

"Why are you here?" he said.

"I had to see you."

She wanted to hug him but he took her arm and escorted her from the restaurant and through the lobby to the elevator. He didn't say a word until they were inside his room on the third floor.

She thought he might kiss her but he crossed the room, a bit unsteadily, she noticed, and stared out the window at the city lights and the crowd of demonstrators in the square below.

"I told you not to come."

"I was worried."

"Have you been vaccinated for dengue, malaria, zika and yellow fever?" he asked, whirling around.

"Why haven't you called me?"

"You shouldn't have come. I mean, you're wearing a sleeveless shirt! It's like you're sending an open invitation to every mosquito in the city... come and get me!"

He'd been drinking. He was slurring his words and his voice was uncharacteristically loud, harsh and sarcastic. She'd never seen him drunk.

"Will, what's going on?"

"I'm busy, Neave. Busy trying to make a living. I know that's hard for you to comprehend – you, the only child of a couple of respectable, overpaid scientists, who never once had to worry about where your next meal came from. You wouldn't know the first thing about having to make a living."

Tears welled up but she blinked several times to hold them back as she crossed the room, reaching out to touch him. But he swatted her hand away, stepping backwards, bumping into a chair and staggering slightly.

"You need to get back on a plane tonight and get outta here," he said, recovering his balance. "I've got meetings all day tomorrow and then I'm goin' to Honduras."

"I can go with you."

"Hell no, you can't!"

It was like a punch in the gut. She swallowed hard, trying to maintain control but the dam burst on her tears.

"Will, talk to me!"

He refused to look her in the eye, lurching past her to yank the door open. With an exaggerated nod of the head, he gestured for her to leave.

She wanted to argue with him but forced herself to keep quiet. The concussion must be worse than the doctor suspected, worse than anyone suspected. Maybe he just needed some rest. A demanding business trip definitely wasn't what the doctor ordered.

She took a step toward the door, then turned toward him again.

"I love you with all my heart. I don't know why you're upset but please give me a chance to fix it."

He stared beyond her, eyes unfocused, weaving slightly as he held the door.

The first flight out wasn't until seven the next morning. She changed her ticket online for the return trip and then wandered outside to the city square. The demonstration was over but small groups of protesters, some still lugging their signs, strolled the sidewalks. She stopped at a coffee shop and sat at a table on the patio with her café mocha. The caffeine gave her the energy she needed to find her way back to the airport. But it didn't fill the emptiness in her heart or calm the fear in her belly.

Chapter 8

Her mother wasn't home when she arrived, which suited her fine. She showered and went straight to bed. She was completely drained and wanted to sleep – to dream of happy times, to dream of Will. But the air in the condo was chilly on her skin and she shivered, like she was back in that cold, dark refrigerator she thought she'd escaped from, which was how she always felt about her childhood home.

She hugged her pillow, pretending it was him, longing to erase those angry eyes from her memory, wishing he would've held her close and kissed her instead of pushing her away. He came to her in her dreams. But when she looked in his eyes, they were no longer blue. Instead, they had huge black irises. Like a frog's eyes.

She wondered if she'd cried out because when she awoke, her mother was sitting on the edge of the bed, her hand on Neave's arm. But there was too much light so she turned away.

"Neave, dear, you've been asleep since I got home last night," Dr. Sullivan said. "And now it's Wednesday evening."

She was confused but didn't care enough to ask for clarification.

"Are you feeling all right?" her mother asked.

Neave covered her face with her arm. Her head was pounding and her eyes were burning.

"You feel so warm," Dr. Sullivan continued.

She closed her eyes but knew she couldn't doze off again until she went to the bathroom. She pushed the covers back

71

and her mother moved out of the way so she could get up. She stood slowly and walked unsteadily across the room. By the time she returned, she was exhausted and nauseated.

"I'm calling the doctor," her mother said.

As she drifted off, she had a flashback to the ordeal in her old bedroom when Nat drugged her and violated her while she was unconscious. Her eyes flew open and she peered around the room, reassuring herself that she was actually in the condo. No view walls, no Nat. But it was unnerving, falling back through time like that.

Maybe that's why Will pushed her away, she thought. Despite her irrational fears that she'd somehow been soiled, he had reassured her that none of that mattered, that he loved her. And she believed him. But maybe it bothered him more than he let on, more than he wanted it to. It was like her brain was immersed in a bowl of Rosa's banana pudding and she found it hard to think clearly, finally succumbing to her body's desire for rest.

By the time the doctor arrived, her head felt like a baseball that had been used for batting practice. The pain was most intense right behind her eyes. And her bones became hot pokers in her legs and arms. Dr. Okonjo did a blood test first thing, then looked her over, noticing she'd developed a rash all over her body. He asked a lot of questions about where she'd been, then announced she'd contracted dengue fever.

"You should've been vaccinated weeks before traveling to Central America," he said, shaking his head as he looked at her mother. "Why didn't you advise her about that, Molly?"

"I didn't know she was going," Dr. Sullivan replied, a rare tone of irritation in her voice.

Neave closed her eyes.

"It probably won't kill you but you'll be very sick for a

couple of weeks," he continued. "And it'll likely take several weeks longer to regain your strength. Once you completely recover, I strongly urge you to be vaccinated, especially if you're planning on traveling. Because if you contract dengue again, it'll be much more serious. I have to admit I'm disappointed, Neave. I'm surprised that you, of all people, would be so careless since your own mother is a geneticist who knows all about the mosquito gene modification program. Seems like you would too. And although it's true we've made good progress reducing mosquito populations, that doesn't mean they've been wiped out. Not yet, anyway."

He turned to her mother then.

"Lots of fluids, analgesics for pain. I'm transmitting a list to you now. I'm also transmitting a list of symptoms to watch out for – symptoms of severe dengue. If she exhibits any of those, you need to get her to the ER and call me pronto."

"Right," Dr. Sullivan said.

In a perverse way, Neave was glad to know Will wasn't using the line about not being vaccinated as a brush-off. She still believed he was intent on sending her away for other reasons, but there was some small reassurance that he did at least have her physical welfare at heart.

"I think someone should stay with her for the first several days," he continued.

"I'll call Rosa," Dr. Sullivan replied.

"How's her fiancé doing?" he asked as they headed for the front door.

Neave didn't hear her mother's reply.

~~~

Rosa came every day, but nothing she did made Neave feel any better. She now understood why the doctor called it "breakbone fever" because it sometimes felt like her legs were being used as boards in a karate demonstration. Her headache was intense, her eyes hurt, she had fever and chills, and she was nauseated and disoriented. She felt worse with each passing day. And while the initial rash faded away, an even uglier rash took its place – bright red spots with white patches. She told Rosa not to let anyone visit. The thought of talking was too much to bear.

But on the fifth day, Rosa carried a bowl of soup in for lunch.

"So, chica, tell me what happened in Guatemala," she said.

Neave rubbed her eyes.

"So it didn't go well?"

"It's like he hates me," Neave replied, her voice wobbling.

"I know for a fact he doesn't hate you. I think he's got something troubling him. Angela thinks it's the concussion. She says Will's behavior is very strange, that it has to be the concussion. He'll come around. You'll see."

Neave stared into her soup. Lifting her spoon would take too much energy.

"Jaz and Charlie got back yesterday," Angela said, sitting down and taking the spoon. "They say the storm damage is unbelievable. Jaz says they saw a boat sitting on the road near the house and old caskets were piled up, helter skelter, where the warehouse used to be. But we're not telling Isabel about the coffins. They say the house is a total loss, just like Will predicted – a pile of sticks. Which makes Angela so sad. Que frustrante." She paused, shaking her head. "Here, eat." And Rosa fed her the soup.

Sometime during the night she woke up in a cold sweat. She'd dreamed again about Will turning into a poison dart frog and she thought for a moment she was back in her bedroom with Nat holding her prisoner. She thought maybe she'd called out but no one came.

The next morning Rosa knocked on her door, then opened it just far enough to peek into the room.

"You've got a visitor."

"No."

"It's Will."

But there was no smile on Rosa's face.

"Give me a minute," Neave said, struggling out of bed.

She washed her face, brushed her teeth and combed her hair. Exhausted, she returned to bed and pulled up the sheet. She had intentionally avoided looking in the bathroom mirror, hoping she didn't look as horrible as she felt. A moment later Rosa opened the door, and seeing she was ready, ushered Will into the room.

He looked positively grim as though he was sick too, and stood silently so long, she wondered if he would ever speak.

"Hope you're feeling better," he finally said.

"I'll be all right."

Her voice was so soft she wasn't sure he could hear her.

"I'm really sorry, Neave. Sorry you got sick. Sorry I didn't explain the risks better so you'd know not to come."

She wanted him to sit down on the bed and hold her hand or kiss her forehead or something, but he just stood there looking miserable, hands in his pockets.

"I can't stay," he said. "I'm heading out on another sales trip. Drumming up business."

He cleared his throat and nodded for no apparent reason.

"I just wanted to drop by and tell you in person that I need to call off the engagement. And I'm really, really sorry. The last thing I want to do is hurt you. But I've decided I need to stick to my own kind. Which will be better for me and better for you."

"What kind is that?"

"I met a woman… a woman who's a clone, like me."

His eyes were focused on the floor.

"Is this another ruse?" she said.

"A ruse?"

How could he forget tricking her into dumping him by pretending to have another woman in his hotel room? All because he didn't think she could love a clone.

"No, it's not a ruse," he said.

She almost told him she loved him but there was a huge lump in her throat and she didn't want him to see her lose control. So she turned toward the wall, closed her eyes, and waited for him to leave, wondering what kind of man would kick the woman who loved him when she was down.

~~~

It was easy to distance herself from the Galloways while she was sick. But as she began to feel better she decided to steer clear. It was just too awkward. And she didn't know if she could hide her anger and hurt.

The relationship with Will was like riding a roller coaster – too many negative G's, sharp drops and diving loops. Her doubts about clones bubbled up once again. Maybe he couldn't help being warm and loving one moment and cold and aloof the next. Whatever the reason, she didn't want to be on the receiving end of his on-again, off-again affections. Unfortunately, there was one infuriating problem: she was totally in love with him.

She decided to throw herself into her studies. If she got her master's and PhD, she'd have more credibility to speak out on climate issues. Although she'd grown up despising her father for forcing her into that field, she now realized professional credentials could give her a platform for activism. A part of her wanted to show the world she was a better person than her father, that unlike him, she really did care about slowing the melting. Ironically, she'd never put much stock in family names but now she wanted to repair the damage done to hers.

Too weak to walk very far just yet, she took a hub car to Yong Li's class on the Effects of Land/Atmosphere Interactions on Global Warming. Kwan greeted her as she entered, explaining that Li was on his way. Her attention was drawn to an antique brass bell hanging from the neck of an S-shaped dragon. It was about ten inches tall, with a tiny brass mallet attached, sitting on the instructor's desk. She smiled as she turned to find a seat.

The auditorium held about a hundred students, each row of seats rising higher than the one before it. She found a spot in the back.

A moment later Yong strode to his desk and lifted the little hammer, striking the bell until everyone heard the delicate ringing. When the students were quiet, he returned the tiny mallet and began pacing slowly back and forth across the stage.

"One thing has become clear in the last century. Climatology must include fields of science that were studied separately in the past. We now know that what happens in the oceans impacts what happens in the atmosphere; what happens in the atmosphere affects what happens on the land; changes in the biosphere cause changes in the other spheres. We know that the atmosphere, the land, the oceans and the biota are all linked. Feedback loops involving these interactions accelerated global warming and polar and glacial melting to a far greater extent than experts of the early twenty-first century imagined."

He lectured for about forty minutes, then told his students

to research one example of interactions between the atmosphere, the land, the oceans, and plants and animals, and be ready to discuss it next time.

Neave thought it was a good overview, although he didn't deliver it with any kind of passion. In fact, she noticed a number of students using their iComs or snoozing, which surprised her for a graduate level course.

He put his dragon bell in a wooden box and tucked it under his arm as he headed for the door.

"Li!" she called out, dodging other students as she made her way down the center aisle.

A few steps from the bottom a man in jeans whirled around and bumped her, spilling the contents of his biofoam cup all over her. She cried out in surprise and he groaned in dismay. It was a cup of coffee, nearly full, but fortunately it was room temperature and not scalding hot as she feared.

"I'm so sorry!" he blurted, looking truly embarrassed.

Her cream colored top was sopping wet and now looked more like a sautéed mushroom. She had nothing to dry off with so she pulled the drenched garment away from her body a few inches.

"I've ruined your clothing," he said.

He had a bit of an accent – maybe eastern European, she wasn't sure – a stocky build, brown hair and a closely trimmed beard and mustache. A rarity since few men wore beards anymore because of the heat.

"No big deal," she said. "Don't worry about it."

She pushed past him, anxious to catch Yong, trotting down the remaining steps and toward the door where he nodded his head in greeting.

"Hello," she said, smiling and looking down self-consciously at her coffee-stained shirt. "Sorry, I had a little accident."

"Miss Alvarez," he said.

"Please don't go back to using formal address," she replied, smiling. "Neave is fine."

"Neave."

"He sounds great, doesn't he?" Kwan said, joining them. "I really like the new pacing technique, man. Has a very professorial feel to it."

Yong nodded uncertainly.

"You just lose a mud wrestling match?" Kwan said, noticing the coffee stain.

She rolled her eyes in response and turned back to Yong.

"Your English has improved a lot," she said.

"You can thank me for that," Kwan said, laughing. "I've been teaching him contractions, slang, all kinds of stuff. And he's a quick study, that's for sure."

"I have a meeting soon," Yong said, ignoring Kwan as he looked at his iCom.

"I was hoping to talk with you, if you've got a minute," she said.

"You can accompany me to my office."

Kwan took the hint and headed off in the opposite direction.

As they walked, she told Yong about her father's messages and how upset she was that the government had apparently let him off the hook.

"Do you think the fact that he has access to an iCom means the Chinese government might not put him on trial?" she said.

"He is a special prisoner, not a poor Chinese man locked up for theft or murder."

"True. He's the former American climate secretary. Still, if the Chinese government is serious about prosecuting him for financial fraud, don't you think he'd be detained without communication privileges?"

"I'm not expert on Chinese justice or prisons."

"It really concerns me that he's sending me threatening messages. What if he has unfettered internet access? Who knows what he might be capable of?"

"I think you should not worry," he said, opening the door to his office.

She waited in the doorway as he set the box with his dragon bell on a shelf and picked up a black bag.

"By the way, I like the bell," she said.

He tilted his head slightly before responding.

"The dragon is a benevolent symbol in China, believed to have power over water, rain and storms. My antecedent, Dr. Zhang, used such a dragon bell in his classes as well."

Neave was struck by his use of the word antecedent, meaning the man he was cloned from – old Dr. Zhang was a famous climatologist in his own right. Yong Li was China's rising star until he was brought to Georgia Geosciences University to speak out against the shade ring plan. Dr. Osley sponsored his trip, using the young scientific prodigy's speeches as ammunition to win the climate secretary post. Obviously, Dr. Osley didn't realize Neave's father wanted the post so bad, he was willing to commit murder to get it. That jumble of memories churned around in her brain for a moment as she recalled how Osley was intentionally dumped out of the helicopter to eliminate her father's competition. Which made her cringe.

"How is Mr. Galloway?" he asked.

"Hard at work. I saw him a few days ago while he was in town between sales trips."

She didn't want to tell him anything more than that. Not yet.

"I must go," he said abruptly.

"Right. Kwan says you're very busy, quite the sought out authority. Congratulations on your success."

She stepped aside so he could pass and watched him walk purposely down the hallway, checking the time on his iCom. She wondered if he might've welcomed her more warmly if she'd told him Will had called off their engagement. She and Yong had become close on their desperate trip to New DC to stop the shade ring treaty signing. He'd actually let his guard down, allowing her to see his personality and his sense of humor. But their relationship changed abruptly when she and Will announced they were going to be married. Maybe that was why he was so stiff today. Perhaps he thought he had to be distant if she was committed to someone else. She'd have to bring him up to date sometime. But she didn't want to talk about it now.

Her wet shirt was making her cold in the air conditioning and she reeked of stale coffee. So she hurried home and threw the ruined top in the recycling bin and took a shower. When she came out, she found a message on her iCom. It was from her father.

"Cariño, I need for you to call me. It's about spraying some pesticide on a certain relationship."

"Like hell I will," she muttered to herself.

Chapter 9

"Why didn't you tell me, Mother?"

It was the first time they'd shared a meal since she moved in.

"I haven't seen you, dear. I apologize. I've just been so pre-occupied with my work."

Neave, Dr. Sullivan and Rosa were eating tacos in her mother's spartan kitchen. No pictures on the wall, no decorations of any kind. Just like the rest of the condo.

"But, Rosa, you could've told me. You were here with me every day. Someone should've let me know. This is serious. Have they called the police?"

"Of course," Rosa said, "Angela contacted the police several days ago and gave them every scrap of information she had about Toni and Gib's trip."

"I assumed they'd gotten back while I was sick!"

"I'm sorry, but you were very ill," Rosa said. "And then there was, you know, what happened with Will."

Neave understood they were trying to protect her but there was no need to treat her like a child.

"Where were they the last time Angela heard from them?" she asked.

"They flew to Oklahoma City but no one knows where they went from there," Rosa explained.

"Anyone for a glass of wine?" Dr. Sullivan said.

Rosa nodded but Neave declined. She was already weak. A glass of wine might do her in.

"Tell me everything you know," she said to Rosa as her mother poured two glasses of Cabernet.

"Charlie and Jaz flew out to Oklahoma City and they talked with the same museum curator Toni and Gib met with. But that curator said he told Toni they weren't interested in what she had to offer. You know, a lot of the best stuff was lost when the truck washed away. Anyway, Jaz says Toni told her before she left that she wasn't coming home empty-handed. She said if the Oklahoma City people didn't buy something, she and Gib would find another client to pitch. But Jaz thought Toni was just angry at Will about wanting to quit the antiques business and didn't really think she'd take Gib on an extended fishing expedition. And she figured if they did go somewhere else, they'd tell Angela."

"Are the police searching?"

"The Oklahoma City Police Department, the Oklahoma State Bureau of Investigation, the FBI and police in Seattle, Las Vegas and Salt Lake City are all looking. Those are the cities Jaz thinks Toni might've had on her list. They all have museums she's dealt with before. But no leads so far."

"And they checked out of their hotel?"

"Yes. Police found an e-trail showing they paid for the train to the airport. But that's where the trail disappears. No sign of them after they touched the pay pad for the train."

Neave had lost her appetite. Her stomach was in knots and her headache had returned. She couldn't believe Gib and Toni had vanished without a trace.

"Does Will know?" she asked.

"Yes, he's contacting people they've worked with at some other museums."

Although she hadn't fully recovered from her bout of dengue fever, she couldn't sit still. She paced around the kitchen, trying to figure out how she could help. She had no contacts, no special know-how that would be of any use.

"I'm flying to Oklahoma City," she announced.

"To do what?" her mother asked.

"To look for them."

"Neave, dear, Charlie, Jaz and Will are already doing that. And so are the police."

"Your mother's right, chica," Rosa agreed. "We know you're worried – we all are – but it won't do any good for you to fly out there and walk the streets searching for them. And I'm pretty sure you'd keel over in the heat if you did."

"I'm sure between the family working on it and the police working on it, they'll be found," Dr. Sullivan said. "I really think there's just been some kind of miscommunication."

"I've changed my mind," Neave said. "I think I'll have one of my wine chillers."

Rosa jumped up to get it.

She didn't want to say it out loud, but it was hard to believe a miscommunication, as her mother put it, would go on this long. There was also another matter that seemed more troubling now.

"I haven't mentioned it yet, but Father's been sending me threatening messages," she said.

She told them she was starting to think he might actually have spies keeping tabs on her. She also told them about her conversation with Barry King – how he seemed unconcerned and treated her like she was overreacting.

"I'll call Stan Mintz," her mother said.

"I don't think that'll do any good. I doubt even the secretary of state has any clout with the Chinese government now. It's like Father was a birthday present to China from the United States, gift-wrapped in shiny paper with a giant bow on top."

~~~

She was running through a deserted city, looking down every street and alley, peering into every doorway, every window, frantically searching for someone. But she had to find him before he succeeded in hurting... hurting who? She didn't know. And she couldn't remember what he looked like but knew she'd recognize him when she saw him. She ran and ran through valleys of tall buildings until she saw two people in the distance just as a mountainous wall of water crashed through the street, heading straight toward them.

Her mouth was open in a silent scream when she awoke, clutching the sheets.

~~~

The next day she stopped by the university cantina on the way to her graduate seminar in Accelerated Polar Melting, which was one reason the earth's albedo effect was suffering. Less ice meant less sunlight reflected back into space, and thus, more warming of the oceans. She was in line to buy a cup of coffee and a fruit bar to take with her when a man stepped up behind her.

"Allow me," he said, indicating he wanted to pay for her purchases.

It was the student who splashed coffee all over her the day before.

"I would feel much better if I could make it up to you in some small way for ruining your blouse," he said.

"There's really no need."

"Please? It would reduce my feelings of guilt and shame."

He gave her a mock hangdog look. So she reluctantly let him pay.

"Okay, now don't give it another thought. We're even," she said.

He laughed but then his brows furrowed as he noticed something across the large dining room. She turned toward the wallscreen he was staring at and was stunned to see Yong Li standing with President Rachel Cohen. There was another man and two women also standing with the president in the White House briefing room. The graphic said it was a live news conference. Neave couldn't hear the sound for the noise in the cafeteria so she clicked her iCom to find a news site and popped her earbud in.

"If there's one thing I've learned in my long public career, it's not to throw the baby out with the bathwater," the president said, looking her usual borderline frumpy self, in a blue power pantsuit topped by a grey poof of hair. "As you all know, I dismissed our former climate secretary after learning he had a vested interest in launching a shade ring, but that does not mean the shade ring itself isn't a viable plan. We do, however want to make sure there's complete transparency in how we choose the companies, agencies and nations that participate in its launch and maintenance. My administration has now consulted with a number of top climatologists, including some who, in the past, spoke out against the plan. And, after consultation with these experts," she said, gesturing at Yong and the others, "we feel strongly that a shade ring would help shield the earth from the sun and reduce the warming of the oceans and, thus, decrease the melting and the very alarming rise in sea level. We've formed a coalition to finalize plans. Some members of the coalition so far: China, Australia, Kuwait, Saudi Arabia and Iran – just to name a few."

"It looks like Big Oil might want to delay clean energy," her new friend said. "And I thought Yong Li opposed the shade ring."

"He does," she replied. "Or, at least, he did."

She was shocked that Li had apparently switched sides. The president said she'd consulted with opponents of the shade ring, but surely Li wouldn't be standing with her before a bank of cameras if he wasn't on board. So that's where he was rushing off to the day before. His meeting was in New Washington with the President of the United States!

"It makes you wonder whether Dr. Yong was bought off," the guy said.

She gave him a sharp look, finding the idea preposterous. The Yong Li she'd come to know would never sell out.

"I'm just speculating. It's just that I'm very surprised."

She turned to the wallscreen again where the president was ushering Yong to the microphones to answer a reporter's question. He stood stiffly in a suit and tie.

"Dr. Yong, you spoke out against the shade ring as recently as a few weeks ago, supporting your late mentor's position that it would only cause a delay in the transition to clean energy. Why the sudden change of heart?"

The question came from a striking Asian woman wearing camera glasses.

Yong squinted into the bank of lights and cleared his throat.

"At the time, I thought Dr. Terrance Osley was correct, that a shade ring would encourage nations to continue polluting the environment. But since President Cohen contacted me, I've done extensive research and I now believe we need to act with urgency to decelerate polar and glacial melting. I have also now adopted an American frame of reference. I still urge countries to transition to clean energy but if we don't move with haste, we could see the pace of melting increase beyond human capacity to intercede."

Neave was amazed but she wasn't sure she wanted to talk about it with a stranger. She headed for the exit, but he kept pace beside her.

"You're Neave Alvarez," he said.

"How do you know my name?"

"I saw you on the news."

It made her uncomfortable to think people would recognize her now.

"You're not American, are you?" she said, a part of her wanting to put him on the spot as well.

"I'm a graduate student from Russia. Alexei Sokolov."

"I've gotta run, Alexei. I'm heading to a seminar."

"Polar Melting?"

"Uh, yes."

"I, as well. We can walk together."

Which irritated her because she wanted to be alone with her thoughts.

~~~

She left a message for Will telling him how upset and sorry she was, and asking if there was anything she could do to help find Gib and Toni. She messaged Kwan, telling him she had to talk with him that very afternoon. No reply from Will, as expected, but she got a response from Kwan telling her to meet him at the gym at four o'clock.

She found him in the weight room, lying on his back, doing bench presses. He grunted at her, then remounted the barbell and sat up. He was dressed in neon workout clothes, which showed off his physique.

"You're getting awful pushy in your graduate student phase," he said, grabbing a small white towel to wipe the sweat from his face.

"I saw the president's news conference today and lo, and

behold, guess who was standing by her side? Yong Li! What...?"

"Don't ask me. I'm not his keeper. I'm just his graduate assistant. He tells me what to do, not the other way around."

He took a swig from a green sports bottle.

"He was opposed to the shade ring, totally opposed," she said.

"Well I guess he changed his mind."

"Did you know he was going to do this?"

"Listen, Neave," he said, standing up to face her, "you need to talk with Li, not me. He's been, like, hard to keep track of the last couple of weeks. He disappeared on some kind of trip, never telling me where the fuck he was going. Then he's been in a zillion meetings, telling me nada about any of them. He pops out of town and then, presto, he's back. I was as surprised as anyone. But I get paid to do his bidding, not vice versa."

He picked up a couple of large dumbbells and began a set of bicep curls.

"He's so changed," she said.

"Yeah, but you know, he's under a lot of stress now that he's a full-fledged prof. The bigwigs expect him to step into Osley's shoes ASAP. Faster than ASAP, actually. And those are some damn big shoes to fill. He's gotta teach class again tomorrow and he hasn't told me to fill in for him, so I'm guessing he'll be here. Maybe you can talk with him then."

He stopped lifting and looked directly at her.

"And, by the way," he said, "you need to chill a little. I mean, no offense or anything – you're still the best looking woman I know and I still occasionally wish you'd recognize my brutally macho Korean charms – but you've turned into one bossy, bitchy babe."

Part of her wanted to punch him and part of her wanted

to laugh. She opted for the latter, preferring to make peace with her good buddy. With Lena gone, he was her only good friend. And she suspected they were both feeling the loss more than cared to admit.

She was checking her iCom as she walked out of the gym, hoping for a message from Will, and was taken off guard by a crowd of people on the sidewalk. It appeared to be a spontaneous flash mob moving past her. It took her a moment to realize some of them were chanting "no shade ring." She watched as they streamed toward the center of campus. Then one of the marchers, a dark-haired young woman, pointed at Neave, telling her friends something. Several of them broke off from the main group and ran straight for her.

"You're Alvarez's daughter," the dark-haired girl cried. "He's the asshole who tricked the government into supporting the shade ring!"

"Yeah! And now they've let him go!" someone yelled.

"Special treatment!" a young man behind them shouted.

"Hell, yeah!" another student said.

"And he's your father!" the dark-haired girl said, jabbing her finger in Neave's shoulder.

"For your information, I happen to be against the shade ring," Neave said, surprising herself.

"Well then, get out here and join us!"

She latched onto Neave's arm and a tall, skinny guy took hold of her other arm. They yanked her along with them, chanting "no shade ring" over and over until they reached the courtyard outside the cantina where reporters with head cameras and camera glasses scurried around like ants searching for food. They were broadcasting live, waiting for a spokesperson to step forward – someone they could swarm with their cameras and microphones to keep their viewers glued to their coverage.

As they drew closer, Neave made a break for it, twisting away from her pushy escorts.

"You chicken shit!" the girl bellowed after her.

Neave zigzagged back through the throng of demonstrators until she broke free of the mass of bodies, as though the crowd had excreted a turd on the sidewalk. Which is pretty much how she felt.

Chapter 10

Speaking out against the shade ring was actually what she hoped to do, but on her own terms. She wasn't going to allow herself to be shanghaied, even if it was by a group she was sympathetic with. Still, as she trotted towards the MARTA station to catch a train, part of her took the fiery young woman's put-down to heart. Maybe she was a chicken shit.

Someone called her name. Looking over her shoulder with alarm, she spied Alexei hauling ass to catch up.

"Neave, wait!"

She reluctantly slowed to a fast walk.

"Have you seen what's happening?"

"Yeah, I saw them."

"I mean what's happening around the world."

"What're you talking about?"

He clicked his iCom and turned up the volume. A Canadian news site was broadcasting a live report of a massive demonstration, much bigger than the one on campus.

"Where's that?" she asked.

"Montreal. And look at this."

He clicked again. Another huge march.

"London," he said.

"Protesting the shade ring?"

"Yes. Here's another one."

He clicked again to a report of a giant demonstration with minarets in the background.

"Moscow?" she said.

"Moscow."

"Whoa."

"Your president badly misjudged world reaction if she thought people would lie down like doormats so she could wipe her shoes on them. Because once we head down the geo-engineering path, it would be like an addiction that's impossible to give up. And while some countries might benefit from blocking sunlight, others would suffer."

She clicked her own iCom, looking for a report on the campus protest. It only took a moment to find. She watched the small screen and listened as the dark-haired girl spoke directly into the camera.

"This is the only planet we've got!" she thundered. She was sweating profusely, her voice as loud and insistent as her personality. The graphics identified her as Haseya Roanhorse, with the Georgia Chapter of Indigenous Americans for the Environment. "We need to get rid of dirty energy like coal once and for all and make everyone use clean energy. You need to know the United Nations does not endorse geo-engineering because it's pretty damn obvious some countries will make out like bandits while others have to foot the bill. And why would the president take the word of our worthless ex-climate secretary that launching bits of space junk is the right thing to do? I mean, maybe we need to investigate the president to make sure she doesn't have some kind of vested interest in this solar shade ring bullshit. I wanna ask everyone watching me right now to speak out against this phony baloney coalition she cooked up."

Neave turned it off.

"I saw what happened back there," Alexei said, nodding his head in the direction of the protest. "Not that I agree with their methods, but it might help the cause if you did speak out.

Being the daughter of Robert Alvarez would get you a lot of media attention."

His eyes were intense and, for some reason, they suddenly didn't look like the eyes of a graduate student. They looked like the eyes of a man on a mission, the crinkles she now noticed at the corners suggesting he might be older than his early twenties.

"Who are you?"

"My name *is* Alexei Sokolov. But let's get out of this heat so we can talk."

"Not sure I want to go with you."

"The big food court three blocks from here. Lots of people. Out in the open."

She studied him for a moment, weighing whether she should join him. And weighing whether three blocks was a bit much for her. Once they left campus, there were no cooling centers on the way.

But he had piqued her interest. So, despite the uncharitable sun baking the city, they walked to the busy Centro Food Court where two dozen establishments lined a curved, air conditioned space jammed with white plasteel tables. The din of voices bounced off the tile floor to a high ceiling dotted with skylights. Sunshine streamed in from the west.

She got a blended juice, hoping it would help her cool down, while he bought an iced coffee.

"You're not really a student, are you?" she said, once they were seated at a tiny table she'd chosen in the center of the huge dining area.

"Yes, I am a graduate student. I'm enrolled in classes, seeking a master's degree in Climatology."

"But..."

"But I'm not *just* a student," he said, lowering his voice and leaning across the table. "I also work for the Russian government."

"You didn't accidentally spill coffee on me."

"No, I planned it."

"So you could meet me."

"Yes."

He glanced around like he was doing a security sweep.

"Before I go on," he said, "please understand my safety could be compromised if you reveal who I work for. Even to someone you trust. I'm not doing anything illegal and I'm not spying, but some people might perceive it differently."

She retwisted her hair into a knot on top of her head, desperate to cool the back of her neck.

"As you know by now," he continued, "my government strongly opposes the shade ring. It would not be in my country's best interests, or the best interests of most countries around the globe. So I'm hoping to convince you to speak out against your government's plan, which we knew was still on the table, even if you didn't."

She cleared her throat before responding.

"You say being the daughter of the ex-climate secretary would attract media attention but I don't believe there's anything I could say that would make a difference. Besides having the Alvarez name, which I'm not exactly proud of right now, I'm a nobody."

"You're wrong. If the daughter of Robert Alvarez – a daughter who also has a degree in Climatology – criticized the shade ring and reminded us why he was removed from office, that could make a big difference."

She sipped her raspberry/banana juice, trying to absorb everything. But her brain was fuzzy. She wasn't sure when she'd last eaten. She surveyed the food court until she spotted what she was looking for – a NeoBurger restaurant. She realized what she needed for her brain to function was protein. Her eyes lingered on their sign: "No animals killed, no rivers polluted to produce fresh, lab-grown meat."

"I need some protein," she said, scooting her chair back.

He jumped up.

"I will buy us both a burger," he said, noticing where she was looking.

So she let him do the honors, deciding maybe he owed her a little. He trotted over to get their sandwiches, looking over his shoulder, no doubt, to see whether she was making tracks behind his back.

It came to her as she waited that there was something about Alexei that made her want to trust him. She wasn't sure what it was exactly. She would have to tread cautiously though. She'd been fooled before.

~~~

She waited up for her mother that night, too anxious to sleep anyway, scanning news sites on her iCom, transmitting images to the wallscreen. There was more coverage of all the protests, in addition to statements from world leaders. Among them – Russian President Ania Kupchenko, who appeared before reporters to express her strong disapproval. Neave watched Kupchenko's statement with interest, especially after her talk with Alexei. She spoke in Russian, with her comments translated into English graphics that scrolled across the bottom of the screen.

"This is not space exploration. This is a unilateral initiative by the United States that would impact all nations without their consent. This program could harm agriculture and solar energy generation. The shade ring plan was an effort by former Climate Secretary Robert Alvarez to become rich and powerful. It is unconscionable that America's president would continue to pursue such a plan which has been exposed as pseudoscience."

Pseudoscience? Not exactly. Geo-engineering wasn't pseudoscience. It was based on a lot of research. The real question was whether it would produce the results that people – and nations – desired. But she knew in politics, if you say something often enough, people may eventually believe you. So she had to give it to President Kupchenko for her political savvy.

Her statement was followed by angry comments by Canadian Prime Minister Leo Habib, his dark eyes flashing.

"Canada has long been a good neighbor to the United States. We would like to continue that relationship. But relationships are a two-way street and it's time President Cohen faces up to the fact that she cannot dictate to the rest of the world. This solar shade ring is pure folly and Canada will not sit idly by and allow the US to lead a handful of countries down this path – a path that has serious implications for every nation around the world."

She powered down as he began making the same statement in French, wishing she could discuss it with Will. He was the person she could talk with about everything. She wondered what he would say. She almost clicked on his code. How silly of her. He wouldn't answer. He'd made it perfectly clear he didn't want her.

A scratching sound drew her eyes to the living room window. No doubt, a small animal rustling around in the yard. The darkness outside turned the window into a mirror and she didn't like the reflection staring back at her. Rounded shoulders, the corners of her mouth drooping.

She was suddenly transported back to kindergarten when

her school held its father-daughter dance on Valentine's Day. She remembered running into the dining room where her father was reading the evening news on his tablet and having his before dinner Tom Collins, to give him the hand-made invitation she'd colored. He laughed and told her he didn't have time for such nonsense. He said he wasn't like other fathers who held less important jobs. Then he told her to run along. That was her first real inkling that he might not be a nice person. She'd hurried back to her room and removed the sparkly silver tiara she'd put on her head, looking at her reflection in her vanity mirror – all prune-faced and wet with tears. Rosa, who was cooking supper, must've overheard everything, and appeared in her room a moment later, hugging her close, reassuring her that everything would be all right. The next day, her best friend J'nai invited her to go to the dance with her and her daddy. J'nai's dad took turns dancing with his own daughter and with the little white girl whose father wouldn't lower himself to waste his time on such a meaningless event.

She straightened her shoulders and gathered some cleaning supplies from the hall closet, deciding to make herself useful. She started a load of laundry, cleaned the bathroom, and had just begun dusting the furniture when she heard the front door open.

It was after midnight but Dr. Sullivan was more animated than Neave had ever seen her. And despite the streaks of grey in her auburn hair, she looked like she'd taken a sip from the fountain of youth.

"Mother, you look like you're on top of the world."

Which would've been impossible to imagine a few short weeks ago.

"Would you like to join me in a celebratory glass of wine?"

her mother said.

"What're we celebrating?"

Dr. Sullivan uncorked a bottle of Sauvignon Blanc and poured two glasses, handing one to Neave.

"To success!" she said, beaming.

Neave clinked her glass and they both took a sip.

"You've done it?" Neave asked.

"Yes."

"Really?"

Dr. Sullivan nodded and took another swig, her green eyes flashing.

Neave knew what she was talking about. She'd been working for years on cloning a human heart inside the chest cavity.

"Congratulations, Mother! I'm so proud of you."

"Thank you, dear. I don't think I've ever been happier. I'm holding a news conference tomorrow morning. I hope you can attend."

"I wouldn't miss it."

They talked for some time about the two patients Dr. Sullivan had successfully treated, both of them with newly regrown hearts. Her mother told her they were thriving, no complications. Neave knew how long she'd toiled in the lab, never giving up despite numerous setbacks.

Finally, Dr. Sullivan yawned and put her wine glass in the dishwasher.

"I've been talking non-stop," she said. "How was your day?"

"Interesting. I was dragged into the middle of a protest against the shade ring. One of the leaders tried to shame me into speaking out once she found out who I was."

"Oh dear."

"The thing is, I've been considering doing just that – coming out publicly against it. Some people think, as the daughter of the shade ring king – as he's known in some circles – I might actually have some influence."

Her mother planted her hands on her waist and closed her eyes for a moment.

"What do you think?" Neave asked.

"The news media would certainly jump all over it. It's possible a statement from you might carry as much weight as a big protest. I saw the news about all those demonstrations, by the way."

"What would you do if you were me?"

"I can't imagine being you, dear. That's beyond my ken."

"Sometimes it seems like it's beyond my ken too."

She added her glass to the dishwasher and pushed the start button, then showered, hoping to wash away all the adrenaline and cortisol pumping through her body. Her mother had called her brave back when she broke into the shade ring treaty signing, bringing a halt to the proceedings. But she didn't feel brave now. With her father sending her intimidating messages about not fraternizing with the enemy – Will and his family – she wondered how he would respond if she criticized the shade ring plan, using her famous last name as a PR tool. Because if there was one thing that had become obvious over the last few weeks, it was that her father was mentally unstable.

~~~

The media turned out en masse at Pioneer Genetics, reporters jockeying for position for the big announcement. Neave wore a grey outfit, trying to blend into the background, but noticed some cameras trained on her before her mother appeared.

"Wonder what the commentators are saying right now," she whispered to Rosa, beside her. "I wish they'd focus on

Mother, not me. She deserves the recognition."

"Cierto," Rosa said. "And I wish I could take a peek at Roberto's face when he sees all the news reports on her achievement. He always put Molly down, telling her she would fail, that she didn't have an original thought in her head. Estupido! Sad to say, though, that this will be something else for him to be jealous about."

"I know his mother was a drug addict who abandoned him, but..." Neave said, shaking her head.

"It's true, his mama was a terrible person. I was lucky – two loving parents. Sometimes I used to feel guilty that Roberto didn't have more affection when he was little. Our grandparents tried to love him, tried to help him, but he didn't seem to want love by then. He wanted..."

"Dominance," Neave said.

Their whispered conversation ended when Dr. Sullivan swept into the room, leading her researchers and assistants to a bank of microphones. She'd always been a punctual woman and that's one thing that had not changed. She looked radiant in a short green jacket with large black buttons and black slacks.

"Muy bonita," Rosa said, nodding in approval.

Dr. Sullivan waited a moment until all the reporters were ready.

"Thank you for coming out today on short notice," she began. "We've got some thrilling news. My team and I have succeeded in cloning a human heart inside a patient's body. Two patients, actually."

There was a stir as some reporters tapped away on their iComs.

"We've been working on this project for nearly twenty years," she continued. "We're excited to share our news with

101

the world and pleased the FDA has agreed to expedite the approval process for the procedure. And now we'd like to introduce one of our patients."

She looked past her team as a side door opened.

"This is Tom Benevidez," she said, "who suffered a massive heart attack last year. But we successfully cloned his heart and regrew it in situ – inside his chest. His newly regenerated heart muscle is now functioning normally."

Benevidez was average height with thick black hair that was greying at the temples. He and the two attendants on either side of him joined her center stage as Dr. Sullivan and her staffers applauded.

"Thank you, Dr. Sullivan," he said, smiling nervously. "And my thanks to your team and to all the medical staff who helped make this a success. I can't tell you what this means to me and my family."

Then the reporters with their camera glasses and lights were calling out questions, some to Dr. Sullivan and some to her patient. It was a rare moment of triumph for her mother, and Neave couldn't help but feel a sense of pride.

But then Rosa tapped her on the arm.

"I've gotta go," she whispered. "I told Angela I wouldn't be long."

Neave followed her to the lobby.

"Everything all right at the house?"

"There's a lot of stress and worry. Angela's muy preocupada."

"I'll go with you."

They rode together in a driverless hub car. Neave found it comforting being with Rosa again.

"How are you and Angela doing?" she asked as they made their way through the city.

"In some ways it's like we've never been apart. But she's been a mother all these years while I haven't."

"You mothered me. And you certainly mothered Lena."

Rosa smiled sadly at the mention of her troubled niece.

"I wish I had done a better job with Lena," she said. "Sometimes I feel like I opened the gate for her to the lion's den, leading her directly to Roberto and the drugs he used to control people."

She held her hands out, palms up, as though she were asking for forgiveness.

"You did your best," Neave said softly.

Rosa snorted.

"I don't have a great track record," she said. "And they're Angela's children, not mine. I have to be careful not to overstep my bounds, if you know what I mean. I try to lend a sympathetic ear without offering too much advice." She clasped her hands in her lap. "There's just been so much ansiedad – anxiety – about the storm, the house, about Toni and Gib, and Will's concussion. I just try to be there for her."

"I'm sure having you close means a lot."

When they got to the house, they found Angela slumped over at the dining room table like a dying sunflower, Charlie and Jaz on either side of her.

"What is it, mi amor?" Rosa said.

Angela looked mournfully into her eyes.

"Will has disappeared too."

Chapter 11

"What are *you* doing here?" Jaz hissed, giving Neave the evil eye. "You're not a part of this family!"

She remembered the first time she laid eyes on Jaz in Charleston. The big laugh, the smartass comments. She was still the same snarky person, but any sense of humor was long gone.

"I..." Neave started.

"Get out!"

"Jaz, stop it," Charlie said. "She *is* a member of our family."

"Not anymore," Jaz said, glaring at Neave. "Bad shit started happening when you showed up. And now Will's gone missing. You need to leave us alone!"

Rosa stood behind Angela, placing her hands on her shoulders.

"Enough, Jaz," Angela said, her voice barely above a whisper, focusing on Neave. "I don't suppose you've heard from him?"

How different she looked now, Neave thought, with dark circles under her eyes, in a faded robe – no longer the cheerful matriarch.

"No," she replied, then addressed herself to Jaz. "You're right." And she marched out the front door.

She turned off her iCom as she slid into the hub car, heading first for the bank where she withdrew most of the money in her account. Then she drove to the Fernbank Museum of Natural History. She used cash for a ticket and made her way to the indoor waterfall.

Wooden park benches and fake tree stumps provided visitors somewhere to sit and soak up the beauty. They'd gone to great lengths to recreate the falls and ponds like those that used to exist in the Atlanta area back when rivers and streams were full. The waterfall tumbled from a precipice about twenty feet high, creating a spray of droplets that wet your hair and eyelashes if you got too close.

She studied the smooth rocks and pebbles and the lovely green moss that covered the wet soil, where pretty ferns and orchids made her feel, for a moment, like she was in a rainforest. The sound of splashing water drowned out people's voices and she could hear the twittering of birds above her. A recording, no doubt, but a nice touch, nonetheless.

She was twelve years old on her last visit here. That was when her father left on one of his mysterious trips. As usual, he made a mean game of it, saying it was top secret – that he was not allowed to reveal his destination. Which only made Neave more curious. After he left, she was so upset that Rosa suggested they go on a mystery trip as well, just the two of them. She said their mission was classified and they were not to tell anyone their destination. Rosa brought her to the museum and they sat on one of these very benches, watching the water plunge onto the polished stones below. Neave was about to take a picture with her iCom but Rosa said that would be evidence of where they'd been which might reveal their clandestine operation. Neave smiled, remembering the fun she and Rosa had. Afterwards, they stopped by her favorite ice cream parlor and pigged out on butter pecan ice cream. And they never told her mother or her father – especially not her father – about their undercover operation.

Rosa knew what she was talking about when it came to evidence. After her father got back from that particular trip, he told Rosa one evening as she was serving dinner that he wanted her to make some Navajo tacos, made with Indian fry bread.

"No sé cómo," Rosa said. "That's not something I know how to make."

"I'm sure you can learn," her father said, using his most imperious tone.

When Neave got home from school the next day, Rosa was hard at work in the kitchen, grousing under her breath about having to figure out how to make Indian fry bread.

"He must've visited New Mexico," Rosa muttered. "That's where they make Navajo tacos. But I'm not from New Mexico."

A couple of years later, after another of her father's trips, she was helping Rosa make sweet concha buns.

"Did you see the Indian pottery your father brought back?" Rosa asked.

"He put it in his office. And since I'm not allowed in there, I never got to look at it."

Rosa made sure no one was within earshot and lowered her voice.

"Well, when I dusted his office this morning I noticed the bottom of that bowl and it's signed by the artist. It also says Jemez Pueblo. You know where that is?"

"Where?"

"New Mexico."

Neave remembered those conversations vividly now. Because at the time, it solved a great mystery she was keen to get to the bottom of. She also remembered overhearing a conversation between her mother and Rosa a few days after one of her father's trips when she was in high school. She'd been in her room studying but decided to get a snack. Just as she was walking through the dining room she heard their voices in the kitchen.

"It's none of our business."

"I know, Molly, but I thought you'd be interested that the laundry bag he brought home with his dirty clothes says Gran Hotel Albuquerque."

"I'd just as soon not know," Dr. Sullivan replied.

She closed her eyes as the water cascaded onto the rocks and the make-believe birds sang happy songs in the branches of giant artificial maple trees, whose leaves were programmed to simulate the changing seasons. They were just beginning to turn from summer green to a showy reddish orange. She relaxed for a moment, knowing it might be her last chance to do so for quite a while.

Then she drove to the condo, changed into her light green climate suit and stuffed some clothes and toiletries in her backpack. She left her mother an old-fashioned, handwritten note on the kitchen table – to guarantee it wouldn't be found till later – that she was going on a brief research expedition. Next, she returned the hub car and used cash to rent a scooter at the trans station. She drove to the Airport hotel where Will had parked his EV when he flew out of Atlanta. He'd added her fingerprint to the security app so she was able to open the door and start the car without a problem. First, she checked the battery. Thankfully, it was ninety percent charged – good for a cross country sprint. She popped the hatch and loaded the scooter in the rear, drove to the nearest trans station and returned it. Next, she visited the library where she used a computer to do a bit of last-minute research. On her way out of town she stopped by a discount store and picked up a few supplies. It was nearly three o'clock when she passed the city limit sign, traveling west on I-20.

She was sure she knew where Will, Toni and Gib were. She was also certain her father was behind their disappearance. And she was positive he had somehow tapped into her iCom and was probably monitoring the Galloways with cameras or microphones installed in the house years before. He always knew if she'd had contact with Will or any of his family. He seemed to know everything she was doing. So she wouldn't even turn her iCom on as she drove across the country. That way no one could track her.

There was no time to waste because when it became obvious she was gone, everyone, including her father, would be looking for her. So she would drive non-stop, using the driverless mode when she had to. Flying or taking the JetTube would be faster but would require an iris scan and fingerprint payment, which meant leaving an e-trail.

As she passed through Alabama's parched terrain she wondered why it took her so long to put two and two together. It was Jaz's angry comment that finally opened her eyes. How did she put it? Bad shit started to happen when Neave arrived in their midst. She was sure Jaz didn't blame her for the hurricane. But ever since Will took Neave home to introduce her to his family, Jaz had been openly hostile, holding her responsible for her parents. She'd been particularly skeptical about Neave's mother, but it turned out it was her father she should've been worried about.

She didn't know what she would do once she arrived at the American Climate Institute's Albuquerque research station. It all came together as she remembered Rosa's clues about her father's secret trips. That was the one destination he never shared with his family, his top secret port of call, so to speak.

That's why she used the computer at the library – to find the exact location of the facility – without using her iCom or a computer at home that might be hacked. One tantalizing bit of information she discovered online was that the station had been temporarily deactivated, probably because of funding problems stemming from her father's absence. Making it a perfect place to hold people prisoner.

The Institute had placed Dr. Alvarez on a leave of absence after his arrest. Someone else was Acting Director now. But she didn't know if all ties had been severed or whether her father still had his tentacles in the organization. He had likely corrupted at least some of the staff, possibly getting them hooked on Discretion, the same drug he used to control Nat and Lena. She focused on the solar roadway panels ahead of her, not really wanting to revisit the distressing events of the past couple of months.

She was driving directly into the setting sun. If she hadn't been in such a hurry, she would've stopped and gotten a bite to eat and waited for the sun to drop below the horizon. But there was no time for that, so she just squinted through her shades and pressed on until she reached the Mississippi River at Memphis before making a pit stop.

She crossed the once mighty Mississippi, now reduced in width and depth by decades of drought. The freeway bridge was busy with cars and trucks but the river channel wasn't deep enough for giant barges anymore.

The Arkansas Welcome Center was welcome, indeed. She and several other travelers exited into the rest stop. Although it was dark now, the rest area was well lit. She parked the vehicle and walked quickly to the ladies room. She stretched as she walked, well aware she wasn't quite a third of the way to her destination and already fatigued, at least partly because she hadn't fully recovered yet from dengue. She didn't want to be reminded of that unpleasantness either.

Heading back to the EV, she'd just stepped down from the curb and reached to touch the keypad on the door when she realized someone was close behind her. She whirled around to find a man and a woman only a few feet away, both of them tall and slender with small backpacks dangling from their shoulders. But with a streetlight behind them, she couldn't make out their faces, only their silhouettes.

"You drive like a maniac," the woman said.

Her husky voice had a familiar ring to it. For a split second she thought it was Toni and Gib, but immediately realized it was Jaz and Charlie. It must've been obvious Neave's heart was in her throat.

"Don't worry," Charlie said, "nobody knows we're here."

She couldn't decide what to say. She didn't want to say anything. This was not part of her plan.

"I've gotta go," she mumbled. "No offense."

"We wanna help," Charlie said. "We've got a sneaking suspicion you know where they are."

She flinched as though he'd threatened her. What if her father was tracking them? All her precautions would be for naught.

"Dammit," she finally said.

"The feeling is mutual," Jaz shot back. "But three heads are better than one."

"You don't understand."

"Explain it to us," Jaz said.

"I don't have time!" She slapped the hood of the car. "I've gotta get back on the road! And I really need for you to turn around and go home."

"No can do," Charlie replied. "So fill us in."

"The short version," Jaz added.

"Did you tell anyone you were following me?" Neave asked.

"No," they both said.

"Are your iComs on?"

Jaz stared at her like she was a dimwit.

"Have you been using them?"

"We haven't made any calls," said Charlie.

"Just looked up a couple of things," Jaz said.

Neave let loose with a low growl of frustration.

"Spit it out," Jaz snapped.

"My father's been spying on me. And I think the house you guys are living in is wired. So he's been spying on all of you as well. It didn't come together in my brain until this morning."

Which took the steam out of Jaz's cockiness.

"And the iComs?" Charlie said.

"I'm pretty sure he's got mine tapped because he always knows about my conversations and messages. So I turned it off this morning. I'm only using cash, not making any calls, not accessing the internet, nothing."

"So where you headed?" Jaz asked.

"I've gotta get back on the road," Neave said. "No time to lose."

"We're going with you," Jaz insisted.

"I don't think so."

"Three is better than one for a rescue mission," Charlie said. "Let's hit the road."

Neave hesitated a moment, but the logical part of her brain convinced her they were probably right.

"What about your car?"

"We'll retrieve it later," Jaz said.

"Then turn off your iComs," Neave ordered.

Charlie started to sit in back but Jaz said she wanted to take a snooze, so he sat up front beside Neave. She was relieved, although she suspected Jaz opted for the back to keep her distance.

"Have you been trailing me since I left the house this morning?"

"No," Jaz said. "We wouldn't've come at all except the GPS alarm on Will's vehicle alerted us someone was driving it. If it was Will, he would've deactivated the alarm."

"Yeah, we didn't know who took off in his car," Charlie explained. "But we were able to follow it because all our vehicles have GPS tracking devices on them. We started doing that a few years ago when one of our trucks was stolen. Of course, it took us a while to catch up because you had the pedal to the metal."

"So where we going?" Jaz said.

"Albuquerque."

Chapter 12

As the baked flatland that once boasted rich cotton fields flew by in the darkness outside their windows, the conversation centered on their mission.

"So why Albuquerque?" Charlie asked.

Neave wasn't sure that sharing memories of her father's secret trips and the clues Rosa uncovered would sound terribly convincing to her new teammates so she opted for a more concise response.

"The American Climate Institute, which my father led for many years, has a research station there. And I believe that's where they're being held."

"You got some evidence?" Jaz said.

"Circumstantial."

"Such as?"

Naturally, Jaz would want more.

"It's a gut feeling based on my father's secret trips when I was growing up."

"We're driving all the way to Albuquerque based on a gut feeling?"

"I'll pull over and let you out right now if that's what you want," Neave snapped, taking her foot off the accelerator as she eyed Jaz in the rearview mirror.

"Don't pull over," Charlie said. "You must have a good reason to suspect that's where they are, otherwise you wouldn't be wasting your time driving across the country when it would've been a lot quicker on the JetTube."

He peered at Jaz in the back, obviously trying to send her a message to chill out as Neave sped up again.

"Iris scans," Neave said. "Didn't want to be tracked. Although, obviously, I didn't totally succeed."

Charlie gave her a friendly shrug.

"Did you tell anyone you were doing this?" he said.

"No one."

"You got a plan?" Jaz asked.

"Yeah. Get the lay of the land and play it by ear."

"Killer strategy. And if you don't mind my asking, how you planning to protect yourself?"

"I bought a Swiss army knife on my way out of town."

"Whoa, that'll definitely scare the shit out of the bad guys!"

"Stop it, sis," Charlie said. "You're not helping. If you wanna help, zip it."

Jaz opened her mouth to speak but closed it again.

"You guys have weapons?" Neave asked.

"Real guns," Jaz said, dripping with sarcasm.

Which made Neave more anxious or less anxious. She couldn't decide which.

Finally, Jaz went to sleep, or pretended to. A relief either way. And Charlie stopped trying to make conversation. Neave refueled on a banana and some peanuts, sharing her feed bag with him.

But it wasn't long before the roar of tires on pavement made her eyelids heavy. She stifled a yawn, intent on driving as long as possible. Maybe a little more conversation would help.

"You think it's a good idea to focus on the energy business?" she said, keeping her voice down.

Charlie peeked over his shoulder, checking on Jaz before responding.

"Yeah, I think Will's right," he said quietly.

"Why?"

"You know how many climate refugees there are?"

"Well..."

"Do you have any idea how many there'll be if warming continues and oceans keep rising?"

"Millions."

"Billions, with a B. And it's not the rich and powerful who lose their homes and businesses. They can afford to move inland. It's marginalized people being ignored, mistreated and left behind, just like in a Charles Dickens novel. So Will's right. We should focus on the clean energy business."

"Dickens."

"Don't get me wrong – Dickens wasn't perfect. Far from it. In fact, if he were alive today, he might very well be anti-clone. He was in many ways a man of his time. But one thing he excelled at was painting vivid pictures for the masses of the unfairness and brutality of the economic chasm between rich and poor."

Interesting, she thought, being the namesake of the British author apparently helped mold his outlook on life. Here she'd been concentrating on global warming's impact on the earth, while Charlie saw it in terms of its consequences for humanity.

"I'm impressed, Charlie."

"Likewise."

She tossed him a questioning glance.

"Well," he said, "it was you who convinced Will he deserves to be treated like a full-fledged human being. Before you came along, he was 'Mister Lay-Low Galloway,' hoping nobody would find out he was a clone, staying on the periphery so people wouldn't notice him. Not anymore."

Which just stirred up all of her emotions.

"And I've gotta say," he continued, "I really respect clones who aren't afraid to stand up and be counted. Like Will. And your mother. I saw her on the news saying you were the one who taught her to speak out. So maybe you're the common denominator here. One thing's for sure, it takes cojones to publicly admit you're a clone and demand respect."

She couldn't talk about Will right now.

"Well, I hope it doesn't cause a family rift," she said. "The two businesses, I mean."

"Nah. Something like that would never happen in our family. If the others want to continue with antiques and demolition, it's all good. Jaz has already made it clear she's gonna head up the demolition work. She loves sitting in the cab of those giant machines and knocking down all those old buildings."

He chuckled, sneaking a look into the back seat again.

"Just part of her personality, I guess," he added.

No amount of conversation could keep her awake forever, though. And when they were about two thirds of the way through Arkansas, she gave in and let Charlie drive. She shifted to the back seat and Jaz moved up front. It only took her a few minutes to drift off.

Maybe it was because Charlie was at the wheel that Neave slept so soundly. He was the kind of person you trusted. When she opened her eyes, it was still dark and she had no idea how much shut-eye she'd gotten. She was too tired to move and lay there listening to the hum of the engine, the tires whizzing over solar roadway panels and low voices in the front seat.

"I've already lined up a crew," Jaz said. "I'll be the foreman now."

"Where?"

"Houston. A ton of buildings to demolish."

"When?"

"Coupla weeks."

"What about insurance?"

"Don't need it."

That's when the highway suddenly became unusually rough. At least that's what Neave thought as the vehicle began to vibrate.

"Charlie!" Jaz cried. "Stop, stop, stop!"

Neave was thrown against the back of their seats as Charlie slammed on the brakes and the tires skidded. Jaz cursed and Charlie groaned as the car shuddered to a halt.

Neave slowly raised herself off the floor.

"Don't move!" Jaz whispered.

Her heart was in her throat as she watched a long span of the bridge they were on collapse into the river below them with a horrifying screech of metal and concrete. It seemed to fall in slow motion, their vehicle only a couple of feet from the ragged edge. The street lights winked out and they were plunged into darkness. But the streetlamps on the other side of the yawning divide provided just enough light to see that the only thing in front of them was air. And there was a very real possibility the span on which they were perched might buckle as well.

"Shit!" Charlie cried, eyes glued to the rearview mirror.

Neave whirled around to see a pair of headlights approaching fast. Charlie switched on the flashers and sounded his horn, trying to warn the unsuspecting driver. There was the piercing sound of rubber scouring the roadway as the other driver braked hard. They braced themselves for impact, waiting helplessly to tumble over the precipice into the river. But the car veered to the right to avoid them and skidded to a halt beside them.

Charlie jammed the car in reverse and backed up, all three of them watching the road behind them for more vehicles. Then he rammed it in drive and turned the wheel sharply to make a U-turn. The other car did likewise. But then they spotted a big truck approaching from the east, its double headlights and cab lights visible in the dark. Charlie honked the horn repeatedly and flashed his headlights, trying desperately to signal the trucker to stop. The other car did the same. They watched as the driver of the big rig downshifted and hit the brakes, causing the semi to jackknife, folding in half and sliding directly toward them. Charlie veered as far to the right as he could while the driver of the other car swung to the left. Neave felt like she was in one of those car crash compilations you could watch on the web where you knew, unlike in digital games, real people died in the crashes. And she was afraid that's what was about to happen to them, that they were on the verge of becoming the latest dead web stars who went out with a bang. In some ways, it was like time slowed down but it all happened in the blink of an eye – the big truck grinding to a halt between the two cars, coming to rest at the edge of what was left of the mangled freeway bridge.

Charlie didn't pause to look, accelerating until they were back on solid ground, on the shoulder of the eastbound lanes. The driver of the other car followed suit.

The operator of the big truck jumped down from the cab and ran toward them, already on his iCom. Neave, Jaz and Charlie got out of the EV and stood on the dirt with the woman who'd been driving the other car.

"It was an earthquake, six-point-five on the Richter scale," the trucker shouted. "I contacted the cops but they'd already been alerted by sensors on the bridge and they've started diverting..."

He stopped speaking, distracted by yet another approaching vehicle. They all turned to look as headlights appeared out of the darkness. Charlie jumped in the car and flashed his lights and honked the horn as the rest of them waved their arms frantically, trying to signal the driver. But a small EV swept past them at a high rate of speed, no doubt in autonomous mode with the driver asleep. The brake lights turned red way too late as the car's sensors belatedly detected a problem. They watched in horror as it slammed into the abandoned semi, sending the big rig and the smaller vehicle plunging over the edge into the water below.

Neave clapped her hand over her mouth as the truck driver called police again to tell them what they'd just witnessed. She, Charlie and Jaz started toward the bridge to check for survivors but stopped in their tracks when another section collapsed into the river. They stared helplessly at each other. And that's when they heard the first siren.

A dozen police, fire and rescue vehicles roared to a halt in front of them. Flashing lights were placed across the freeway to stop traffic while firefighters and EMTs scrambled down the river bank.

Neave and the others were asked to give brief statements. The truck driver, a middle-aged guy named Gio, told them he probably would've ended up at the bottom of the river except he drove this route every week and knew the bridge was jinxed. He explained that the Webbers Falls Bridge collapsed more than a hundred years before, killing fourteen people whose vehicles plunged into the Arkansas River. He said it wasn't caused by a quake that time, but a barge that slammed into bridge supports.

"I always override driverless mode and slow down when I reach this section of I-40," he said. "I'm kinda superstitious."

Neave knew it wasn't uncommon for a bridge to collapse during an earthquake. Especially here. Oklahoma came late to upgrading its built environment to withstand seismic activity after fracking for natural gas reactivated local fault lines in the early twenty-first century. Another contributing factor was global warming, which exacerbated the problem as melting shifted the earth's weight load, increasing stress along all geological faults. There was also the sinking of the landscape, caused by depletion of underground aquifers.

Although they were shaken, they knew they had to get back on the road. The State Patrol advised them to head south, staying off I-40 until they were well on the other side of Oklahoma City, which had suffered damage from the quake as well. Jaz took a turn driving with Charlie beside her while Neave sat in back, trying to calm her nerves. They were in a line of vehicles on the detour route, which meant, in addition to adding extra miles, they were losing time because they had to drive more slowly.

"We should've avoided I-40," Jaz said. "Everyone knows Oklahoma has too many quakes."

"It's the fastest route," Charlie replied.

"Not anymore."

Charlie's shoulders drooped.

"I wonder how many people were in that car," he finally said, shaking his head.

"And we nearly…" Jaz began, but Charlie interrupted her.

"I guess it was a good thing it happened in the middle of the night. If it had been during the day, who knows how many lives would've been lost."

"A patrolman said two cars went into the river on the other side."

"Damn," Charlie said.

Neave closed her eyes, letting her head rest on the back of the seat.

Everyone got quiet then, lost in their own gloomy thoughts after a close call that seemed to reinforce the theory that life was a crap shoot. Eventually, she dozed off. And when her eyes opened again, they were driving through Amarillo. She actually gasped when she saw the sign.

"You okay?" Charlie asked.

She nodded. She wasn't going to tell him how she really felt. If she were a yellow jacket, she'd be releasing an alarm pheromone, alerting her fellow wasps to a threat. Then again, maybe she'd actually emitted some kind of signal and Charlie already knew her heart was racing and her blood was pumping through her veins so forcefully, she could hear it.

Chapter 13

After a brief pit stop, Neave got behind the wheel for the last leg of the trip. The vista was like something out of a western – dry as the bleached skull of a steer from back in the day. Accelerating onto the freeway, her eyes were drawn upwards. Huge black birds circled above them, their wings spread wide as they soared on warm thermals. She cringed, recognizing them as vultures.

As they crossed the state line into New Mexico, her hands ached from clutching the steering wheel like it was a weapon. The danger of their mission now seemed excruciatingly real.

It was late afternoon as she drove through Tijeras Canyon into Albuquerque, then headed north on I-25 for another fifteen minutes until she came to the exit she was looking for. Although it might not be the best time of day for a rescue operation, they couldn't risk waiting. The element of surprise was critical.

She parked two blocks from the research station on the outskirts of Rio Rancho and slid her roll of sensor tape onto her left wrist like a bracelet. Then she tucked her new Swiss army knife in her pocket.

Jaz looked at her like she was pathetic as she and Charlie pulled their handguns from their backpacks and tucked them in their waistbands.

It was a warehouse district. Lots of trucks, large, nonde-script buildings, rocks and cacti. It was about 115 degrees but ominous thunderstorms darkened the western sky, meaning it might get a little cooler rather than hotter.

When they spotted the Climate Institute sign in front of a tan brick building, they slowed their pace.

"Let's slip around back," Neave said, pocketing a handful of rocks from a landscaped area along the driveway.

When Jaz took the lead, Neave suddenly remembered thinking she was Toni at the rest stop. They were twins, for all intents and purposes, and that might just give them an edge.

"Jaz, you pretend to be Toni," she said. "We'll make some noise and see if we can get someone to open the back door."

"And shoot me dead on the spot."

"I'll cover you," Charlie said.

"Mucho reassuring," Jaz replied.

There was a loading ramp leading up to the back door, in addition to some steps. A green van was the only vehicle in the small parking lot.

"Stand at the bottom of the ramp," Neave said, nodding her head at Jaz.

Neave and Charlie positioned themselves close to the building on either side of the door, Charlie with his gun drawn. Jaz held hers behind her. When they were ready and her heart was about to explode from her chest, Neave tossed one of her rocks at the door.

It made a small plink. They waited. She lobbed a second one, harder than the first. Again, no response. She withdrew two rocks from her other pocket and threw them as hard as she could. They heard a noise from within and the door opened a couple of inches. Neave flattened herself against the bricks.

"Shit," said Jaz, shaking her head.

"Hey!" a man cried, opening the door all the way. He stared

in confusion at the tall, slender black woman looking up at him from the parking lot. He was a Latino guy, the size of a football player. "How'd you..." he said, waving a large hand-gun with a silencer as he rushed toward her.

The door started to swing shut but Neave moved quickly and blocked it with her foot.

"Drop it!" Charlie yelled, aiming his weapon at the guard who whirled around in surprise, his gun extended.

"He said drop it," Jaz barked, pointing her own pistol at the man's back.

He froze, his eyes darting from Charlie to Neave to a point above them. She figured that's where a security camera was mounted and braced herself for another guard to burst through the door.

"Drop your weapon!" Charlie said.

Finally, the guard lowered his gun.

"Toss it over there," Charlie commanded, nodding toward Neave's side of the ramp.

The guard did as he was told.

"Hands up!" Jaz said.

He slowly complied.

Neave placed one of her shoes in the door to hold it open and hurried over to the guard, telling him to lie face down and put his hands behind his back. She used her sensor tape to bind his wrists tightly together and then she taped his ankles and knees together. Finally, she put a large piece of tape over his mouth.

"Let's go," she said, retrieving his weapon and running for the door.

It was at that moment the door flew open and another guard appeared, a burly Asian guy with a shaved head. He aimed his weapon right at Neave's chest. She instinctively hit the deck and rolled off the ramp onto the parking lot, landing hard on her butt.

"Drop it or I'll shoot!" Jaz cried at the top of her lungs.

Like the first guard, he was obviously confused about one of his prisoners suddenly appearing outside with a gun in her hand. But he didn't look inclined to give up.

"Don't even think about it," Charlie warned.

Neave jumped up and moved behind him, pulling her big roll of tape off her wrist.

"Toss the gun on the ground," Charlie cried. "Now!"

He reluctantly followed orders and Neave soon had him bound and gagged a few feet from his compadre. She retrieved his gun and her shoe as they entered the building, Charlie and Jaz holding their weapons in front of them.

"Don't shoot any Galloways," Charlie cautioned his sister, who grunted in reply.

Neave ditched the guards' guns right away, dropping them in a garbage chute by the back door. They were useless to anyone besides their owners since fingerprints were required to shoot them.

They moved quietly down a central hallway, scanning each room as they came to it, waiting for a hail of bullets. They had no clue how many guards were in the building or whether reinforcements might be closing in from another location.

Then there was a noise. Jaz hid in a room on the right while Neave and Charlie slipped through an open door on the left. They held their breath, listening. Neave pulled the last rock from her pocket and showed it to Charlie and Jaz, who both nodded. She tossed it down the hallway. Then a tapping noise came from one of the rooms.

They eased out of their hiding places and stepped lightly, pausing to listen. There was a second sound. A cat maybe?

There were four closed doors at the end of the hallway, two on either side. They tiptoed ahead, checking behind them with every step. When they came to the first closed door, Charlie waved Jaz to the right while he moved to the left. He gestured for Neave to hang back. Then he nodded at Jaz who turned the knob. With the door ajar, they could hear a tapping and a muffled noise that sounded like a voice. Neave sat down on the floor, sliding on her butt until she was close enough and kicked the door open as Charlie and Jaz leapt in front of her, brandishing their guns.

From her position, she could see between their legs to the far side of the room where Gib was seated in an office chair, tape over his mouth, his arms pulled behind him, his legs bound to the chair with wire, his ankles tightly strapped together with more wire. His eyes filled with tears as he looked up into the faces of his brother and sister.

"Shh," Charlie whispered. "We'll get you out of here."

Jaz moved back to the doorway to stand guard while Neave hurried into the room. First she removed the tape from his mouth but held her finger up to caution him to be quiet. Then she pulled out her new knife and used its handy little wire cutter to clip the wire tying his wrists together behind the chair. She cut through the wire on his legs and ankles as well and then looked him in the eye.

"You all right?" she whispered.

"They drugged me," he said in a hoarse whisper, as more tears welled up. "Kinda woozy."

"Can you walk?" Charlie asked.

"Yeah."

They repeated the procedure in the next room and freed Toni.

"Hurry," Toni whispered. "More guards will be here soon."

"Did they drug you too?" Neave asked.

Toni nodded in reply.

They moved to the closed door across the hallway, but when they opened it, no one was inside. There were several video monitors, a couple of chairs and half-eaten Chinese take-out. On the monitors they watched the guards in the parking lot for a second, wriggling with all their might to break free.

They moved quickly to the last door. Neave kicked it open and Charlie and Jaz rushed into the room, guns drawn. This time it was Neave whose eyes filled with tears. Will was bound to a chair as Toni and Gib had been, but he was also blindfolded.

"Hey, brother," Charlie whispered. "We're busting you outta this joint."

Neave rushed to his side and removed the blindfold first. He squinted at her, a fleeting gaze of tenderness, or was she just imagining things? Then he looked around the now crowded room. Jaz and Charlie stood guard in the doorway. Toni and Gib were startled at the sight of their brother as Neave pulled the tape from his mouth and moved behind him to cut the wires on his wrists.

"I didn't..." Gib started, but Toni shushed him. He lowered his voice to a whisper. "I didn't know you were here too."

Will rubbed his wrists, but said nothing as Neave cut the wires on his legs and ankles.

"Let's go," Charlie said, leading them out the same way they came in.

The guards stopped struggling and lay motionless on the pavement as the former captives and their liberators hurried through the door. Everyone trotted around the side of the building except Neave. She stopped at the green van parked out back and used her knife to slash two tires before jogging to catch up with the others.

They hurried the two blocks to their vehicle as the sky got darker and the wind picked up. Will's EV wasn't actually big enough for six but it would have to do.

"You wanna drive?" Neave asked him.

"They gave me Discretion," he said.

Which explained his slow responses.

Just as they were opening the doors, a green van flashed by them, then screeched to a halt.

"Get in, get in, get in!" Neave cried, jumping behind the wheel and cranking the engine. "That's just like the van parked behind the research station."

"We're in, let's go!" Jaz shouted from her spot in the cargo area in the back.

Neave slapped it in reverse and backed up to the intersection behind them. Then she slammed it in drive and did a sharp U-turn. She looked in the rearview and saw the van turning around, tires squealing, coming after them.

Chapter 14

Neave knew she needed to go southeast to get back to the interstate. But she was headed to the northwest. Fast. Glancing in the rearview mirror, she couldn't tell if the two guys in the van behind them had guns but based on their experience at the research station, she could only assume the worst.

She kept looking for a street on the right, hoping to double back, but there wasn't one. All she could see was a road coming up on the other side. So she made a hard left and gunned it, giving the rearview a quick glance.

"Oh my God," Gib said from his spot directly behind her.

"Damn," Toni said.

"What?" Neave cried.

"That's not a thunderstorm," Will said from the back seat. "It's a monster dust storm."

A towering brown cloud was sweeping toward them like a desert tsunami. She'd seen images and videos of dust storms, but facing one in person made her throat dry.

"Neave! Look out!" Charlie squawked.

She yanked her attention back to the road in front of her just as it came to an end. She hit the brakes hard, throwing everyone forward before bouncing off the pavement onto the bone-dry mesa. She picked up speed again with the green van close behind them, the driver obviously undeterred by the rough terrain.

"Make a loop and head back the way we came!" Jaz cried.

"Quick, before we run into a giant friggin' rock."

She swooped to the right, preparing to make a wide turn toward the left.

"He's closing on us!" Jaz yelled.

When she checked the rearview and saw the van was only a couple of car lengths behind them, she accelerated again, careening over small cactus bushes, rocks and gullies, jolting everyone so violently, their heads hit the ceiling.

"Turn, turn!" Charlie barked.

The maps she'd studied online weren't topo maps and she didn't know she was driving along the edge of a canyon. She swung around sharply to the left, causing the vehicle to tilt, threatening for a second to roll over, before landing again on all four wheels.

"Can you shoot his tires out or something?" Neave cried.

Jaz opened the rear window partway and fired off several shots, one of them striking the pursuing van's windshield. Someone screamed – Neave wasn't sure who it was, might've been her – and watched in horror as the van swerved sharply to the right and launched into the air like an Olympic swimmer exploding off the block. Only there was no water to land in, just the canyon below.

"Turn, turn, turn!" Charlie yelled.

She yanked her foot off the accelerator and hit the brake just as the EV headed down a washed-out ravine. Panicked voices filled the vehicle as she struggled to keep them from turning over, the car bouncing so hard she feared the axles might come off the chassis. But finally, finally… they came to a halt, the vehicle leaning precariously to the left.

"Quick, everyone out on the right side," she whispered. "Don't open the doors on the left."

Charlie hopped out first, holding the front passenger door

as he opened the back door as well.

"Damn," he said. "Mucho static electricity."

Toni, Will and Gib exited through the back door while Neave crawled over the console in the front to step out on the passenger side. Then Jaz shimmied from the cargo area over the back seat, preparing to follow the others. But without their weight to hold it down, the vehicle began to slip.

"Jaz!" Toni cried.

Will and Gib pulled her from the car just as it tipped, then slid down the ravine, bumping into rocks and lurching over fissures on its rough descent. Jaz grunted, landing on her knees, then wheezed and rolled onto her back, lying there with her eyes closed for a moment. Gib sat down beside her and held her hand.

"Are you all right?" he asked.

"No thanks to Neave, the fucking race car driver," she said, her eyes still closed.

"Come on, Jaz," Charlie said. "If it weren't for Neave…"

"No time for that," Will blurted.

Everyone followed his gaze. The giant dust storm was closing fast. It towered thousands of feet in the air, a huge wall of swirling brown dirt and sand that looked like thick, billowing smoke. It extended as far as the eye could see from north to south – a dangerous leviathan. And it was about to swallow them.

"Can you suffocate in one of those things?" Gib asked.

"It's called a haboob," Charlie said.

"Good to know," Jaz sniped.

"We have two choices," Will said. "Slide down the gorge and get back in the vehicle or huddle behind a big rock. But we've gotta move fast."

Neave remembered learning about dust storms and how

131

dangerous they could be. In big storms like this one, some people stranded outside actually did choke to death. Shelter was critical, but this time there were no safe rooms nearby.

"The car," she said. "We need to get back in the EV."

"Are you out of your mind?" Jaz cried.

"The fact of the matter is you *can* suffocate in a dust storm of this magnitude," Neave replied.

And she headed down the ravine, sliding on her butt when it got too steep.

"How about we just hunker down beside that boulder up there?" Jaz said.

"I'm getting in the vehicle," Gib said, scurrying down the hill after Neave.

The others followed, Jaz bringing up the rear, grumbling every step of the way.

The car had come to rest, right side up, the front end lodged against a large boulder, its tires flattened. It looked like an old heap in a junkyard ready for the crusher, but only the back window was broken out.

"We need to cover the rear window," Neave called out as the others arrived. "We can use the floor board in the back that's over the spare tire."

She withdrew the Swiss Army knife from her pocket, handing it to Charlie, who jumped back when he touched the door.

"Dangit," he said. "That static electricity is not nice."

"It's part of the storm," Neave explained, using her shirttail to pull the driver's door open.

"My hair's tingling," Gib complained.

Charlie perched on the back seat, leaning over with the knife to remove the thin flooring. Gib followed Neave's lead, covering his hand with his shirt to avoid being shocked. He gingerly opened the opposite door, which creaked loudly, and slid in beside Charlie to help with the makeshift window covering.

"Here's my tape," Neave said, passing it to them. "And can you hand me the emergency road kit?"

When they did, she gave it to Will. She didn't mean to, but accidentally touched his hand, causing an intense spark of electricity between them, shocking them both.

"Damn," he said, looking into her eyes for a second.

"Might be some stuff in there we can use," she said, immediately averting her gaze.

A disorganized flock of birds cawed above them, flying east – away from the massive, roiling dust cloud racing across the canyon. She watched as one of the birds fell from the sky, probably from exhaustion.

"Everyone needs to get in the car," she said. "Now."

"Hopefully, the windows will hold," Will said, as the others piled inside. "But, just in case, we still need to cover mouth, nose and eyes. The locals keep a good dust mask and goggles in the car. Obviously, we don't have the right equipment. But wet cloth would be helpful."

"We don't have any cloth," Gib said.

"Yeah we do," Neave said. "Hand me my backpack. And there's a case of water behind the seat."

Gib gave the water bottles to Toni so she could pass them out, then handed Neave the backpack before helping Charlie finish taping the makeshift window covering in place.

"We've got a Mylar blanket and a disposable poncho," Will said, removing the items from the emergency kit. "And a flashlight."

Daylight faded like they were in a time lapse sunset, darkness swiftly enveloping them. Will turned on the flashlight as the wind picked up, blowing dirt and sand against the windows.

"Charlie, you through with the knife?" Neave asked.

He handed it to Toni who passed it to Neave, once again in the driver's seat. She used the scissors in the Swiss Army Knife to cut a couple of shirts from her backpack into pieces, distributing them to everyone.

"Wet those pieces of cloth and hold them over your eyes, nose and mouth to keep the dust out," she said.

"Oh my God," Gib said, staring wide-eyed.

"Turn away from the windows," she added, "just in case they break."

The darkness deepened so they could no longer see the rocks nearby. It was like the sun was a candle that had been snuffed out for lack of oxygen. The dust cloud enfolded them in its unwelcome embrace, the wind churning dirt and sand through the air.

"It looks like the apocalypse," Gib whispered.

"But it's not," Toni reassured him. "Now cover your face."

She wasn't going to say it, but Neave agreed with the frightened fifteen-year-old. Now she understood those descriptions from the Dust Bowl era when people in Oklahoma and Texas thought Black Sunday was the end of the world.

She wet her piece of cloth and covered her nose and mouth as she anxiously watched and waited. It was like they were sitting ducks but she knew the risk would be much greater if they were outside. The wind howled through the canyon, rocking the car from side to side. Then something crashed into her window, causing her to yelp liked a startled child. A quick inspection revealed a marble-sized hole in the middle of the window with cracks radiating outward in all directions.

Dirt was already seeping through the opening.

"Pass the tape," she said.

After some quick rummaging around, someone slapped it in Will's hand. He unrolled a piece, using his teeth to rip it off while she used the scissors to cut a large piece of the Mylar blanket. He helped her tape the metallic blanket to the window to seal the hole and the cracks. Just for a second, his hand touched her arm, which gave her another shock. But there was no time to think about that now. She coughed before she could cover her mouth and nose again, realizing the air vents were open. So she slid the floor mat on the driver's side up over the vent, motioning for Will to do the same on his side.

Leaning so far forward, she was overcome by a feeling of vertigo, but realized it wasn't her – it was the car rocking. The wind was blasting the vehicle with pebbles, in addition to all the dirt and sand. Then something larger smacked into the EV – a rock, a branch – she had no idea, causing everyone to jump.

"I'm getting out of here!" Gib cried, opening his door.

A whoosh of dirt-filled wind rushed inside as Charlie and Toni struggled to pull him back.

"Close the damn door!" Jaz bellowed.

"I can't take it!" Gib croaked, but then suffered a fit of coughing that made it impossible for him to speak.

"Get back in here," Charlie roared, wrangling his little brother into the car.

Toni managed to wrench the door shut. But when she did so, a big crack appeared in the window. Charlie called for the tape, sealing the cracks as Toni wrapped her arm around Gib's shoulder, shushing him like a baby.

They draped their protective masks back over their faces

but the air inside the car was now thick with dust and sand. Gib was coughing and crying. The rest of them were just coughing. Everyone was coated with dirt.

When the hacking finally died down, Gib apologized.

"I'm sorry, guys."

"We're fine," Toni said.

"But why are there so many dust storms?" he said. "It's like we're turning into Mars."

"Neave, you're the climatologist," Toni said.

"Well," she began, then paused to clear her throat and take a sip of water. "There were times in the past, like the Dust Bowl of the 1930s, when drought and over-farming caused some awful dust storms. During what was called the great plow-up, farmers plowed up the grasses so they could plant wheat and other crops. When the next drought hit, with the grasses gone, the wind just picked up the soil and blew it away. Some of that dust even settled on snow at the poles, reducing the planet's albedo effect. Which means the sun's rays made it that much hotter. And then farmers started sucking all the water out of underground aquifers. That was called the great pump-up. Nowadays farmers can't just drill a well anymore to water their crops because a lot of aquifers are mostly empty. So the ground got drier and drier, and the earth got warmer and warmer, and it was like an ultra-long drought. That's why dust storms and sand storms are so common now."

"I..." Gib began, but succumbed to a coughing fit and the conversation died.

She lost track of time as the storm went on and on, allowing herself to daydream about Will touching her arm. Had he caressed her arm, or just accidentally brushed against her? Maybe it was just wishful thinking on her part. But she couldn't help imagining holding him again the way she used to.

Just when she was being lulled into thinking everything might be all right, there was a cracking noise from the back and a sudden, harsh blast of dirty air rushed into the EV once more. Jaz grunted from her spot behind the back seat.

"Quick, pass the tape," she rasped, her voice gravelly and anxious. "And point the flashlight this way."

Neave twisted around to hold the flashlight for them, watching Jaz and Charlie reattach the piece of plastic flooring over the busted back window, accompanied by the familiar sound of tape being ripped and applied. In a moment, the flow of air ceased, although it was decidedly more difficult to breathe.

"How long will this last?" Gib asked, a childlike whine in his voice.

"Hard to tell," Toni replied, her words muffled by the cloth over her mouth. "But we'll be all right. Don't worry."

He huffed several times but finally got quiet.

After what seemed an interminable length of time sheltering in the beat-up car, the wind gradually died down and the volume of sand and dirt lessened.

"Can we get out now?" asked Gib.

"Not yet," Will cautioned.

His voice seemed to reverberate through Neave's body.

"I need to stand up," Gib whispered.

"We all do," said Charlie. "Hang on, dude."

Finally, the wind diminished and a bit of light pierced the eerie darkness so they could survey their otherworldly surroundings. It was like they were in a thick brown bubble. The sun was a dim orange smudge to the west. And the car was covered in a three-inch layer of brown.

"Armageddon," Neave whispered.

"I told you, it's like we're on Mars," Gib said, triggering another coughing spasm.

"Pour some more water on your rag and keep your mouth and nose covered," Will said.

Dirt also blanketed every surface inside the vehicle – the dashboard, the seats, their clothes, hair and skin. Neave's eyes were red and sore, her nose hurt and there was grit in her teeth.

"Thank you, Neave, for keeping us safe," Toni said.

Neave looked her way, not knowing what to say. While she was relieved they'd survived the dust storm, she knew they were not yet out of harm's way and wondered if they ever would be. She didn't mean to, but she heaved a tired sigh. This time, it was not her imagination. Will reached over and patted her arm in a reassuring way, letting it rest there longer than he needed to – she was sure of it.

After waiting another hour or so, they finally piled out of the battered car.

"Damn," Charlie said. "Your paint job is toast."

"The whole vehicle is toast," Will replied.

The blue paint was gone in some places – sanded off by the storm – and the windows were sandblasted, so scratched, they were now opaque.

Gib had no interest in the car. He just wanted to get out of there and started up the hill immediately. Everyone followed, a bottle of water tucked in their pocket or waistband, holding their moist rags to their faces – first Jaz, then Charlie, Neave and Will, with Toni bringing up the rear, coughing.

"Try rinsing your mouth out with some of your water," Neave suggested.

Toni swilled and spat on the ground.

"It really does look like Mars," Gib said. "And look behind

us at the sunset. The sky is blood red."

"Enough with the Mars business," Jaz said.

Neave looked over her shoulder at the sky and sure enough, it was a hazy reddish orange. Gib was right – it was like they'd landed on Mars. Then she noticed Toni lagging behind. She tapped Will's arm, gesturing behind them, and he turned around to go back.

"You all right, Toni?" he called.

"Tired," she mumbled. "Probably the drug. They called it D."

"Yeah," he said, "D is short for Discretion. Nasty stuff."

"I need more water, I think," she said. "Dehydrated, I guess."

She stumbled a little as she lifted her bottle to her mouth, stepping on a small mesquite bush, and then cried out.

"Toni?" Will said, hurrying toward her.

She shrieked and stamped her feet as Charlie rushed over as well.

"A snake!" she cried. "A snake just bit me!"

"Where is it? Where is it?" Charlie yelled.

She pointed to a spot by the bush she'd just stepped on. Charlie aimed the flashlight and pulled the gun from his waistband, took aim and fired. The retort was muffled by the dust hanging in the air. Jaz squatted down to examine the fang marks on Toni's calf as she winced in pain. Charlie scanned the ground for more snakes.

"Charlie, you need to turn on your iCom and call 911," Neave said.

"We've gotta get her to the hospital fast," said Will.

"Jaz, you call 911," Charlie said. "I'll carry her."

He squatted down so Toni could climb on his back. With Will's help, he stood up and began walking back toward civilization. Jaz clicked the emergency number repeatedly but got no answer.

"Dammit! All I get is a busy signal!"

"It's the dust storm," Neave said. "They must be overloaded with calls."

"She's not looking too good," Will said, aiming the flashlight at Toni's face.

"Do we have any idea what kind of snake it was?" Neave asked.

"Some kind of rattlesnake," Charlie replied. "Kind of a green tinge to it. Diamond shapes, you know, and stripes."

"If you reach 911, Jaz, tell them it was a pit viper," Will said.

Jaz nodded as she clicked the number over and over again.

Charlie handed his iCom to Will so he could call as well. While it had only taken them a few minutes by car to get so far from the edge of town, it was a long way by foot and every minute of delay put Toni in more danger. Complicating matters, it was hard to breathe and walking was more of a challenge with the ground soft underfoot. And with each passing moment, it became harder to see as the sun set behind them. The small flashlight didn't help much.

"Try social media too for police and EMTs," Neave said.

Will nodded, focused on the iCom as they trudged across the barren mesa.

She was afraid that firing up her own iCom might draw more of her father's henchmen but she was terrified Toni might die from the snakebite. She wrestled with her fears as they walked, hoping against hope that a rescue vehicle might come racing toward them at any moment, sirens blasting.

"Is this the snake?" Jaz asked, holding her iCom in front of Charlie.

"Looks like it."

"That's a Mojave Green Rattlesnake," Jaz said. "One of the deadliest snakes in North America. She needs antivenom right away, and lots of it."

That's when Toni moaned and vomited over Charlie's shoulder.

Chapter 15

"Is she gonna be all right?" Gib asked, his voice quivering.

"We just have to get her to a hospital," Will said, still trying to reach the EMTs.

"At this rate, it'll take forever to get back to the road," said Charlie.

"Well, then, let's pick up the pace," Jaz snapped, moving faster than Charlie could possibly walk with Toni on his back.

"While Jaz tries to reach Rescue, I'm gonna call for a hub car," Will said.

Neave was glad he seemed to be recovering from the effects of the drug.

So he worked that angle while Jaz continued calling repeatedly for an ambulance, pulling ahead of them in a futile effort to force Charlie to speed up. Finally, Will got a company to dispatch a hub car to the edge of the mesa. They couldn't send it beyond where the pavement ended. Then Will said he was strong enough to take a turn carrying Toni, so Gib and Neave helped make the transfer. Charlie joined the effort to reach the Fire Department. They'd been walking for nearly an hour when Jaz finally got through, after reluctantly slowing down to walk with the others.

"We think it was a Mojave Green Rattler," she explained. "She needs antivenom as soon as possible." She paused for a second, then moved closer to Toni, squatting down to look closely at her leg. "It's swollen and bruised looking." Another pause. "No, she passed out." She paused and listened, huffing in frustration. "Jesus Christ, can't you come any sooner? She could die!" Then she waited again. "Okay, okay, I understand. Can I send you my GPS coordinates so you'll know where we are?" Another pause. "Done. We're walking as fast as we can but I don't know how long it'll take us. Which hospital has the antivenom? Got it."

She lowered her head, pinching the bridge of her nose for a moment before briefing them.

"Could be a while before they can send a unit. They've got our coordinates. If we get to the hub car before they reach us, we should take her to Jameson Memorial Hospital. I'm getting directions now."

"Is she gonna die?" Gib whispered.

"Not if we can help it," Charlie said, patting him on the shoulder.

It took them another twenty minutes to reach the street where they found a hub car parked and waiting for them under a streetlight. No ambulance. As it turned out, the car was a tiny subcompact – not enough room for everyone. So they loaded Toni in the back seat, Jaz slipped in beside her, wrapping her arm around her unconscious sister's shoulder. The rest of them looked at each other uncertainly.

"Me and Gib'll call for another car," Charlie volunteered. "Now, get going!"

Will rode shotgun, forcing Neave into the driver's seat again – something she didn't really want – but she didn't say a word. She programmed the vehicle using Jaz's iCom and the car turned around and headed for the hospital.

Neave looked in the rearview mirror at Charlie and Gib standing forlornly behind them under the streetlamp, covered in dirt, looking for all the world like they were being left behind on an alien planet. Then she glanced at the two sisters in the back seat. They didn't look like identical twins now. Toni's head rested on Jaz's shoulder, her mouth hanging open like an old woman who'd fallen asleep in her chair, her skin ashen and splotchy. Jaz's eyes were clamped shut and her features were contorted with fear.

Albuquerque resembled a city coated with volcanic ash. A cloud of dust rose as cars made their way slowly along streets so thick with dirt, you couldn't see the pavement. A scooter on the side of the road looked like it had sunk several inches into a mudflow, although there was no mud. The few people outside wore high-tech masks, which made them look like astronauts. A siren wailed nearby and then another. No one said a word for the duration of what turned out to be a forty minute trip, until the little car finally pulled into the Emergency Room driveway clogged with rescue vehicles. Jaz used her iCom to pay the car fare and Will carried Toni inside.

The ER was a madhouse – overflowing with patients and medical personnel. Jaz grabbed the arm of the first staffer she saw, announcing that her sister needed snake antivenom immediately.

"Listen, lady," the orderly snapped, "we've got victims in here from a sixteen car pile-up and..."

"You listen, buster, my sister's been bitten by a fucking rattlesnake!"

Fortunately, a triage nurse appeared at that moment to defuse the situation, and helped lay Toni on a gurney. A harried doctor took a quick look and ordered an IV. And within a few minutes the antivenom was flowing through her veins.

But Neave didn't have a good feeling. She was anxious. And she was angry.

They were allowed to stay with Toni in her curtained off area of the Emergency Room. It looked like they'd be there a while. So Will asked Jaz to call their mother and brief her.

"And tell her not to answer any calls from our missing iComs," he said. "They're long gone and might be used to hack into our security system and maybe even Mom's iCom."

She gave him a look that was a mixture of irritation, fatigue, worry and understanding before going in search of a private space to make a call.

Then he sat down in the chair beside Neave and leaned forward with his elbows on his knees. He was so disheveled and dirty that he looked like an old brown shoe left behind in a sunken city.

"So you saved my butt again," he said.

She wanted to hold him tight and cry on his shoulder but swallowed hard instead. He had dumped her, after all. She ordered her heart to shut up. But she couldn't speak. She knew if she did, her voice would crack and she'd be damned if she let him see her all teary-eyed.

"I owe you big time," he said.

Why didn't he just stop it and leave her alone? She would probably be in love with him for the rest of her life but she wasn't a masochist. Self-torture was definitely not her idea of a good time. Besides, she had other things to worry about – like whether her father knew where they were and whether he had more of his goons on their way right now to the hospital.

"Neave?"

Now was a good time to take a walk down the hallway. Her mind was racing. If her suspicions were true, her father would know about the escape. He would know she was in Albuquerque. Will said their iComs were gone and might be used to gain access to the family's other iComs. What if her father had already hacked into Charlie and Jaz's devices? What if he knew they were at the hospital? They had to get out of there. But they couldn't leave, not with Toni in critical condition. The doctor said if they'd been able to start the antivenom right away, her prognosis would be better. She said the drug Toni had been forced to take during her captivity may have weakened her, or the rattler may have injected a large amount of venom.

Who could help them? She'd called on Yong Li last time she was in a bind but this was way more complicated. And it infuriated her that the president and her administration just let her father go, treating him like a white collar criminal. He was a murderer, even if he forced others to do his dirty work, and he was a traitor. Barry King's dismissive attitude really galled her now – now that her father's messages had proven to be anything but idle threats. Would Mr. King understand the urgency now that three members of the Galloway family had been kidnapped and her father's armed guards had chased them into the desert? But since the Cohen administration had washed its hands of its former climate secretary, what chance was there that they would step in now to bring him to justice? For that matter, with his release to the Chinese government, what could the American authorities do to rein him in?

She pulled her iCom out and looked at it, figuring as soon as she turned it on, her father would have a fix on her exact location. But, hell, he already knew where she was, didn't he? What did she have to lose at this point?

She stood up to leave. There was business to attend to and she wasn't going to sit here and let Will manipulate her. There was no time for that.

"Neave?"

God, his voice made her ache.

"Your father threatened to kill Gib and Toni if I didn't break up with you."

She whirled around.

"He called you?" she said.

"And then he said he'd kill you too, if necessary, to keep his daughter from marrying a clone. He..."

His voice trailed off as he buried his face in his hands. She sat down next to him.

"I was trying to save them, thinking if I could just get them home, then I'd go to the authorities," he continued. "But he told me he would know. He's a monster. A monster."

"It's all right," she whispered.

"I'm sorry," he said. "I'm sorry. I kept thinking I'd find them, and then I'd tell you. But it's like he knew everything."

"I know."

"There was never anyone else," he said, finally lifting his face to look at her. "Never."

It was as though he'd removed a vise from her heart, a vise that had been squeezing it to the breaking point. Looking into his glistening, bloodshot eyes, she wondered how she could've doubted him. Why hadn't she considered that her father wasn't just threatening her, that he was calling and messaging Will too? Who else was he threatening?

She leaned close and kissed his lips, holding his dirt-streaked face in her hands.

"He's not gonna win," she said. "I won't let him."

She wanted to wrap her arms around him and hold him close, but there was no time. She fired up her iCom and found a number of messages. At the top there was one from Dr. Alvarez. She was so angry, she had a mind to call him right this minute and tell him what an animal he was. What would

147

it hurt since his men were probably already closing in on them?

"I'll be back in a few," she said, giving Will's hand a squeeze.

She clicked on her father's code before she could change her mind as she hurried down the hallway.

"Cariño, you woke me up. It's morning where I am. But that's all right. I've been wanting to talk with you."

"Don't ever call me cariño again, Father. I am not your little sweetheart! I never have been! You have violated every rule of decency in the book. And it's time to stop trying to hurt me and the people I care about."

"Now, now, sweetheart. I made sure my men never fired their weapons at anyone. I was adamant about..."

"You drugged them. You bound and gagged them. All because you don't want me to marry a clone?"

"You're young, Neave. And you obviously don't realize..."

"I realize you're vicious!"

"I've been very patient so far. But my patience is wearing thin. You seem to be forgetting, by the way, that two of my men were killed today when they crashed into a canyon. I hold you responsible..."

"You hold me responsible? You're insane."

"And I might just have to tell my men they can fire their weapons in the future if you don't cut all ties with that clone and his..."

Her mouth opened, preparing to launch a verbal attack, but she came to her senses and hung up. She paced furiously to and fro, shaking her head and grinding her teeth. People were staring at her but she didn't care. It was obvious there was no way to reason with him. She shouldn't have called him. It galled her, holding her responsible for the deaths of his men. They were two more deaths on *his* hands, not hers. Still, it hurt her for anyone to die. They were his victims too, whether they realized it or not.

Finally, she sat down in a waiting room chair and closed her eyes for a moment. She had to calm down. When she opened them again, she noticed a message from Alexei – all caps: CALL ME NOW. I CAN HELP YOU. When she opened it, it said "I'm en route to your location."

If he was an operative for his government, like he said he was, then maybe he might really be able to help them. In fact, he might be their only viable option. Jaz said they needed to call the police or FBI, but Neave could only imagine their lack of urgency. In fact, they might actually make things worse, not understanding who they were dealing with.

She clicked on Alexei's code.

"Are you all right?" was the first thing out of his mouth.

"Yes, but..."

She stopped, not wanting to say anything more.

"Call me from a public iCom."

So she clicked off.

She followed the signs to the main hospital entrance where there were a couple of pay iComs. He answered right away.

"Where are you exactly?"

"Jameson Memorial Hospital."

"Are you hurt?"

"No, but Toni's in critical condition. She was bitten by a rattlesnake and it took us a long time to get here."

"Who is Toni?"

"Will's sister."

"Who is Will?"

"My fiancé."

149

"Okay, so who's with you?"

"Will and his sisters, Toni and Jaz. His brothers, Charlie and Gib, will be here shortly. We had to leave them on the mesa. But Toni can't be moved. She's hooked up to an anti-venom IV."

"My plane lands soon. I'll come straight to the Emergency Room. Keep watch for me."

"Alexei?"

"Yes."

"My father hacked my iCom, which means he now has your code."

"Mine is encrypted. He can't hack mine."

By the time she got back to the ER, Jaz was telling Will about her call to Angela, about how frantic their mother was.

"Who did you call?" Will asked, immediately turning to Neave.

"A friend who can help get us out of here."

"Can we afford to trust him?" Jaz asked.

"The question," Neave said, "is can we afford not to?"

Chapter 16

She was just heading for the ER entrance to wait for Alexei when the rhythm of the heart monitor changed. She looked at Toni, whose face was half covered with an oxygen mask. Ever since they hooked her up to the monitor, it had been beeping steadily. But now those beeps suddenly became irregular, sometimes closer together, sometimes farther apart.

Jaz noticed it too.

"Shit!" Jaz cried, pulling the privacy curtain back. "Hey, can we get some assistance here?"

No one seemed to hear her plea over the din of the Emergency Room. Doctors and nurses were overwhelmed with patients, a number of them with serious injuries from multi-car crashes during the dust storm, some suffering breathing problems and some with heart problems. But then the monitor emitted a high-pitched, ear-splitting buzz and a woman doctor turned from the patient she was treating nearby to rush to Toni's side, immediately starting chest compressions. A nurse hurried over to assist.

Neave, Will and Jaz watched helplessly as the staff performed CPR and then used a defibrillator to shock Toni's heart. It was like a long drawn-out, nightmare version of a hospital scene in a movie with another nurse relieving the exhausted doctor, to continue the chest compressions. It was painful to watch so Neave studied the tile floor instead, slipping her hand into Will's. But the shriek of the monitor persisted, so that everyone within earshot knew a patient had flatlined. And when it was finally over, the doctor gave them a crestfallen look, shaking her head sadly. Toni was dead.

"Keep trying," Jaz cried. "Don't stop now!"

"I'm sorry," the doctor said.

"You've gotta keep going!" Jaz wailed.

"There's nothing more..." the doctor said.

"You're wasting time!"

Will stepped forward then.

"Jaz..." he said, putting his hand on her arm.

"Don't touch me!" she growled. "They have to keep trying! They can't give up so easily."

It was heartbreaking watching Will try to embrace his sister only to have her shove past him so she could continue chest compressions herself. The doctor and nurse waited until the hospital social worker arrived. Then they returned to other patients and Neave moved away as well.

She had to get to the entrance to wait for Alexei. But she couldn't help wondering what would've happened if she hadn't turned left on the dead-end street that dumped them onto the mesa. She checked a map on her iCom as she waited by the door. The map showed no street where she could've turned right, no way to double back to the freeway unless she'd done a U-turn and tried to get past their pursuers. Could they have escaped and avoided the scary drive across the mesa, losing their vehicle, being trapped in a deadly dust storm and forced to hike back across the desert with a poisonous snake lying in wait? If she hadn't turned left, Toni would still be alive. But what if their pursuers had crashed into them as they tried to make a mad dash to the freeway? And it occurred to her that if she'd known her father had ordered his men not to shoot, she would've reacted differently. But what if her father lied to her? What if he never gave that order? Because it certainly looked like those guys were serious, tailgating them at high speed. And the guards at the Climate Institute had waved their guns at them. She didn't think they were just pretending. And what if they'd actually made it to the freeway and then got caught in one of those chain reaction wrecks where vehicles suddenly slowed down in the blinding dust only to have cars plow into them from behind? She'd heard that at least three people had been killed. But she would never know. Because she turned left. And she couldn't stand thinking she was to blame for Toni's death.

She stood by the automatic doors, watching every car that pulled up, fearing more of her father's mercenaries would pile out of a van any minute, intent on taking them captive. She wished she could talk with Rosa. Comfort is what she desperately wanted. Someone to tell her everything would be all right.

"Neave!"

Charlie and Gib were standing right in front of her. She hadn't seen them walk through the door. Where was her mind that her eyes couldn't see what was before them?

"We got here as fast as we could," Charlie said. "How's Toni?"

She choked up, unable to break the news to them. Her silence confirmed their worst fears.

She pointed to where Will was now holding Jaz in his arms. Gib took in a sudden breath and his face crumpled. Charlie wrapped his arm around his shoulder and guided him to Toni's hospital bed. A huge lump grew in Neave's throat as she watched them grieve.

"Are you all right?"

Someone was talking to her. It took a second to register that it was Alexei, two men who looked a lot like federal agents right behind him.

"No."

He paused, giving her time to explain. She replied by gesturing toward where the Galloways were gathered around Toni's lifeless body. Then a staffer drew the curtain around them.

"I'm very sorry," Alexei said.

Neave took a deep breath, trying to clear her mind. The danger was far from over. She couldn't let herself collapse now from grief and guilt. If they didn't make tracks quickly, it's possible they could all be kidnapped and drugged. Or worse.

"What's the plan?" she asked.

"We have vehicles waiting outside to transport everyone to a suburban airstrip where a private jet is waiting."

"Not the JetTube?" she asked.

"The earthquake damaged a section in Oklahoma. I also want to avoid iris scans and fingerprinting. And your father would certainly have his men at the station, watching for you."

"Why does your government want to help us?"

"I will explain once we are safely on our way."

She looked at his men, wondering who they were and whether they were armed.

"The danger grows with each passing moment," he added.

Which awoke her from her daze. But she deeply dreaded what she had to do next: convince Will, Jaz, Charlie and Gib they had to leave. Now.

As she walked through the crowded ER, she wished she could rewind her life. Where would she rewind to, though? Yes, to that magical time when she and Will were together in Atlanta, falling deeply in love – reveling in the feel and smell of each other, talking about everything, hanging on each other's every word. Or maybe to the time they spent at his family's Florida home when they realized they wanted to spend the rest of their lives together. She craved the feeling of belonging, of happiness.

She drew the curtain aside so she and Alexei could step into the small enclosure. Sorrow hung in the air like dirt from the dust storm that clogged their windpipes on the treacherous walk across the mesa. Gib was holding Toni's limp hand, Charlie close beside him. Jaz stood with her arms crossed angrily over her chest, Will in front of her, a hand on her shoulder.

Neave paused before speaking.

"This is Alexei Sokolov," she announced. "He's got a jet waiting to fly us out of here."

Charlie looked confused but Will shook Alexei's hand.

"I'm very sorry for your loss," Alexei said, nodding at each of them. "And I regret that we have to move swiftly. But Dr. Alvarez has armed men heading to the hospital and we need to leave before they arrive."

"Who the hell is this guy?" Jaz asked. "And what kind of accent is that?"

"He's a friend," Neave replied.

Jaz looked at Will, her eyes like saucers.

"You mean they're still coming for us?" Charlie said.

"Yes," said Alexei.

Jaz glared at Neave. "It's all because of you! Toni's death is because of you!"

"That's not true," Will said softly. "You can't blame Neave for her father's actions. You can't blame anyone for who their parents are or what they've done. You, of all people, should know that."

"I'm sorry, Jaz," Neave said. "Deeply sorry. I wish I could undo what happened."

Jaz scowled at her.

"We need to go," Alexei said.

"We can't just leave Toni here," Jaz objected.

"I don't wanna be locked up again," Gib blurted.

"Me neither," Will said. "That's why we've gotta clear out. Jaz, no one's going to hurt Toni now. We can arrange for her body to be flown back to Atlanta once we're underway."

He nodded at Alexei who gestured for everyone to follow him, telling them to power down their iComs. There were two black EVs waiting, both with dark tinted windows and covered with dirt. Alexei directed Charlie, Gib, Jaz and one of his bodyguards to ride in the first one, while he, Neave, Will and the other guard jumped in the second one. Drivers were already behind the wheels of both vehicles with the motors running.

Neave couldn't help but look behind them once they were underway. Although it was dark, there were lots of street-lights.

"We expect to be followed," Alexei said. "But we have an escape plan."

He was sitting on her right, with Will on her left in the back seat.

"How far is this airstrip?" Will said.

"Not too far. But first we have to evade Alvarez's men."

"Are they already behind us?"

"We're verifying that right now," Alexei replied, tapping on his iCom.

The driver turned right on a street that was virtually empty. They drove a few blocks, then turned left. A short distance down the road, they turned right again in tandem with the other vehicle.

"We've detected a vehicle pacing us," Alexei said. "And a drone is following us from above."

"Shouldn't we speed up?" said Neave.

"At present, no."

They watched as the guard in the front passenger seat pulled out an anti-drone rifle, rolled down his window, quickly leaning out the side of the EV and aiming the weapon skyward. No noise was emitted but a moment later, the guard rolled up the window and stowed the weapon in a case at his feet.

"The drone has been forced to the ground and disabled," Alexei said.

They turned a few more times until they were on a four-lane street in a commercial district. The muscles in Neave's back were in knots. A part of her feared she'd been rash putting her trust in Alexei. What did she really know about him? She'd taken him completely at his word. A creeping sense of paranoia made her skin crawl. Surely, it couldn't be possible he was actually employed by her father. No. She scrutinized him out of the corner of her eye. What if, by trusting him and going with him, they'd already been kidnapped? No way, she told herself. It was just a bad case of nerves. They couldn't possibly be evading the good guys.

As they approached the next four-way intersection, two EVs crossed in front of them, going from left to right – a white one and a silver one. Like all the others on the road, they looked like they hadn't been washed in years. Then the black vehicle carrying Charlie, Gib and Jaz turned right, close behind the white and silver cars. Neave's hands were sweaty as their own vehicle followed. Immediately after turning, there was a moving van parked in the outside lane, forcing them to swerve around it. A flagman waved them on but then stepped into the road as they drove by. She twisted around and watched as he waved at a green van behind them to slow down for a moment while the big truck backed up a few feet. When they merged into the right lane again she was confused because directly in front of them, where the black car had been a moment before, there was a white EV. Then she noticed that in front of the white vehicle were two black vehicles. She suddenly became aware that the hood of their own car now appeared to be silver, not black. The guard sitting in front and Alexei both slid down in their seats so they wouldn't be visible.

"The paint," Will said. "You used para-magnetic paint."

"Yes," Alexei replied, looking up at them from his supine position.

They watched as the two black EVs, which used to be white and silver, streaked away at a high rate of speed, clouds of dust billowing up behind them like race cars barreling along a dirt track. Then the green van hightailed it past them in hot pursuit of the decoys.

"Nice switcheroo," Will said.

The white EV transporting Jaz, Toni and Gib turned right on the next street and they followed, accelerating as they headed out of town. When they reached the airstrip, a jet was waiting on the runway, just as Alexei promised. But it was much bigger than Neave expected, which made her even more curious about why the Russian government was willing to foot such a hefty bill to get them out of there.

They took off into the night sky weighed down by Toni's death. When Neave began her perilous journey, she had hoped to bring everyone home. Although she'd known the cards were stacked against her, she hadn't actually considered that someone might die. She was shell-shocked.

One of Alexei's guards offered everyone bottled water and sandwiches. She quenched her thirst but had no desire to eat.

She was startled when she saw herself in the lavatory mirror. Her face was dirt-smeared, her hair was matted and her climate suit looked like a used cleaning rag, so covered with dirt that you couldn't make out is original color. She did her best to tidy up but it wasn't much of an improvement. She also realized she smelled like a mangy street dog, but didn't really care.

When she got back to her seat, Alexei invited her and Will to join him in a private conference room toward the front of the plane. They sat in plush chairs facing each other across a polished table.

"Okay, tell me why the Russian government is spending a wad of rubles on this fancy business jet to help us escape," she said.

Will looked at her and then at Alexei.

"You're..." Will began.

"Not a spy," Alexei replied. "But I do work for the Russian government, which wants to find Robert Alvarez and bring him to justice." He nodded at Neave. "And my superiors think you can lead us to him."

"So you're hoping to use me as bait."

"Correct."

Chapter 17

"You said you talked with your father today?" Alexei said.

"We had words," Neave replied.

"And?"

"Same old thing – telling me not to marry Will."

"Because?"

"Because I'm a clone," Will said, his voice filled with exasperation. "And it would sully the Alvarez name."

He popped his knuckles as if to express his disgust.

"Your best course of action is to call him back and tell him you'll do as he asks," Alexei said.

She stared at him incredulously.

"It would give us some time and possibly make Will and his family safer," he explained. "The two of you should not be seen together. You need to make people think you have severed all ties."

Will chuckled softly, giving Neave a look. It did seem ironic that Alexei was suggesting what had already happened.

"It would be helpful if you let Dr. Alvarez believe you're coming around to his point of view," he added. "It would also be useful for you to keep using your current iCom so we can try to get a fix on his location. That means you'll have to be careful about the calls you make and the messages you send. We'll supply you with a second iCom to use for more sensitive communications."

Then he turned to Will.

"Your family should move to a different home that's not

being monitored. Right away."

Will rubbed his hand over his face.

"If your family needs money," Alexei continued, "my government may be able to assist."

Will gave him a tired nod.

"I want him stopped," Neave said.

"That's what we hope to do," Alexei said. "We want to bring him to justice as well."

"Why?"

"For the death of Mikhail Gagarin, a graduate student at the university who worked for your father."

"The one who OD'd?"

"His death was classified as an overdose."

She remembered Dr. Osley insulting Nat, saying he was even worse than Dr. Alvarez's previous graduate assistant who overdosed.

"But it was not an accident," he added.

She didn't tell him she'd already decided to contact the FBI because she didn't want to put all her eggs in one basket, as Rosa said.

When they returned to their seats with the others, Neave and Will held hands as they sat side by side. Finally, he leaned closer so their heads were touching.

"I need some time with you," he whispered, kissing her ear softly. "After I see my mom."

She squeezed his hand.

"But where?" she said.

"The Hummingbird Motel. Meet me at nine tomorrow night in the lobby."

~~~

Her mother was asleep on the couch when she walked through the front door in the wee hours of the morning. But she sat up immediately and studied her through bleary eyes. It was obvious she was taken aback by her daughter's appearance.

"Neave, dear, are you all right?" she said, her words half swallowed.

"I..."

But her voice got stuck in her throat. She didn't know who was more surprised, her mother or herself, as a big sob racked her body. Her mother sprang from the sofa and hugged her close while she cried, neither of them saying a word. Finally, the tears slowed and Neave told her she had to shower and sleep, asking if they could talk in the morning.

"I'll be here," her mother said.

It took half a bottle of shampoo to get the dirt out of her hair and a long shower before she finally felt clean. But no matter how hard she tried, she couldn't wash away the deep remorse over Toni's death. Life was so fragile. It could be over in a minute. She mourned for Toni. For Lena too.

And when she checked the newswebs, she was saddened to learn that five people died in the I-40 bridge collapse when their vehicles plunged into the river. Three more were killed when the quake caused a building to collapse in Oklahoma City.

Sorrow pressed her body into the mattress. Despite being bone-tired and emotionally drained, she didn't think she could fall asleep. But she closed her eyes to rest them for a moment and sank into slumber so deep, she didn't move a muscle all night.

When she awoke the next morning, it was very late. But her mother was waiting with fresh coffee and warm bagels. Dr. Sullivan looked odd, dressed casually in capris and a summer top. Neave sat down at the kitchen table in her robe, certain it was the first time her mother had ever stayed home from work. She doctored her coffee, took several sips and recounted her story from beginning to end.

When she finished, the bagel was gone and her mug was empty. Her mother refilled their cups and sat back down at the table, as unhurried as Neave had ever seen her.

"I called Stan Mintz this morning," Dr. Sullivan said. "I asked him what they were thinking, letting Robert go. I brought up the fact that he was probably involved in the murders of at least two people, including Lena. I also told him he was very likely behind the kidnappings of Will and his brother and sister, and that he's been sending you threatening messages. Stan is a nice man and probably a good secretary of state, but I have to admit, I was disappointed with his response."

"Which was?"

"That there's basically nothing they can do now that he's in Chinese custody. And I had the distinct impression that he views the kidnappings, the threatening messages and even the deaths as unimportant in the larger scheme of things. Stan is focused on politics, on maintaining a partnership with China, and on pleasing his boss."

"I was thinking about getting in touch with the FBI," Neave said. "But I don't know."

Dr. Sullivan sipped her coffee.

"By the way, Father may have hacked into your iCom. You should get a new device and a new code."

"That's rather irksome."

~~~

"Agent Dudnic, thanks for calling me back," Neave said.

She decided to feel him out before contacting the FBI through formal channels. She thought, just maybe, their personal contact in the capital might make him more honest with her now. Not that they'd developed any kind of bond, but when he questioned her about her father and Nat, she had the feeling he was trustworthy.

"How can I help you, Miss Alvarez?"

"It's about my father."

He grunted in reply.

"I'm sure you know he was extradited to China."

Another grunt.

"Well, in the short time he's been there, he's orchestrated the kidnappings of my fiancé and his brother and sister. His men caused the death of my fiance's sister. And he's been sending me threatening messages, ordering me to break off my engagement. All this, while he's supposedly being brought to trial in China for financial misdeeds. And I'm sick of it."

"So you're calling me."

"Yes."

"What's your question?"

"My question is: how does a man who's supposedly being prosecuted by Chinese authorities have the wherewithal to kidnap and threaten people here in the US? I mean, should he have unrestricted use of an iCom?"

"Miss Alvarez..."

"Agent Dudnic, our lives are in danger and I'm hoping the FBI can stop him."

"Have you gone through official channels with your request?"

"Not yet. I wanted to get your take first."

"My take is that there's nothing we can do to help you. With Dr. Alvarez now in the custody of the Chinese government, the FBI has no standing."

"So going through official channels would be a waste of

my time?"

"Correct."

"Do you think I'd have more success contacting the CIA?"

There was a long pause before he answered.

"I believe that would probably also be a waste of your time."

"Sounds like federal agents have been told to butt out."

There was no reply at all. Not even a grunt.

~~~

She twisted her hair up on her head and tugged a curly brunette wig into place before leaving the condo that evening to walk to the trans station. She'd never worn a disguise, but precautions were necessary. She paid cash for a transit card to rent a scooter. Interesting, she thought, that she was now using her father's tactic for avoiding an e-trail. She also didn't want to make it easy for someone to follow her so, after donning a helmet, she took a circuitous route to the motel. At length, satisfied she wasn't being trailed, she parked and entered the lobby.

There were two men sitting on couches. She pivoted nervously to look through the glass doors to see if Will was coming, then jumped when she realized someone was approaching her from behind. It was him. He was one of the men in the lobby. In her effort to avoid looking at anybody, she didn't recognize him in shades and a baseball cap.

"This way," he said, leading her past the elevators to a stairwell.

She followed him to a room on the fourth floor. Once inside, he tossed his hat on a table beside a bottle of red wine, then gently lifted the dark wig from her head, dropping it on the table as her hair tumbled to her shoulders.

"How's your mother?" she asked.

"Not good. No one's good." His voice was just a whisper. "They're planning a funeral. Lots of crying going on."

She slipped her arms around him and held him close, laying her head against his chest.

"And we're moving into an apartment tomorrow," he continued. "So it's crazy and messy and depressing as hell."

"Jaz is right," she said. "It's my fault."

"That's not true."

"Yeah..."

"No, it's not," he said, pulling away so he could see her face. She averted her eyes.

"If you and I had never met..." she started.

"Stop. Don't go there. We can't change the past. And I'll say it again – say it till I'm blue in the face, I guess – no one is responsible for who their parents are. Not you. Not me. Not Jaz. No one."

He pulled her close again and kissed her forehead.

"And besides," he said, "I need you."

He lifted her chin and kissed her – a slow, gentle kiss.

"And I love you," he said.

"Oh, Will..."

"And remember: 'the course of true love never did run smooth.'"

"From?"

"*A Midsummer Night's Dream*. And, believe me, it *is* true love."

He kissed her again more deeply, his arms enveloping her as though trying to fuse their two bodies into one. She felt the same urgent need and pressed her hips against him. He drew her with him to the bed as she unzipped his jeans and slid his shirt over his head. He groaned as he shed his pants, then pushed hers down as well. He started by kissing her breasts but mounted her urgently. Their lovemaking was fast and intense, like a violent thunderstorm that ends as quickly as it begins.

Holding her on top of him, he kissed her ear and her neck, caressing her lightly with his fingertips.

"God, I've missed you," he whispered, kissing her again and again. "I'm so sorry I hurt you."

"Shh."

They lay quietly for a moment, their eyes locked as if in a trance.

"I had imagined romantic lovemaking," he admitted. "But... "

"The feeling was mutual."

"The hunger," he said. "Like Hamlet to Ophelia: 'That's a fair thought to lie between maids' legs.'"

"You may lie between this maid's legs."

She kissed his mouth, a kiss of sultry invitation. And his caresses grew more ardent as his hands sought out the most sensitive parts of her body. They made love again, more deliberately this time, like an autumn shower where the rain falls slowly, but continues for hours, drenching the soil. Afterwards, they nuzzled, their thirst finally quenched.

"I don't think I can stand being apart," he said.

"So we'll figure out how to be together."

"Do you know how much I need you?" he whispered, kissing her again.

"About as much as I need you, maybe?"

After they rinsed off, she slipped on a shorty nightgown and he, a pair of boxers, and they drank wine from hotel water glasses.

"I should've known you wouldn't leave me," Neave conceded. "I should've guessed it had something to do with my father."

"Not your fault."

"But why didn't you just tell me the truth? Why didn't you just tell me what my father was up to?"

"Neave, he threatened to kill my sister and brother. And damn, if he didn't succeed!" He swallowed hard. "He even threatened to kill you. He ordered me to break up with you, or else. I was scared he'd know what I was doing and..."

"I know, I know," she said. "But maybe in the future..."

"In the future, I think we'll both know to trust each other."

~~~

The Galloways moved into an apartment the next day. They hired some movers to help but everyone was involved. Except Neave. For one thing, she couldn't be seen with Will's family, and for another, Jaz wouldn't want her there.

So she headed to campus for her class on Dynamics of the Atmosphere and Oceans. Although Yong didn't teach that class, she was hoping to catch him in his office. She wanted badly to ask him about his endorsement of the shade ring plan. She still couldn't believe he'd changed his position. But his door was locked, the lights were off and, as usual, no schedule was posted so she had no idea when he might show up. She called his code and left a vague message about taking a few minutes of his time.

When she got to class, Alexei was seated in the center of the room, surrounded by other students. She sat in the back, making a point of not looking in his direction, not sure if they should be seen together. She found it hard to concentrate as Dr. Irick, a middle-aged blonde woman, delivered her lecture, despite her lively, down-to-earth style. There was lots of talk of fluid dynamics, stratification and circulation, but Neave knew she would have to read the text closely to make up for her inability to focus.

The extremely unpleasant phone call she had to make weighed heavily on her mind. She hoped she could be a good enough actress to pull it off.

As Dr. Irick wrapped up, Neave's new secure iCom vibrated. It was a message from Alexei. "Library study room #8."

It was closet sized, no windows, and had two chairs on either side of a black table. It was also soundproof. Alexei was already there, two biofoam cups of coffee on the table, along with an electronic device that looked like a cross between a sophisticated computer and a commercial recorder.

He smiled in greeting and waved her to the other chair, sliding one of the cups across to her.

"Have you recovered?" he asked.

"Yes. And I want to thank you again for coming to our rescue. I don't know what we would've done without you."

"Obviously, it was more than just altruism. But on a personal level, I was gratified to assist you. So, have you thought about what you're going to say?"

She gave him a resigned nod.

"While you are talking with him, I'll be recording your conversation and trying to pinpoint his location. I would urge you to remember how important this is to your fiancé and his family."

Despite his formal speech – he was obviously a good English student in Russia – she knew what he meant: don't lose her cool.

He nodded, indicating he was ready. She took a deep breath, pulled out her old iCom and clicked on her father's code.

"Cariño, to what do I owe this honor?"

"I've been thinking about our last conversation, Father, and I want to apologize for losing my temper. I was totally freaking out. I also need to tell you that after a great deal of thought, I've had a change of heart about your request that I not marry Will Galloway. I've decided it's not worth it to continue our relationship. For one thing, I don't want to cause him or his family any harm. I also just don't want all the complications in my life. It's just way too much stress to deal with. I need to focus on my studies."

"I can't tell you how pleased I am to hear this, sweetheart. I'm also delighted you're following in your father's footsteps – getting your master's and PhD in my field of study. I think I can safely predict that, with my help, you'll have a very successful career."

"I've broken my engagement to Will. I think he understands my feelings. Now I'm just hoping my life can calm down so I can concentrate on my classes."

"Excellent. But remember, cariño, I'll be watching."

Chapter 18

"Did you get a fix?" Neave asked.

"Regrettably, no. He's obviously using advanced encryption software."

She pounded the table.

"We're not giving up," Alexei assured her.

"God, you mean I have to call him again?"

"Not yet."

He slid his computer into a black bag and stood up.

"You've got to find him," she pleaded.

"Believe me, I want that as much as you do."

She drummed her fingers on the table in frustration.

"I'll be in touch," he said. "Wait ten minutes before you leave."

So she was alone with her fears – fears that her father would be allowed to continue intimidating her and Will. And that he'd be allowed to continue influencing climate decisions. Which was infuriating.

While she waited, she used her new iCom to surf the news sites. She was surprised to see more protests of the shade ring announcement, including demonstrations in Germany and Japan. There was also a statement by the International Union of Climate Scientists denouncing the plan, saying "it would most likely delay substantive change needed to reduce the carbon footprint of nations around the globe." She finally exited the study room and was making her way through the library when someone called her name.

"Neave Alvarez!"

She looked over her shoulder and there was the dark-haired activist. She was prettier than Neave remembered. Of course, her long black hair was now shiny and clean and she wasn't sweating up a storm, yelling slogans under the hot sun.

"I was hoping I'd run into you!" she called, prompting dirty looks from students studying at nearby tables.

She trotted over and they walked out the door together.

"First," she said, "the name's Annie."

"Annie? I saw you identified on the news as…"

"Haseya is my professional name. Means 'she rises' or 'to rise up.' Which, you've gotta admit, is a cool name for an activist."

"What about Roanhorse? Is that made up too?"

"Hell, no. That's my real last name. Annie Roanhorse."

"And you're Navajo?"

"Along with a fourth of a cup of Arapaho, a tablespoon of Hopi and a pinch of self-important, land-grabbing, culture-killing European immigrant. Maybe two or three pinches."

Neave nodded, not sure what to say to that.

"Now that we've got that out of the way," Annie continued, "I want to apologize for being so pushy during the march. I shoulda talked with you ahead of time. Kinda got carried away, if you know what I mean. I was very 'in the moment,' you might say."

It was only a short walk to the Climatology building where Yong's office was located. Neave wanted to stop by again, on the off chance he might be there. She paused when she reached the front steps and looked up.

"Weird looking sky," Annie said, noticing it too.

Neave stared for a moment, realizing she was witnessing the remnants of the Albuquerque dust storm arriving in

172

Atlanta. A brownish haze hung over them, causing the Atlanta skyline to look as though they were viewing it through a glass of dirty water. Which made Neave want to get inside.

"So..." she said.

"So, we're planning a rally," Annie replied. "Wondering if you could make an appearance. You'd be a big draw."

"I don't think so."

"You said you're opposed to the shade ring. Or was that a lie?"

"Listen, Annie, I've got a lot on my plate right now and I don't have the time or..."

"Well, excuse me! How dare I ask someone to help stop a crime against humanity, a crime against the Earth? Especially when it's possible her support might actually make a difference. I'm sure all that bullshit on your plate is way more important than the future of the planet!"

She stalked off, calling over her shoulder: "Hope you sleep well tonight!"

Neave trotted up the steps and hurried through the front door, eager to get out of the dust. She also wanted to get as far away as possible from that pushy, know-it-all, self-righteous, judgmental activist who obviously had no clue what Neave was going through. The more she thought about it, the angrier she got. She decided the next time she saw Annie Roanhorse – or whatever her real name was – she'd tell her to go screw herself! Come to think of it, was she really an American Indian? Or was that just a put-up job?

"Really, who does she think she is?" she muttered, as she barreled around a corner toward Yong's office, bumping into the very person she was hoping to see, causing him to stumble.

"Li!" she cried, stepping back. "I'm so sorry."

"It was my fault. I was not looking where I was going."

"No, it was all my fault. I was distracted and walking too fast. I was actually on my way to your office, coming to see you."

He looked like a trapped animal, desperate to get away.

"Do you have a few minutes?" she asked.

"Certainly. We can talk in my office."

He led the way and offered her a cup of tea, but she declined, knowing it would just make her hotter than she already was.

"I have to tell you," she began, "I was amazed when I saw you standing by the president, supporting the shade ring plan. You were strongly opposed last time you and I talked about it."

"I was," he admitted. "But I had a change of mind. President Cohen made a strong case for the plan and I concluded it would be in the best interest of the country."

"But what about the best interest of all the other countries?"

Was the expression on his face one of guilt? Or was it just extreme discomfort? She wasn't sure, but it was obvious he didn't want to talk about it.

"We must do what is necessary for the greater good," he said.

"The greater good? Is that what the Cohen administration is saying? Remember when you used to say it was urgent that countries switch to clean energy? As I recall, you agreed with Dr. Osley that a solar shade ring would discourage them from doing that."

"Switching to clean energy is not enough," he said. "It will not slow the melting quickly enough."

"You know, a fellow student asked me if you were bought off. I said 'no way.' Because the Yong Li I've come to know could never be bribed. I certainly hope I was right."

He looked truly shocked by the suggestion.

"I am not purchased."

~~~

Toni's service was held at Herrero Memorials, a modern funeral home that specialized in view walls and themes "to create the kind of atmosphere the deceased would've wanted," according to their brochure. Neave had been to two funerals there. One was in a large room where view walls created a 3D effect of being on the rim of the Grand Canyon, so visitors could look in any direction and see what you'd actually see from the spot where the video was shot. They had recorded sounds too, and created a breeze, making it feel like you were actually sitting in chairs along the edge of the canyon, looking down on what was left of the Colorado River below. The other funeral was in a room that recreated camping out under the stars. There was a campfire with logs to sit on, a viewscreen on the ceiling showing actual footage of the sky, shot in some isolated spot with no light pollution, and a video of a tall pine forest on the wallscreens. A soundtrack of crickets made it seem almost real.

The Galloways had chosen a nineteenth century sitting room for Toni's memorial service. It was a combination of view walls with baby blue wallpaper, a bannistered staircase, and flowing draperies on windows that appeared to look out over manicured gardens. To sit on, there were antique settees, covered in cream-colored brocade. A recording of a string quartet played in the background.

Will told Neave that Toni often said she wished she'd lived in another time and took every opportunity to visit historic places as she traveled the country.

She'd called Angela to make sure it was all right if she attended the service after Will told her Jaz had calmed down. It was still dicey, though, because she didn't want her father to find out. So she wore her short, brunette wig again, and used cash to rent a hub car, leaving her old iCom at home.

She hugged Angela when she arrived.

"Neave, it's so good to see you, honey, although you do look odd without your auburn hair. I want you to know I don't blame you. I know Jaz was upset, but we all know you were the one brave enough to go and find them."

"I'm so sorry," Neave said, doing her best to hold back tears.

"And I told her it's not your fault your father is evil, that anyone who gets close to him gets burned – including the family of the man you're engaged to."

Although Angela may have intended to smooth things over, Neave was troubled by her words. No, she wasn't responsible for her father, but there was such a thing as guilt by association.

Everyone hugged her, except Jaz, who sat stony-faced on one of the settees. She was dressed in a form-fitting black climate suit and a black headwrap in the Yoruba fashion. Isabel was nestled between Angela and Rosa, holding her Patty Jo doll in her lap. Neave and Will sat on the other side of the room, holding hands. Charlie and Gib were behind them, along with a few of Toni's friends.

A woman Neave had never seen before made her way to the front. She was draped in a royal blue sari appliquéd with ornate white flowers. She had dark eyes and short black hair with thick bangs.

"Salaam aleykum," she said in a friendly, melodic voice.

"Peace be upon you. My name is Nora Chatterjee. I'm honored you invited me to speak today.

"I'm wearing the traditional Bangladeshi sari to show my respect for the past, something Toni had a passion for. We became good friends through our mutual interest in history. Both of us belonged to the International History Society. We used to visit every week online, eventually deciding we should meet in person.

"Toni told me how much she loved her family. In fact, I feel like I know each of you through our conversations. She was always curious about my family as well, and how I was connected to my relatives in Bangladesh even though I've never visited the home country, now so terribly devastated by rising seas. She studied her family history in Nigeria but took the most pride in her American family.

"Angela, I must tell you that Toni loved you deeply and revered you as a role model for your generous heart and loving spirit. She told me she wanted to be like you as she went through life. She said you saved her and Jaz from a miserable existence, expecting nothing in return besides love."

Angela blotted her eyes.

"And little Isabel," Nora continued, "Toni was so proud of you and said you were exceedingly smart and talented, with a kindhearted nature, and that she expected great things from you."

Which caused Isabel to smile and nod her head.

"She told me she was very close to you, Jaz, and that she loved growing up as your twin sister. I'm so pleased to finally meet you, although I wish our meeting had come under happier circumstances. She said you and she are proof that genes do not necessarily dictate personality, describing the two of you and as yin and yang. She said you are a truly caring person, although sometimes you don't want other people to know that.

"And she described her three brothers in such detail, that I think I would've known you if I'd run into you on the street. Will, the leader and the romantic; Charlie, the peacemaker and humanitarian; and Gib, the gentle soul with a big heart and big dreams. She loved each of you and celebrated your differences and your loyalty. And she was right: you don't often see such a diverse family, which, once again says a great deal about you, Angela, and the kindness of your heart.

"We Skyped a week before the hurricane and she said the family was about to gain two new members. She said she was thrilled for her mother and Rosa, and for Will and Neave."

She paused, taking a moment to look each family member in the eye.

"If there's one thing I know, it's that Toni would want each of you to have a happy life. She would not want you to drown in your grief. She would want you to continue on a path of helping others and making the world a better place. Which is what Angela taught her by example." She nodded her head and said: "Khoda hafez, God bless you."

Then Rosa stood and read an essay Angela had written about Toni, describing her inquisitiveness and her loving nature, recounting what she was like as a three-year-old when she adopted the twins, and how she grew into a young woman, mature beyond her years. Angela blew her nose as she listened and watched images and video on a wallscreen of Toni and the family.

Afterwards, the family was headed for Atlanta's historic Oakland Cemetery to scatter Toni's ashes to the wind. Neave wouldn't accompany them, not wanting to intrude, and not wanting to risk being seen.

"Tomorrow night," Will said, kissing her goodbye.

But as she turned to leave, Jaz blocked her path, giving her a start.

"Although we were the same age, and despite being twins, sort of, I always looked up to Toni as my big sister. It's true – we were yin and yang. I was yin – the shady side of the hill – and she was yang – the sunny side of the hill. I loved her more than she knew."

"I think she knew," Neave said.

Jaz swallowed and closed her eyes.

"At any rate, I wanted to tell you I don't blame you."

"Thank you, Jaz."

"Although I still wish you hadn't turned left."

"Me too."

Neave almost hugged her but decided that would be pushing her luck.

As she drove home, she couldn't help but think about what the mystical Nora Chatterjee said, that Toni would want the family to help others and make the world a better place. Which is what Neave wished she could do. One of the items on her to-do list was to take her father out of the climate debate altogether and to disarm the Robert Alvarez time bomb. She told Annie she had too much on her plate to get involved right now with a demonstration, but was that true? Or was she just being a coward?

As soon as she was back at the condo, she found the website for Indigenous Americans for the Environment and sent Annie a message.

Chapter 19

"A protest?"

Will was standing behind her, brushing her hair at the bathroom vanity, a towel wrapped around his waist. They'd taken a leisurely shower together after making up for lost time in each other's arms at another motel.

"It's important," she said, adjusting a white hotel robe to make sure she was covered. "Very important."

"But so is your safety. And my family's safety."

"I'll ask Alexei if he can provide bodyguards."

"Everybody's getting back to work. I'm leaving for another sales trip."

"Where to?" she asked, meeting his gaze in the mirror.

"Kenya."

"Alone?"

"Charlie's going with me."

"Will..."

She whirled around.

"We have to make a living," he said. "I can't just sit on my hands."

"I know," she said, cringing at the memory of him practically shouting that very same thing at her in his Guatemala hotel room. "It's just that I worry."

"Tell me about it. I worry too. Especially if you speak at a protest. I don't know how your father's gonna take it."

"I told him we broke up. That's what he wanted."

"I don't trust him."

She didn't trust him either. But, like Will, she just couldn't sit on her hands and do nothing. It would take her a couple of years to get her PhD if she worked as fast as she could, without any distractions. And a lot could happen in a couple of years.

"Neave."

He set the brush down and wrapped his arms around her. His eyes were mesmerizing when he looked at her this way. She found herself wishing, yet again, that they didn't have to sneak around to spend time together. The subterfuge was already wearing thin and the separation was agony.

"I don't want you taking unnecessary risks," he said, "which you have a tendency to do."

"I'll be careful. And Alexei's working on finding Father."

She didn't tell him about Agent Dudnic's brush-off or that the government had apparently washed its hands of its former climate secretary.

He gave her a soft, sweet kiss.

"You look beautiful in white," he said. "You gonna wear a long, white wedding gown when we get married?"

She returned his smile. But since their wedding was on indefinite hold, she avoided daydreaming about it. She understood what he was trying to do – to remind her they should go on planning for the future.

"I've never worn a tux," he said, giving her a delicious smile as he swayed with her from side to side. "How do you think I'll look?"

"I think I might faint from your gorgeousness."

He laughed and held her close.

"But," she continued, "I'm so afraid there's no such thing as a fairy tale ending."

"We don't need a fairy tale ending. Fairy tales were never real anyway. Doesn't mean we can't have an awesome life together. Even before the seas rose, people like you and me had challenges to overcome." He kissed her again. "Her passions are made of nothing but the finest part of pure love."

"From?"

"*Antony and Cleopatra.*"

Then he untied her robe, sliding one hand inside, caressing her smooth warm skin. But this time, it was Neave who led the way, making love to him, savoring every moment, every sensation.

"Making the beast with two backs," he chuckled afterwards.

She laughed too, understanding the meaning, if not the exact reference.

"*Othello*," he added.

She messaged Alexei as soon as she got home about protecting the Galloways. He promised to make it happen.

~~~

"You're kidding," Neave said.

"We had such a huge response, we decided it just made sense to join forces with other groups for a big protest in New DC," Annie explained. "We've got people coming from all over. It's gonna be mind-blowingly spectacular!"

They were sitting in a funky bar just off campus – a student hangout that reeked of beer, pizza and incense. Although it was only late afternoon, the joint was already crowded and noisy.

"But we were talking about a demonstration here in Atlanta. That's what I..."

"We can pay your travel expenses, if that's an issue."

She didn't want to tell her what she was really concerned about. Namely, her father. When she agreed to speak at the rally, it was supposed to be a modest affair in Atlanta, something that wouldn't necessarily attract a lot of media attention.

"Listen, I'm totally chill with whatever you wanna say, as long as it's anti-shade ring," Annie said. "I mean, you just spit out whatever pops into your head. We'll fix a pitcher of mimosas that morning. A couple of drinks'll help you relax. That's what I used to do when I first started out."

Neave just stared at her.

"I think part of it," Annie added, "is that having a drinkie-poo helps keep you from feeling self-conscious."

What the hell had she gotten herself into, Neave wondered.

"Oh, and by the way," Annie said, "the chairwoman of the International Union of Climate Scientists accepted our invitation to speak. Isn't that brilliant? She signed on after I told her you'd be there. She was super impressed I got the daughter of Robert Alvarez to come out against the shade ring. And once she said yes, we were able to get commitments from three top international environmental groups. I'm, like, totally stoked."

Will, Charlie and their new bodyguard left on Thursday for Kenya and Neave boarded the JetTube on Friday for New Washington. She had to stifle uncomfortable feelings of déjà vu as the capsule accelerated through the tunnel. Digital images of the landscape they were traveling under appeared on the wall of their compartment, giving the impression that they were looking out the window of an old-fashioned train chugging slowly along antiquated railroad tracks through the picturesque countryside. Part of her wished Yong Li was with her. He'd been her rock when she went to DC in a last-minute, mad dash to stop the shade ring treaty signing. But this time she was seated next to a woman named Katya Zhurov, her new Russian bodyguard. Katya had the gentle face of a young pre-school teacher, framed by soft, brown hair. Neave hoped she was more experienced than she looked.

"Smooth," Katya said.

Her Russian accent was much more noticeable than Alexei's. And she had a schoolgirl's voice.

"Pardon?"

"My first time on JetTube," she admitted. "I was fearful pneumatic tube would be painful."

Which only reinforced Neave's perception of Katya as a country bumpkin. Russia only had one JetTube line and tickets were expensive.

Annie had gone ahead the day before. Which was fine with Neave because, despite admiring her gumption, she didn't think she could stand spending too much time with the young firebrand. She figured maybe it took someone on the edge of crazy to throw herself into activism like Annie did. Neave sometimes wished she could do the same. But the thought of taking center stage at what was shaping up to be a major media event left her feeling like she was scrubbing up to do brain surgery without even attending medical school. She had yet to figure out yet what she would say. It was easy to be a virtual activist, quite another matter to do it in real life as reporters recorded your every word, flashing them to audiences around the globe.

She hadn't told Will about the change in plans. Didn't want him to worry – he had enough on his hands. And she hadn't dwelled on the possible repercussions of her public statement, knowing if she did, she might chicken out. Of course, if she'd had any idea how the demonstration would balloon in size, she might not be in this tiny pod right now, hurtling along at six hundred miles an hour.

~~~

The view from the steps of the Lincoln Memorial was like something out of a history documentary, with crowds of people all along the reflecting pool. Unlike the original, there were solar panel trellises on both sides of the fountain, designed to provide much-needed shade for visitors, while at the same time generating power for the nation's modern capital. Below the solar panels, the trellises were also equipped with misters to help keep visitors cool, and air conditioned cooling centers were scattered around the National Mall.

She was standing under a temporary decorative awning a short distance from the statue of Abraham Lincoln. The magnificent marble sculpture was painstakingly moved – at great expense – from the original District of Columbia to the inland site of New DC. The relocation of the nation's capital was forced by flooding along the Potomac River, backing up from the rising waters of Chesapeake Bay.

She was thankful for the chiller fans on either side of the dais. New Washington was in the middle of yet another heat wave. It was mid-morning and the temperature was already 114 degrees. She was dressed in a pale blue climate suit, a matching floppy hat and dark sunglasses, a cooling cloak wrapped around her. She sipped nervously on a water bottle, looking over remarks she'd hastily written that morning on her iCom.

Annie had reassured her that she wasn't expected to deliver a historic speech filled with soaring rhetoric that would be studied by future school children. She said Neave's presence was her real contribution, that having her name on the official lineup was the leverage organizers needed to attract a high-profile roster of scientists and environmental activists, along with a bigger turnout.

Still, as the program got underway with a brief welcome by a guy named Tito Sosa and a couple of songs by a popular group called Ski Slope, Neave's stomach was turning somersaults.

The huge audience listened politely to the first scientist, who criticized the shade ring plan as being untested and risky. They applauded when the first environmentalist attacked geo-engineering of any kind as thwarting the shift to green energy. They cheered when Sara Karimi, chair of the International Union of Climate Scientists, blasted the credentials of Neave's father as the primary supporter of the shade ring. It was no surprise that her father was the butt of intense criticism, but still, she thought his scientific credentials were respectable enough. It was his morals Neave objected to.

And then Annie was at the microphone, full of confidence and energy, tossing out tasty nuggets the crowd could sink its teeth into.

"Are we gonna stand by and let the president get away with this?"

"No!" the huge throng responded, their voices rippling from the first row, all the way back to the Washington Monument.

"Do we want our government spending billions of our tax dollars on this boondoggle?"

"Noooo!"

"Do we trust the Chinese government to do the right thing?"

"Noooo!"

"Do we remember who sold the president a bill of goods about a shade ring?"

Some cried "yes," while others called out "Robert Alvarez."

"That's right," Annie cried. "Former Climate Secretary Robert Alvarez, who was exposed as a fraud by his own daughter at the treaty signing! Remember that?"

"Yes!"

"Damn right, we remember!" Annie crowed. "Well, guess what! We've got Alvarez's daughter here today. She joined our movement to send a message to our leaders that we're not gonna stand for this bullshit!"

Which was met with thunderous cheering. Annie pumped her fist in the air and signaled Neave to step to the microphone.

It was like trying to walk through quicksand. Her steps were slow and labored, and she wasn't certain she would ever reach Annie's outstretched hand. Her mind was racing as she realized all the cameras and lights were trained on her. The networks and newswebs would all have graphics on their screens, announcing she was the daughter of the disgraced former climate secretary. Her father would, no doubt, see her speech before the protest was over. She hadn't brought her old iCom with her, not wanting to tip her father off. How naïve. If he didn't stumble on the coverage himself, one of his flunkies would quickly alert him. She realized from the start he would know about it, but somehow, it seemed less risky in the abstract. Now that it was concrete, now that she was in front of tens of thousands of protesters and a bank of cameras broadcasting the event to the far corners of the globe, she fully understood Will's anxiety.

Annie pulled her to the mic, holding their entwined hands above their heads in a gesture of victory as the cheering grew louder. Neave struggled not to throw up, glad now that her new friend had forgotten the mimosas.

"I give you Neave Alvarez!" Annie exclaimed before trotting back to take her seat.

She nervously faced the sea of demonstrators, many waving signs saying things like "No Shade Ring" and "Clean up our planet." The roar gradually died down as they waited for her to begin. It occurred to her then that the die was cast. She'd committed herself, she was here, she wanted to add her voice to those fighting her father and she would not back down.

She cleared her throat and pulled up the speech on her iCom, then lifted her eyes toward the enormous assemblage.

"The die is *not* cast," she said, stuffing the iCom in her pocket. "It is *not* too late for the president to come to her senses."

Cheering interrupted her and she waited for it to subside.

"A few moments ago you heard Dr. Karimi question my father's credentials, raising doubts about his scientific qualifications. But what brought a halt to the shade ring treaty signing between the US and China was my father's financial interests. It was obvious he had a quid pro quo with the Chinese: he supported their pet project in exchange for big bucks as a board member of the companies getting the shade ring contracts. So what I question is his ethics and his motives. And I have to say it's obscene that the President of the United States is apparently still listening to him."

The crowd hooted its approval.

"You have to ask yourself why our leaders decided to extradite my father to China rather than bring him to justice here. He faced serious accusations of fraud that could even be viewed as treasonous."

She paused as people whooped again.

"But I also find it unforgiveable that the Cohen

administration let him off the hook before authorities could investigate his possible involvement in the deaths of my cousin Lena Ruiz and Dr. Terrance Osley. I'm sure you remember Osley was strongly opposed to a solar shade ring and died under suspicious circumstances just before the president was scheduled to announce whether Osley or my father would be her new climate secretary. My father got the job."

There was sustained booing.

"So I now add my voice to the growing chorus urging the president to rethink committing American dollars to a questionable technology when it could spend that money on helping countries cut the umbilical cord to dirty energy. Thank you."

There was loud cheering as the cameras caught the fleeting look of defiance in her eyes. Annie ran forward and raised Neave's hand again as though she'd just won a boxing match.

"Let the chips fall where they may," she mumbled to herself but no one heard.

She waited until the next speaker had everyone's attention and whispered to Katya to follow her, and they slipped away, heading for the transit station. Her iCom had buzzed as soon as she finished her speech but she waited till they were on the train to check for messages. She read Alexei's first.

"My government is pleased."

Which explained why the Russians were so agreeable about footing the bill for the Albuquerque rescue and providing security guards.

Then there was one from Will: "You're all over the news. Please be careful and call me when you can."

And another from Rosa: "Thank you, chica." She knew Rosa was referring to Neave's call for justice in Lena's death.

Annie messaged her too. "You're gonna miss one helluva celebration party tonight. But thanks a ton for helping out. I'm totally blissed out!"

Later, as she and Katya waited to board the JetTube back to Atlanta, the protest was everyone's top story. She was amazed watching herself on a viewscreen attacking her father and the president. She didn't have Annie's natural gift for stirring people up, but she thought she'd accomplished her goal of calling the Cohen administration on the carpet about her father's extradition. Obviously, people were listening, including Congressional leaders. She saw a report on the Speaker of the House talking about an investigation of the Cohen administration's release of her father to the Chinese. She also saw an interview with Senator Latasha Jefferson, who she'd met at the White House. Jefferson chaired the Committee on Commerce, Science and Transportation that had confirmed her father as climate secretary. Now the powerful senator was discussing possible hearings on the new coalition to launch a shade ring.

"Horosho," Katya said softly as she scrolled on her own iCom, looking at news reports as well.

"What does that mean?" Neave said.

"Oh," Katya said. "It means 'good.'"

"I hope so."

She was filled with dread on the trip home, apprehensive about what she'd find on her old iCom. But it was the last thing she really wanted to ponder at the moment.

"So how does a pretty young woman become a Russian spy?" she whispered.

Katya laughed heartily.

"Not spy," Katya whispered back.

"Well, you know what I mean."

"Not have jobs at home," she said. "This position pays good salary."

"You don't have children, do you?"

"No. But my boyfriend and I hope to get married soon."

"I know the feeling," Neave said. "Any sisters or brothers?"

"Just my mother. She cannot work because of health problem. So I am what you call family breadwinner."

Neave lowered her voice again.

"You've been trained for this job?"

"Oh, yes. Much training. Also, I am strong like Olympic weightlifter and fast like silver medalist in hundred meter dash."

"Not the gold medalist?"

"Dishonorable to boast, Mama says."

Neave laughed. She liked Katya.

When she set her bag down in her bedroom, the first thing she did was to check her old iCom. Her fears were born out. There was a voice message from her father.

"Neave, Neave, Neave... what are you thinking? How could you all but accuse your own father of being a murderer? And treason too? Really, cariño. I thought we had an understanding after our last conversation. You seemed to finally be coming around to a sensible point of view. But I guess I misjudged you. I never imagined you would drag the Alvarez name through the mud like you did today. So now, you will find out just how much influence I have. And I'm afraid you'll regret your rash decision."

Chapter 20

"Alexei says you need a bodyguard too."

"Neave, dear," her mother replied, "I'm not going to be shadowed by a Russian guard, or any other kind of guard, for that matter. I'd rather die on my feet than live on my knees. Have you ever heard that quote?"

"No."

"It's from Emiliano Zapata, one of the leaders of the Mexican revolution of the early twentieth century. And I must say, he had a point."

Neave took the last bite of her toast, nodding thoughtfully.

"I appreciate your concern, but I don't think your father will bother me. I really don't. Although I must admit, it's reassuring that you've got Katya."

"Da?" Katya said, strolling into the kitchen.

Dr. Sullivan had bought a twin bed for the guest room, in addition to the queen bed Neave was sleeping on. Cramped quarters, but it was temporary and fortunately, her new bodyguard was a considerate, compatible roommate. And there was also the loneliness factor: she was glad to have a friend.

"Good morning, Katya. I was just telling Neave I'm glad you're here. Would you like a cup of coffee?"

"Da, spasiba. Yes, thank you."

~~~

Neave was surprised when Kwan messaged her, inviting her to lunch with him and Yong Li. She wondered if the

Washington demonstration had anything to do with it.

Arriving at the Lucky Panda a few minutes late, Katya took a small table near the door as Neave proceeded to the booth where Yong was already seated, looking ill at ease. He was dressed formally in a sport coat and tie, which made Neave feel a tad underdressed in her celery green climate suit.

"Kwan's not here yet?" she asked, sliding into the seat across from him.

"He is not coming. He received a message as we were leaving the office and said he had family business to attend to."

"I hope it's nothing serious."

A waiter set glasses of water in front of them and two menus.

"So," Neave continued, "is your schedule easing up a bit?"

He paused as though translating from English to Chinese. "No."

"Has the job turned out to be too demanding?"

"The job is acceptable but I am required to go to Washington for meetings."

"Isn't that over now?"

"No, I must go again tomorrow," he said, studying his glass.

"Really? I thought you'd already given your advice."

"I must give more."

"If you don't mind my saying so, you don't look very happy."

"I..."

But the waiter reappeared, his iCom in front of him.

"One check or two?" he asked.

"One," said Yong, gesturing for Neave to go first.

"Hot and sour soup, a veggie spring roll and mint iced tea, please."

"I will have the same items," Yong said.

The waiter collected the menus and hurried off.

"I am satisfactory," Yong continued. "Except for one issue."

She took a sip of water and watched as he struggled. Because it did appear he was wrestling with something, maybe a language barrier.

"I want to ask you if you would accompany me..." He paused, as though searching for the correct word. "...if you would accompany me... to a play. A music play."

Which was the last thing she expected him to say.

"Are you looking for someone to show you the ropes, so to speak?" she said.

But that prompted a confused expression.

"I mean," she tried again, "are you looking for someone to give you guidance on going to the theater?"

"No."

He nodded his head toward her, like he was bowing.

"You're inviting me on a date?" she said.

She suddenly felt awful, contemplating what to say. There were several choices. She could say yes and go with him to a play. But that would unfairly lead him on, which she couldn't do. She could say no, and not explain why – just let him think she didn't like him. Which she also rejected. She could make some lame excuse about being too busy with her studies and other activities. But he wouldn't believe her and she couldn't be that shallow. Or she could tell him no and explain the real reason. She and Will had told him and Kwan they were going to get married. But he must've heard they'd broken up. Otherwise, he wouldn't be nervously asking her out.

She took a deep breath and looked him in the eye, or tried to look him in the eye. He was staring at his napkin.

"Li, I'm flattered. Truly, I am. But I can't go on a date with you because I'm engaged to Will."

His head jerked backwards as though an invisible hand had slapped his face.

"Sorry," she added.

"But... he told me..." and he knocked his glass over, spilling water on the table, creating a waterfall onto the carpet.

She laid a cloth napkin on the expanding puddle and waved a server over to deal with the mess. Yong's face turned pink as he apologized profusely to the waitress. Finally, when she'd finished blotting up the water and refilling his glass, they were alone again. He swallowed hard before speaking.

"Kwan told me the engagement was... concluded."

"Well, there was a brief period of time when that was true. I'm really sorry you were misled."

"Don't worry," he said. "I am untroubled."

He might be untroubled, but she felt like she'd just bullied a toddler. And having to sit there and make small talk while they ate lunch was torture. An American guy would've waited till they were through eating lunch before springing something like that on her. But he was definitely the furthest thing possible from an American guy, even if Kwan had been coaching him.

By the time she got home after class that afternoon, she had a message from Kwan.

"I am sorry I missed lunch today at the Chinese restaurant. I am on my way to Korea to take care of unexpected family affairs. I will post on social."

Not much of an explanation. She didn't remember a lot about Kwan's family. Lena would know. But then she realized she couldn't call Lena. It shocked her anew, realizing her cousin and friend was gone. She could never call Lena again.

She also had a message from Annie saying the demonstration had been so successful, they were expecting the president to hold a news conference in the next few days. Neave was curious about what might be in the works but bided her time rather than calling Annie for more details. And sure enough, three days later, President Cohen faced the cameras again.

She got to watch the news conference in her Effects of Land-Atmosphere Interactions on Global Warming class. Yong wasn't there, and since Kwan was out of the country, Dr. Irick was filling in. She surprised the students when she got an alert on her iCom and linked it to the classroom viewscreen as the president launched into her remarks. President Cohen was flanked this time by the leader of the scientist group who spoke at the New Washington demonstration and, once again, by Yong Li. Dr. Irick had to shush the class as some students commented on Yong's Washington connections.

Neave thought the president didn't look as confident as she had during her last news conference.

"My administration has listened to the American people and to world leaders who objected to the shade ring plan," she said. "We consulted once again with experts in climatology and geo-engineering, including Dr. Sara Karimi, chairwoman of the International Union of Climate Scientists, and Dr. Yong Li with Georgia Geosciences University. And we have come up with an alternative proposal. I'd like for Dr. Karimi to come forward now to explain what's on the table. Dr. Karimi?"

Neave hadn't paid much attention to Karimi at the protest and didn't realize until now what an imposing woman she was. She had intelligent dark eyes, short wavy black hair and carried herself in a regal manner. She wore a sleek beige pant-suit with a white scarf draped around her shoulders and towered over the president.

"First, Madam President, I want to thank you for listening to what my organization and others had to say. We have long advocated a shift to clean energy and have begged governments to help third world nations and energy companies make the transition. The International Union of Climate Scientists strongly opposes a solar shade ring because it would be extremely expensive, difficult to maintain and the results could be negligible. The best plan would have been to go green decades ago. Unfortunately, most governments refused to do that, mainly for financial reasons. So my organization has advised President Cohen and the leaders of other countries to use another form of Solar Radiation Management: injecting stratospheric sulfate aerosols into the atmosphere to create cloud cover as a shield. It's a much cheaper alternative and one that is easily reversible if we discover there are too many adverse effects.

"Sulfuric acid, which could be sprayed by regular aircraft fitted with the proper equipment, would combine with water droplets to form sulfate aerosols. Once the aerosol cloud spreads around the entire planet, we estimate an additional one percent of sunlight would be reflected back into space, thus increasing Earth's albedo effect, or reflectivity. This would manifest itself somewhat like an ash cloud from a volcanic eruption. There have been many eruptions in the past that caused significant localized, and even worldwide, cooling.

"There is the possibility that such an aerosol cloud could change rainfall patterns. It could also potentially damage the ozone layer. Scientists must monitor the effects closely. To sustain such an increase in albedo effect would require continual spraying of sulfuric acid into the stratosphere. Thus, if we discover that the negative impacts are too great, the program could be discontinued at any time, unlike the more permanent installation of a solar shade ring, which could not easily be dismantled.

"But the International Union of Climate Scientists recognizes this is only a stopgap measure to help slow the warming and that all due haste must be taken toward reducing carbon and methane emissions.

"I want to be clear: this is not a ringing endorsement of Solar Radiation Management. My organization is, instead, endorsing this compromise as an alternative to a shade ring, in the hope that the United States and other countries will move expeditiously toward reducing greenhouse gases. Thank you."

Then Yong stepped forward.

"Dr. Karimi is correct. The optimal solution is no longer available. It is too late to rely solely on expedited reduction of carbon emissions to decelerate melting. I agree with her assessment that aerosol injection is a worthy alternative. It is also urgent that we replenish aquifers that supply drinking water and irrigation for agriculture. Aerosol injection should increase much-needed cloud cover and rainfall."

He bowed slightly and moved away from the microphones.

Dr. Irick disconnected the feed and waited patiently as a buzz of conversation filled the room, finally clearing her throat to speak.

"If you people are not keeping up with what's going on with these proposals for geo-engineering, shame on you. Your chosen field of study is vitally important and you need to pay close attention and get involved. Class dismissed."

Before Neave reached the door, Alexei was by her side.

"What do you think?" he said.

"I don't know what to think. Li has gone from completely opposing the shade ring, to supporting it, and now he's throwing his support behind this aerosol plan. I'm stunned."

"I mean what do you think of the president's announcement?"

The hallway was crowded with students, many of them talking about the news conference. Katya was there too but hung back to give them privacy.

"It's less expensive than the shade ring but it's still spending a lot of money on a band-aid," Neave said. "That's what Dr. Osley called it – a band-aid instead of curing the cause of the disease."

"I'm glad to hear you say that."

Then a woman's voice shouted Neave's name. She looked behind her and saw Annie pushing her way through the clogged hallway.

"I thought I might find you here," she said, slightly out of breath.

"We better keep walking," Alexei suggested since they were blocking traffic. "I'm Alexei Sokolov, a friend of Neave's."

"I'm Annie Roanhorse."

"I recognize you," Alexei said, "from the protests."

"That's exactly why I'm here. Because the shit's about to hit the fan."

"What do you mean?" Neave said.

"Did you watch the news conference?"

"Yes."

"Well, so did the leader of every country around the world.

We knew the president was gonna make this announcement. And we're ready, baby! We've got a ginormous demonstration in the works at the UN headquarters. And this time, we're gonna have some really big honchos as speakers."

"Like who?"

"Can't tell you just yet. Gotta get everything confirmed, but suffice it to say, it'll make our DC event look like an air conditioned, pre-school fun run."

"That sounds promising," Alexei said.

"Damn right, it does!" Annie said, beaming at him.

"And you came searching for me to tell me that?" Neave said.

"Well, I messaged you, but no reply. So yeah, I busted in here trying to track you down."

They reached the front door and started down the steps.

"You're supposed to ask me why," Annie added.

Neave shrugged.

"Well, it's like this. Some of our big cheese speakers wanna know if you'll be there too. So I came to inform you – you've gotta be on that platform."

"Excellent," Alexei said, triggering a scowl from Neave.

"Watch the news for reaction," Annie said. "We're expecting major blowback. I'll call you tomorrow."

She hurried off while Neave and Alexei headed toward the trans station, Katya trailing behind.

"You know, my father hasn't stopped threatening me," she said. "But I'm mostly concerned about Will's family."

"I'll increase their security detail."

She gave him a worried look.

"This is a great opportunity," he said. "I told you people would listen to you."

"How much longer does this have to go on?"

"We've got encryption experts hard at work. We need to set up another phone call soon."

On the train ride home, with Katya beside her, Neave checked Kwan's page and found a picture of the Seoul airport and a brief caption in Korean. She clicked 'translate.' "I am visiting my homeland."

She sent him another message, asking him what was going on with his family.

Then she checked the newswebs for reaction to the president's announcement. Lots of statements attacking the American president as a bully. The UN Secretary-General made a surprisingly confrontational statement, saying the UN Security Council would take up the matter immediately. And then she saw a report where the president of Argentina said President Cohen's announcement was tantamount to a declaration of war on the rest of the world.

Chapter 21

Until recently, it was a rarity that her mother was home in the evening. But since her breakthrough in cloning a human heart, she'd begun allowing herself a little down time. When Neave and Katya walked through the door, Dr. Sullivan was sitting on the couch, feet on the coffee table, a sandwich in one hand and a glass of white wine in the other. As if that wasn't enough to deep-six her image as a serious scientist, she was also wearing a turquoise caftan and a merry smile.

"Come on in, girls," she called, setting the sandwich on a plate and clicking her iCom to turn off a news broadcast she was watching on the wallscreen.

Her mother's transformation stopped Neave in her tracks. Even Katya giggled at the sight.

"Glass of wine?" Dr. Sullivan said, gesturing at a bottle of Chardonnay just a few inches from her bare feet.

"Mother?"

"Looks like you really did have an impact," Dr. Sullivan said.

"Impact?"

"Well, apparently, your appearance at the big protest helped pressure the president into abandoning the shade ring."

"Oh, right."

"Katya, do you know how to fix sandwiches?" Dr. Sullivan asked in all seriousness.

"Oh, yes. I often make them at home for my mother."

"Good. Maybe you could fix a couple of sandwiches and bring another bottle of wine. I think this one's almost empty," she said, pointing with her toe. "We need to celebrate."

She leaned down to pick up the bottle, studying it for a moment.

"Did you drink all that?" Neave asked.

"I believe I did," she replied, bobbing her head and grinning.

Katya scurried to the kitchen as Neave sat in a chair across from her mother. Dr. Sullivan drained the last of the wine from her glass, then refilled it with what little remained in the bottle.

"Good stuff," she said.

"What are we celebrating?"

"For one thing, we're celebrating your political clout."

Then she took a bite of her sandwich.

"Is that peanut butter and jelly?"

Dr. Sullivan nodded enthusiastically as she chewed. After a moment, she took a swig of wine to wash it down.

"I don't think I've ever eaten a peanut butter and jelly sandwich until tonight," she said, bits of food visible on her teeth. "It's quite good. As you know, I have no cooking skills, but I actually made it myself!"

Neave watched as she took another bite. All the years she was growing up, Rosa had done all the cooking and food preparation. Still, she was surprised her mother had never eaten – or fixed – a peanut butter sandwich before.

Katya returned carrying a tray with cucumber and tomato sandwiches, apple slices, a fresh bottle and two glasses of wine.

"You're a multi-talented young woman," Dr. Sullivan said. "Look at those elaborate sandwiches."

Katya chuckled, amused at how tipsy she was.

"Now, for a toast," Dr. Sullivan said, "to my courageous daughter!"

They all raised their glasses and took a sip.

"And," Dr. Sullivan continued, "to my forthcoming divorce!"

She raised her glass and Katya joined her with gusto, but Neave was momentarily frozen.

"Divorce?" she said.

"Yes, indeed! My lawyer uploaded the documents today."

It made perfect sense but Neave was uneasy. How would her father react? Would he view it as another provocation? Another act of rebellion against his authority?

"I should've done it years ago," her mother continued. "But I had to wait until my daughter grew up to show me I didn't have to cower in fear. Oh, and you'll be interested in this – the investigator says Robert drained his accounts to pay for his expensive lifestyle. He also says the board members of the Climate Institute had been asking questions recently about some of his decisions. Definitely sheds some light on why Robert threw his lot in with the Chinese."

"So his world was about to come bashing down on him," Katya said.

"Precisely," said Dr. Sullivan, tittering at Katya's shaky grasp of English. "The one thing I did right was to keep my finances separate from his. We never had joint accounts of any kind and the house was in my name."

She finally noticed Neave wasn't smiling.

"What is it, dear?"

"Just wondering if Father will be notified."

"I'm filing for divorce in absentia. We certainly don't have an address for him."

"My mother did also," Katya said, "after my father departed."

Neave raised her glass.

"Here's to your long overdue divorce, Mother."

~~~

Just as she was leaving the condo the following morning, her iCom buzzed. It was Barry King. Why would he be calling, she wondered. She debated answering, but curiosity got the better of her.

"Mr. King."

"You absolutely, positively hafta call me Barry."

"Right. So... Barry, there must be a reason you're calling me."

"Gonna be in Atlanta today. Thought we could have dinner."

"Dinner?"

All kinds of thoughts ran through her head. Was it possible he'd had some success getting the Cohen administration to do something about her father?

"Yeah. I hear Pamplona's is nice."

She cringed at the mention of the restaurant where Nat tried to give her an engagement ring during a dreadful dinner with her parents.

"Yes to dinner. No to Pamplona's."

He laughed.

It was six-thirty on the dot when a limo pulled up to the door of Siri Thai Kitchen in the old Virginia Highlands area where Neave and Katya were already seated at separate tables. Barry King waltzed into the dining room looking like a hot cappuccino, his brown skin gleaming against a fitted white shirt and brown slacks – his smile, the foamy, decorative topping. She had to admit he looked tempting. And she knew she didn't measure up in her green capris and peasant top.

"You have to be the most beautiful woman I've ever broken bread with," he said, folding his tall frame into the chair on her left.

"If I knew you better, I'd say you're full of it. But I don't, so I won't."

He guffawed like he was at a comedy club, three drinks in.

"You do remember I'm engaged, right?" she said.

"How could I forget since you keep reminding me. Which makes me wonder, you know, whether it's just some kind of ploy."

"It's not a ploy, I assure you."

He laughed again. They exchanged small talk until the server took their order. For some reason it irritated her when he said "ditto" to the waitress after she ordered Pad Thai and white wine. What was with some men who couldn't choose their own entrée?

"So, what are you in town for?" she asked, after the wine was served.

"First, I want to make a toast to the ravishing Neave Alvarez," he said, holding his glass aloft.

She almost blurted what she was thinking, which was: "oh, please." But she bit her tongue and dutifully clinked glasses with him.

"It's been a while since I was in the A-T-L," he said. "I like it."

He was giving her a suggestive look. It was all she could do not to roll her eyes.

"You're here on business, I assume?" she asked, trying to move things along.

"Very pleasant business."

The waitress swooped in with their plates, filling the air

with the delicious aroma of peanut sauce.

"Mmm," Barry said, eyeing the food, then grinning at her. "Mouth watering."

He was full of double entendres. Translation: full of shit. But she forced herself to deliver what she knew was the furthest thing possible from a Duchenne smile. He apparently didn't know the difference. Maybe that's what happened when you lived in New Washington and worked at the White House. Probably all he saw on a daily basis were phony smiles.

He took a bite and pumped his eyebrows.

"Okay," he said, after washing his food down with a gulp of wine, "I came specifically to see you."

She forced herself not to groan, but must not have succeeded in disguising her skepticism altogether.

"No, really," he said. "Admittedly, there's the part of me that wouldn't mind cashing in on your growing notoriety. You know, fame by association. But, as much as I wish it was just for pleasure or my own self-promotion, I'm here on business."

She sipped her wine and waited.

"Actually, my boss asked me to come."

"President Cohen?"

He nodded and took another forkful of noodles, forcing her to wait until he swallowed.

"You see, we were informed that you're on the speaker's list for a demonstration at the United Nations next week."

"I am?"

He nodded playfully as though he wasn't fooled in the least.

"I wasn't informed I was on the list," she insisted.

"Are you planning on speaking?"

"I've been invited, but I haven't accepted."

"All right. Here's the bottom line. President Cohen is respectfully requesting that you decline."

"Fascinating."

He grinned and took another big bite of his Pad Thai, chewing vigorously as she swirled the wine in her glass.

"Pray tell, why doesn't the president want me to participate?" she asked.

"Well, let's just say, she doesn't think you're serving the best interests of the American people."

"You mean, serving the interests of the president."

"Same thing."

"Al contrario."

"That must be Spanish. I don't speak Spanish."

"Listen, Mr. King..."

"Barry."

"Barry... how about telling President Cohen I might be inclined to at least consider her request if she brings my father back to stand trial. I assume you told her about his threatening messages, which, by the way, he's now put into action. My future sister-in-law is dead because of him. But it's obvious he won't be brought to justice in China. And it's also obvious the president is still listening to him. Which would be laughable if it weren't so appalling."

He shrugged his shoulders as though there was nothing he could do, then scooped up more noodles.

She'd lost her appetite altogether but downed the last of her wine.

He dabbed his mouth with his napkin before speaking.

"Neave, you know I think you're gorgeous. If there's one woman..."

"Stop it."

Which took him by surprise. He nodded before continuing.

"I would carefully consider the president's request," he said. "She might not take it kindly if you badmouth her again like you did at the DC rally. She didn't like that one bit."

"My guess is that when you're President of the United States, it's important to have a thick skin."

"She's invested a lot of time and energy in her climate proposals and..."

"I'm beginning to wonder if a certain government on the Asian continent has invested a lot in the Cohen re-election campaign fund."

His eyes grew wide, as though she'd stepped over an invisible line.

"Be careful, Neave."

"Are you threatening me?"

"I would never threaten you. I'm just cautioning you about who you're dealing with."

"Ah. Well, you can tell President Cohen I was leaning toward declining the invitation to speak at the protest, but now I've decided to accept. And, please, thank her for helping me make up my mind."

His cocky, flirtatious attitude evaporated.

"I'll see myself out," she said, slipping her purse over her shoulder.

"Please let me drive you home. I've got a limo."

"Nothing personal, Mr. King."

"Barry."

In the hub car, she was practically seething. Katya asked if she was all right.

"I don't know. All of a sudden, I've got two guys coming on to me. Which is really aggravating, considering they both know I'm engaged. Will only called it off to protect his sister and brother." She gave Katya an exasperated look. "But we're past that now. It's just that we can't let people see us together because of my father, dammit!"

"I'm sorry you cannot be together," Katya said. "It is similar with my boyfriend. I have to make money to pay my mother's doctor bills. Hopefully, the future will be good for all of us."

Neave couldn't stop shaking her head.

"Taking slow breaths is beneficial," Katya said. "You should do yoga."

She found a message from Annie on her iCom, asking her to call right away. So she clicked on the number.

"About time you called me back."

"You're welcome," Neave said.

"Listen, my peeps are pressuring me to confirm my speakers for the protest. You in?"

"That's what I heard through the grapevine."

"What does that mean?"

"I just talked with the president's press secretary who told me I'm on the list of speakers."

Annie cackled.

"Did you already put me down as confirmed?" Neave asked.

"Well, I figured you'd say yes. By the way, who's your good-looking friend?"

"My good-looking..."

"Alexei. Is he, like, Russian, or something?"

"As a matter of fact, he is. We just met recently. Don't know much about him. He's in one of my classes."

"Are you two dating?"

"Please."

"Well, are you?" Annie repeated.

"Definitely not dating. In fact, I'm engaged to someone."

"Well, well," Annie said. "Listen, I've gotta go, but you didn't answer me: are you on board to speak at the UN?"

"Yeah, I'm in."

As soon as she clicked off, she got a notification that Kwan had posted again. She followed the link to find another picture. It appeared to be a Korean grocery store. There was a caption but it was in Korean. She clicked on 'translate.' "I am buying ingredients for Kimchi. I am also buying rice cakes and fish cakes."

What the hell. She was pretty sure Kwan couldn't speak – or write – Korean. He must've used a translator to convert it from English into Korean, which meant that all his friends then had to use a translator to transcribe it back into English. She messaged him again, asking if everything was all right. Then she opened a new message from "call me Barry."

"Neave, thanks for having dinner with me. I'll certainly pass along your comments. Just please don't shoot the messenger. Barry."

Her mother was eating a microwaved sesame chicken dinner at the kitchen table when they walked in. Neave and Katya heated their own dinners and joined her.

"From the looks of your eyebrows, I'd say you're troubled by something," Dr. Sullivan said.

Neave tried to relax her facial muscles.

"I think I need to take Katya's advice and start doing yoga."

"Excellent," Katya said.

"So what's bothering you, dear?" her mother asked.

"Kwan."

"Kwan?"

"Yes, Kwan. I told you he suddenly rushed off to Korea to take care of family business?"

"Mm-hm."

"Well, he's posting on social media. But there's something odd about his posts. And the more I think about it, the weirder it seems that he would suddenly rush off to Korea to deal with some kind of family business. I mean, it's not really his homeland. His family immigrated to the US like a hundred and fifty years ago."

"Sometimes people call the country of their ancestors their homeland," Dr. Sullivan replied.

"Maybe. But I don't think Kwan has any personal connection with Korea. He's got some very distant relatives he's never met, but family business? I don't think so. Unless he inherited some property or something."

"Sometimes we are drawn to our home country," Katya said.

"But Kwan's an American through and through. I'm pretty sure he doesn't speak more than a word or two of Korean. His cussing in Korean routine is purely for laughs. He just likes being the center of attention. It's hard to believe he would suddenly take off for Korea in the middle of the semester while he's in graduate school."

She reread his post. And that's when it struck her. If Kwan was a stand-up comedian wannabe, where were the one-liners? Kimchi without a wisecrack? Rice cakes and fish cakes, but no silly quip? That was definitely not Kwan. Even if he wrote the message in English and used a translator to post in Korean, there would be jokes. The stilted language without any contractions, she'd chalked up to translation. But that didn't explain the absence of his ever-present smartass jokes.

She was officially worried about her friend.

Chapter 22

The next morning she found a message from her father. She thought about not reading it, sick of his threats, but reluctantly opened it.

"Cariño, I must say I'm extremely disappointed. I've just learned you lied to me about breaking off your engagement to the clone. So I'm teaching you a painful lesson. Once you've absorbed this lesson, we must have a face to face meeting to discuss your future."

Good God! Would he never stop? She rubbed her eyes, wondering who else might be able to rein him in. She was about to hit 'delete' when the message disappeared. She didn't even have the satisfaction of trashing the hateful missive.

In fifteen minutes, Will was expecting her to call. She jumped in the shower, letting the warm water massage the tight muscles in her back while she breathed slowly, trying to lower her heart rate. She didn't want to be bent out of shape when she called him. Seemed like that was her modus operandi lately: frustrated, impatient, angry.

She clicked his code sitting on the bed in her bathrobe.

"I miss you," she said.

"I miss you too. But the trip's going well. We're wrapping up two sales here in Kenya and we've got some good prospects in Ethiopia."

He covered the phone for a moment but she could hear him coughing.

"Are you sick?"

"Nah. Just a lot of air pollution here. Most of their cars still run on gasoline, believe it or not."

"So when are you coming home?"

"Not sure yet. Everything okay?"

She paused, trying to figure out how to answer.

"Alexei keeps saying they're working on tracking Father's location but, I don't know, I just don't have a good feeling about it." She decided not to tell him about her father's latest message. "Please be careful."

"We'll be all right. Nick takes good care of us."

"Nick?"

"Nikolai, our bodyguard. Great guy. Knows what he's doing. Don't worry."

"I'm sick of worrying. I want all of this to be over so we can be together."

"Do me a favor. Take Isabel for a fun outing sometime. It's been hard on her, you know. Maybe you could talk Mama into going too."

"Jaz won't mind?"

"Jaz is fine. She's busy trying to drum up sales for the antiques, even though sales is not her forte. That was Toni's thing." He paused for a moment, as if to collect himself. "Jaz likes demolition. But she's trying to help Mama right now. And with all that's happened, I'm not pushing anymore to dump the business. We'll just downsize a bit."

She was going to tell him about the UN protest but he said he had an appointment. So the call was over too quickly and she was sitting on her bed, propped against a pillow, staring into space when a knock at the door roused her.

"Come in," Neave said.

Katya stepped into the room, already showered and dressed for the day, and began loading her backpack.

"Are you… satisfactory?" she said.

"I can't figure out how my father knows Will and I haven't broken up."

"You received another message?"

"Yeah. He says he knows I didn't really break off our engagement. And he says he's going to punish me."

"What do you think he means?"

"Based on what's already happened, my guess is he's threatening to kidnap someone. Last time, he had his thugs abduct Toni and Gib. And then Will too. I'm worried he might know where Will and Charlie are. Will says Nikolai is careful, but still. Or what if he's talking about Mother? Mother says she doesn't think Father would come after her so she refused Alexei's offer of a bodyguard. But I'm not so sure."

"Who knows that you continue to be engaged?"

"Well," Neave said, pausing for a moment. "Too many people, maybe."

She wondered if she could trust Katya and Nick and the other guards staying with the Galloways, Dmitry and Anna. What if one of them wasn't loyal? Or maybe it was just a slip of the tongue by someone in the family. Of course, it was possible spies had seen her and Will at the motel.

She wanted more than anything for her father to be tried for his crimes. And for the threats to cease. It drove her up the wall just thinking about it day after day.

"I believe I hear your blood squirting through your arteries," Katya said.

Neave chuckled.

~~~

She stopped by unannounced to see Angela and Rosa to talk about an outing with Isabel. She hadn't visited them since they moved out of the house and into an apartment in the suburbs. Grieving over Toni would've been hard enough even if they'd still been in their own home, but there was a terrible pall hanging over the family, kind of like the thick vortex of plastic trash in the Pacific Ocean. She hoped that, unlike the floating garbage patch, their grief would diminish over time.

Gib answered the door, gave her a hug and led her to the kitchen, where Angela was busy cooking, obviously frustrated by the unfamiliar appliances. Rosa sat at the table, transmitting real estate listings to a wallscreen and commenting on each one.

"This one looks nice. Five bedrooms, three bathrooms and a spacious, modern kitchen."

Angela grunted as she poured milk in a bowl.

"Neave's here," Gib announced.

"Neave, honey," Rosa said. "So good to see you."

"Yes, it is," said Angela. She stepped forward to give her a brief hug, holding her hands out so she wouldn't get flour on Neave's clothes. "I'm making biscuits and scrambled eggs."

"I'll set another place," Rosa said, jumping up.

"Before Isabel comes in, I wanted to tell you Will asked me to arrange an outing for her," Neave said. "Is that all right, Angela?"

"An outing might be just the ticket," she replied. "What do you think, Rosa?"

"Una buena idea."

She set another plate and silverware on the table, along with a bowl of canned pineapple. Fresh fruit was too expensive with water shortages causing prices to skyrocket.

"Where do you think we should go?" Neave asked Rosa.

"Let me see. You used to like swimming at the city's indoor water park. Can Isabel swim?" Rosa said, turning to Angela.

"Not yet. But it's on my to-do list."

Which gave Neave the heebie-jeebies thinking about their ordeal in the flash flood.

"Well, then," Rosa said, "how about the Old Timey Games Pavilion? You used to love that when you were little."

"Perfect," Neave said. "One day next week."

Isabel appeared out of nowhere.

"What's the Old Timey whatchamacallit?" she asked.

"It's an indoor children's park that's lots of fun," Rosa replied.

"We're going to take you next week," Neave said.

"Will there be other kids?"

"Oh yeah," Neave said. "I loved it when I was your age. You get to play games that children used to play hundreds of years ago."

"Rosa's teaching me Español," Isabel announced.

"Tienes hambre?" Rosa asked.

"Si, muy hungry," Isabel replied, rubbing her tummy.

"Tengo hambre," Rosa prompted.

"Si. Tengo hambre," Isabel said, sitting down at the table.

Angela had popped the biscuits in the oven and was cracking eggs into a large bowl, when, without warning, a huge sob erupted. She clutched a kitchen towel to her mouth as she hurried from the room.

"Dios mio," Rosa whispered, rushing after her. "That woman couldn't grieve any more if it was her own flesh and blood."

Isabel looked up at Neave, a forlorn expression on her face.

"Mama's sad," she said. "And so am I."

Neave squatted down beside her, wrapped her arms around the little girl and kissed her cheek.

"I'll scramble the eggs," Gib volunteered, washing his

hands at the sink.

Neave decided she needed to come up with an outing for Gib too.

~~~

Interesting, she thought, how Annie managed to sit next to Alexei on the JetTube to NY2 while she and Katya sat one row back. As the pod zoomed through the tube, she couldn't help but wonder if she had let her pride get the better of her, committing to speak at the demonstration because President Cohen pissed her off pressuring her not to. When she told Will about it, he was uneasy.

"Yeah, I understand how important it is," he said. "I also understand your father is evil incarnate."

She tried to reassure him they'd be cautious and that Alexei and Katya were both going with her. She knew there might be some risk but felt she had to speak out.

"I have never participated in a protest before," Katya whispered. "I believe I am somewhat excited. Especially because you are speaking."

Which didn't help calm Neave's nerves. The roster at this event was on a whole other level from the DC event. The UN Secretary-General would be speaking, as would the Canadian Prime Minister, the governors of New York and California – who both had presidential aspirations, she was told – several Senators and Representatives, along with a couple of Hollywood actors and the head of Save the Planet, the pre-eminent international environmental group. She wasn't sure why they needed her too, with all those big names, but Annie insisted the organizers wanted the daughter of Robert Alvarez on the dais. She was being used and she knew it. But she hoped the end justified the means.

Katya didn't answer when Neave tapped on her hotel

room door just before midnight. She'd hoped shooting the breeze might help tamp down the stress hormones. So it took her a while to fall asleep. And the next thing she knew, she was gasping for air, trapped inside a refrigerator. It took a moment for her brain to register that she was lying in bed in her cool hotel room. She was having a nightmare.

Even though she left the lamp on, she dozed fitfully, finally throwing in the towel just before five. She was having coffee in the lobby a few minutes after six when Katya joined her. She wasn't her usual perky self and Neave wondered if she'd had a bad night as well. Katya presented her with a big floppy sun hat with black and white circular stripes that made it look rather like a target.

"To keep you from getting sun stroke," she explained.

"I've got a crushable hat," Neave said, pulling a tan hat from her fanny pack.

"Not pretty enough," Katya argued. "I will wear that one."

She seemed unusually serious, Neave thought. Maybe her training hadn't prepared her for guarding someone at a large event and she, too, had a case of nerves.

Neave swapped with her.

"This is very stylish," Neave said, "although it would reflect the sun better if it was solid white. More of an albedo effect, if you know what I mean."

"But it wouldn't be so fashionable," Katya replied in an unusually quiet voice. "Now you must eat. You will need energy."

"You're a real mama bear this morning."

So she ate a banana.

Then the four of them took the subway to UN Headquarters. Annie joined other speakers and organizers on the stage. Neave, Katya and Alexei positioned themselves along the front barricade where tens of thousands of marchers would arrive after walking from New Central Park to the UN. She wanted to experience the march herself – to be a part of the multitude protesting against geo-engineering – while Annie wanted her on the stage with the others. They compromised: Neave would be in place at the appointed time but she would stand at the front and ascend the stage shortly before it was her turn to speak.

It took longer than she expected for the marchers to arrive. When they finally began filling the park and surrounding streets, she was amazed at the size of the gathering. They kept coming, wave after wave, some carrying signs, some shouting slogans, many, like her, wearing large sun hats and carrying umbrellas to protect them from the sun. "There is no Planet B" was her favorite poster. Annie said more than a thousand organizations were listed as organizers of the huge event. It was impossible to tell how many people there were. One thing that was the same as the DC protest was the heat.

"Mid-October in New York," Neave said. "113 degrees and rising. Not like it used to be a hundred years ago when trees turned red and gold and there was a chill in the air. I've seen images and video."

"A hundred years ago, it was like that in Moscow also," Katya said.

"I think you're engaging in what's called wishful thinking," Alexei said.

Annie was seated under the large shelter covering the stage. The marchers weren't as lucky. Although there were cooling centers throughout the city, there were only a few along the perimeter of the park, but the crowds made them virtually impossible to access. And there were very few shade awnings and even fewer trees. Thankfully, there were giant misting fans throughout the park.

Henry Locklear, national leader of Annie's Indigenous Americans group, was first up, welcoming marchers and sharing a few logistics, like what to do for a medical emergency. Swarms of reporters and photographers were already in position in front of the stage and on both sides of the enormous crowd. The networks and newswebs had stationary cameras on risers as well. And there were two drones hovering above them, one marked with a police logo, the other with a news insignia.

Then New York Mayor Jalen Coleman spoke, calling on the president and other leaders to get serious about clean energy. He was followed by the Governor of New York, Gabriela Ortega. As Governor Ortega spoke, Neave noticed the misters that were helping keep the marchers cool suddenly stopped spraying water. She hoped it was a temporary glitch.

Then a short, elegant woman in a gold and black dress and matching headwrap stepped to the mic. Locklear introduced Anita Sawadogo as the first UN Secretary-General from Burkina Faso. She spoke with an African lilt but had a strong voice.

"My country is concluding a painful transition from dirty energy to clean energy," she began. "Burkina Faso is a poor West African country. And I would argue that if a poor West African nation is willing and able to convert to green energy, then the rest of the world should be willing and able to do so. Especially wealthy nations like the United States and China. A hundred years ago, most people in my country burned wood or charcoal. Only a tiny percentage had electricity. Rivers were severely polluted with industrial chemicals. Now, solar power provides electricity, which has helped deliver our population from polluted air and water. And, as the temperatures soared, my people now have clean energy to help cool their homes and businesses."

It occurred to Neave that any country relying on solar energy might not be keen on blocking sunlight to slow global warming.

"It is time for political leaders to listen to business leaders, who have spoken out quite clearly," Sawadogo continued. "The fossil fuel industry is in the process of being relegated to our history books, much as slavery was."

Neave noticed the crowd getting restless, but not because of the speech. People were becoming overheated without the sprinklers, many fanning themselves and sharing umbrellas to block the sun.

"Why aren't the misters on anymore?" she said, lifting her floppy hat so she could see Alexei and Katya beside her. "Someone needs to tell Annie."

"Let's start moving to the side," Alexei said, clicking on his iCom. "It's almost time for you to speak anyway."

The three of them maneuvered through the crush of people, with Alexei leading the way. Despite being shaded by her big sun hat, Neave was suddenly aware of a niggling headache. While she had wanted to stand with the marchers, she was sweating profusely, wishing she'd worn a climate suit instead of the Kelly green top and light green capris Katya had given her, suggesting the outfit would represent green energy. And she had left her cooling cloak at the hotel after Annie assured her there were misters on-site.

Squeezing between the marchers was a slow process and people were in no mood to step aside. As they continued toward the stage, Locklear introduced the next speaker, Dax Rivera, an Oscar-winning actor known for environmental activism. He looked the part of a Hollywood star – tall and handsome, with thick, black hair. He immediately went on the attack, accusing President Cohen of being in cahoots with the Chinese.

Katya was behind Neave, holding tight to her arm, slowing her progress so they couldn't keep up with Alexei. As he pulled away from them, people filled the vacuum behind him like water flowing around a rock. That's when Neave noticed a buzz in the crowd. A woman on her left leaned over, then stood up again. Then she heard a man's voice calling "need an EMT!" Her iCom indicated the temperature had reached 117 degrees and she guessed someone had collapsed. Then a young man raised a small white flag with a red cross on it, signaling for medical assistance.

Rivera continued speaking. Neave wasn't sure if he was aware of the crisis or not.

Two Emergency Medical Technicians threaded their way through the assemblage. Neave noticed another emergency flag waving and two more EMTs wedging themselves between marchers to reach someone in distress. Locklear appeared at Rivera's elbow, whispering in his ear.

"Okay, folks," Rivera said, pausing uncertainly. "I think we've got some medical issues in the crowd. Please make way for the EMTs. And Mister Mayor," he said, turning around to search for Mayor Coleman in the chairs behind him, "can you get your people to turn the water misters back on? They're not working anymore and the marchers are turning into shish kabobs under the blistering sun."

Katya pushed in front of her then, tugging Neave with her. She couldn't see Alexei anymore. That's when she heard a woman scream. Then another. It was like a contagious virus spreading through the crowd. That's when someone snatched her hat from her head. She was about to turn around to try to retrieve it but Katya yanked her forward.

"Come quickly," Katya cried.

People were pushing each other, trying to escape, which only made things worse. They were penned in by the sheer number of bodies.

Suddenly, someone yelled close on her left.

"She's got a gun!"

Chapter 23

Neave hoped it was a false alarm, that no one really had a gun. But it didn't matter whether it was real or not because all around her, people were screaming and crying and shoving each other.

Police officers who'd been standing along the perimeter waded into the sea of demonstrators, but the situation quickly descended into chaos. The reporters who had only a moment before been focused on the movie star, whirled around, training their cameras on the marchers.

Katya was yelling something in Russian, forcing people aside to create a path. Just as they were approaching the edge of the park, a man hollered at the top of his lungs: "She's gonna shoot!"

What started as agitation turned into a stampede with Neave and Katya leading the way.

"Run!" Katya cried. "But do not fall down!"

The orderly marchers morphed into a giant, panicked mob. People tripped over each other in their haste to flee. They charged in every direction, many of them barreling through a phalanx of reporters, climbing onto the stage, and racing through the confused dignitaries who belatedly realized they might be in danger too. She heard someone behind her arguing that it was a terrorist attack.

Katya was beside her as they raced to the street but she couldn't see Alexei anywhere. They literally ran for their lives along with thousands of others, afraid to stop for fear of being trampled. It didn't take long for Neave to suffer the consequences of the oppressive heat as they dashed along streets with skyscrapers rising above them. With so much concrete, the heat island effect meant the temperature was easily 125 degrees. Her head throbbed as they galloped along the crowded sidewalk.

"This way!" Katya cried, leading them down the stairs into a subway station.

They managed to squeeze onto the first train and streaked through the tunnel along with loads of other marchers, all of them sweaty and haggard. So many passengers were packed into the subway car that it seemed as hot inside as it was outside and there was no air movement. She wished she could at least sit down to rest her cramping leg muscles, but she clung to a handrail above her with one hand and to Katya with the other. She didn't know how far they'd traveled when Katya led her from the subway car onto the platform. They rode an escalator up to street level into a very different part of the city. It looked more industrial – no skyscrapers here. She stopped for a moment and leaned against a brick wall but Katya urged her onward.

"This way," Katya said, finally guiding her through the door of what looked like a restaurant.

Hopefully, they could sit at a table and drink ice water and cool off. Once inside, Neave came to a halt, leaning over with her hands on her knees like an exhausted basketball player. She was panting and felt like she'd taken an elbow to the head. She thought maybe she'd cool off now that they were inside, but she felt unbearably hot and slightly dizzy. She sat down on the hard floor, closing her eyes, wishing again that she'd brought her cooling cloak with her.

"Are you all right?" Katya said, squatting next to her.

She didn't have the strength to answer. Instead, she lay down right where she was.

"Too hot," Katya said, her hand on Neave's forehead.

Then there were other voices. They were talking about her but she didn't open her eyes. Katya was telling them she needed water. A moment later, a water bottle was at her lips and a hand behind her neck, lifting her slightly so she could drink. She took a couple of sips but couldn't drink anymore.

"Not yet," Katya said. "We must cool her body. She is too hot."

She heard the voices arguing but the pounding in her head prevented her from concentrating. Sleep would help, she thought, and she tried to relax but it was like there was a bad drummer flailing away on a snare drum inside her brain. She felt water being splashed on her face and neck. Then her arms and shirt.

"Neave?" said Katya. "Drink!"

A bottle touched her lips again and she swallowed. Then more water was sprinkled on her face and arms. This continued for a while – she wasn't sure how long. Finally, she was able to open her eyes.

Katya was on her knees beside her and there were two other people standing nearby – a man with a shiny, bald head and a scruffy blonde beard, and a young woman with half her head shaved, the other half, a thatch of brown curls. They reminded her of bouncers at a nightclub.

"Okay, time for the restraints," said the woman.

"She cannot even sit up," Katya complained.

"Following orders," the woman said.

She pulled Neave's hands behind her back and applied wrist restraints. She also took her iCom, dropping it in a clear bag. It was her secure iCom which was very concerning.

"She might need doctor," Katya said.

"She'll be fine," the woman said. "She just got overheated. Give her some more water. Go ahead, Vin."

"No fucking names," he snapped, glaring at her.

Katya helped Neave sip from the bottle and sprinkled more water on her face and arms.

"Okay, Miss Alvarez," Vin said. "We need you to pay close attention."

She tried to focus. She could tell the restaurant hadn't been in business for quite a while. No staff. No customers. The only smell filling the air was the stale odor of disuse.

"I'm gonna use my iCom to record you while you make a statement," he continued. "You hear me?"

She gaped at him, trying to figure out what he was talking about.

"You're gonna make a statement claiming responsibility for disrupting the demonstration," he continued. "You're also going to defend your father's plan. Capiche?"

"She's clueless," the woman said. "Explain the situation to her."

"All right. Listen up. It's like this," Vin began. "You've been kidnapped. No one knows where you are. We've been informed your mother doesn't have any bodyguards. And, unless you do as you're told, there's a chance your mommy could get hurt. Now... do you understand?"

"She needs more water," Katya said, holding the bottle to Neave's lips again. "She also needs food."

"No time," he said, keeping his eyes on Neave. "We're gonna record your statement."

"Don't tell me," Neave said, "my father got you hooked on..."

"Zip it," he barked. "First thing you gotta do is claim

responsibility for causing the stampede. Lay it out how you helped plan the squirt gun attack – that you and five other people aimed your squirt guns into the crowd to disrupt the protest. Got it?"

She gave him as much of an evil eye as she could muster.

"We don't have all day," he said, pulling his iCom from his wrist and aiming it in her direction. "Go ahead."

"What?" Neave said.

"Tell us how you and your followers scared everyone by pointing squirt guns at them. You wanted to stop the protest because you think all those eco morons are halfwits."

"But…"

"No time for buts! Just say it! Or I'll call my people in Atlanta to go find your mother."

Katya started to speak but Vin held his hand up like a stop sign and gave her a threatening look. Then he signaled Neave to begin.

"I… uh… I was the leader of the people who pointed squirt guns into the crowd today," she said. "I did it because I wanted to ruin the demonstration."

It suddenly occurred to her: why had they not put restraints on Katya? So Katya could give her water?

"And how come you wanted to ruin the demonstration?" he said. "Use a complete sentence."

"Because…"

"Use a complete sentence!"

"I wanted to spoil the demonstration because the protesters were trying to stop the spraying of aerosols into the atmosphere."

She paused again.

"Don't make me mad, Miss Alvarez."

"I support my father's goals. He's right – we need to block

229

the sun's rays somehow."

"And why did you speak out against him before?"

"Because…"

"Complete sentences!"

"I spoke against my father before because I was misled and pressured."

"All right," he said. "That's a wrap."

It was obvious he was editing the video he'd just shot. He and the young woman turned their backs, speaking in hushed tones. But she could still hear what was being said.

"Send Alvarez a message that we'll deliver her to the drop-off point for her flight," he said. "I'm transmitting the video to the newswebs."

Neave struggled to her feet, determined to make a break for it. She mouthed "let's go" to Katya. She wasn't going to allow anyone to ship her off to her father. Katya looked away, but didn't budge. Then Vin turned around and shoved Neave back onto the floor, banging her head in the process.

"She should not be hurt!" Katya cried, her voice filled with anguish.

"Shut your face if you want your fucking money," he roared. "Mia, put restraints on her ankles too."

The young woman shackled Neave's ankles with plastic ties as she lay sprawled on her side.

"Here's your 'D,' now scram," Vin said, tossing a small packet at Katya. "Your money will be deposited an hour from now."

"You must not hurt her," she pleaded.

"We don't need any Russian advice," he said. "Just remember, you say one word and we'll track you down and put you in a dark hole, if your own people don't beat us to the punch."

Neave glared at the mild-mannered bodyguard who she thought had become her friend. She realized how naïve she'd been to trust her, thinking she knew her, thinking she was a good, caring person. She was stunned.

Katya's eyes brimmed with tears. How touching, Neave thought sarcastically. Then she ran out the door, clutching the drug, leaving Neave behind.

"I can't believe you let her go," Mia said.

"She'll be face down on the sidewalk in a few minutes from a drug overdose. You order the hub car?"

"On its way," she replied.

Vin found a news broadcast on his iCom, beaming the image to a bare wall. Neave's statement was already being aired. She could hear herself claiming responsibility for the stampede. Then there was video shot from a drone hovering above the marchers that clearly showed a woman in a black and white striped hat pointing a pistol into the crowd as demonstrators fled in panic. She could see the hat come off the woman's head, revealing shoulder-length auburn hair and a Kelly green top. She realized how thoroughly Katya set her up, giving her the hat and the green outfit. She remembered then that it was Katya who urged her to stand with the protesters so she could experience what it was like. All, so a look-alike could torpedo the demonstration and frame her, in one fell swoop. Katya was bought off, hooked on her father's favorite drug.

Which pissed her off. And she wasn't going to just lie there like a welcome mat and let them walk on her. She squirmed and wiggled until she got her knees under her. She was trying to stand up when Vin kicked her from behind, sending her sprawling once again, this time, face down. She howled in pain and frustration. Her low-life captors acted like they'd just swatted a fly, not a human being, and continued watching the news.

"One person was killed in the stampede and two others died from heatstroke," the news anchor said. "More than three dozen were injured in the crush and dozens more were taken to the hospital because of heat exhaustion. A spokeswoman tells us charges will be filed for sabotaging the sprinkler system as well as causing widespread panic. Several people have already been arrested and an intensive search is underway for the daughter of former Climate Secretary Robert Alvarez."

"I think we'll get our bonus," Vin said, chuckling.

"The car will be here in two minutes," said Mia.

"Let's stand her up."

"I can't walk with these things on," Neave objected, pointing with her chin at the ankle restraints.

She knew she didn't stand a chance of making a break for it as long as her ankles were bound together.

"Well, then, we'll just carry you," said Vin. "You don't weigh more than a six-pack of beer. Where's the tape?"

Mia peeled off a length of tape and pressed it over Neave's mouth.

They lifted her to her feet and Vin hoisted her over his shoulder, causing a wave of nausea. God, what if she threw up? Might be a serious problem with tape over her mouth. Tears welled up, but she knew she had to keep her wits about her. They waited until Mia got a notification that the car was at the door before exiting. Mia opened the door for Vin and the two of them lowered Neave to the sidewalk before chucking her into the back seat.

As Mia programmed the car's destination Neave watched a man walking along the sidewalk, waiting until he was beside the car. Then she strained to hold her arms up behind her, trying to show him she was shackled, trying to make him see that her mouth was taped shut. But he kept walking, oblivious to her plight. She eyed an approaching couple, waiting till they were close enough, then raised her arms again, pleading with her eyes. But they were engrossed in conversation and walked right by the car without even looking.

Then Mia turned around and saw what she was doing.

"Vin," she said, "maybe we should knock her out."

"No bodily harm," he replied, obviously quoting someone.

The car pulled from the curb and merged into traffic.

She grew more frantic with each passing mile. Damn my father, she thought. And Katya too! God, if she just had her Swiss Army knife. But she quickly realized with her hands shackled behind her, the knife would be useless.

"Vin," Mia cried. "There's a cop behind us."

"Can't be," he said, twisting around to peer out the back. "Dammit, take control of the car. And floor it!"

"This little piece of shit can't outrun a police cruiser."

"We can't let him stop us! Let's go!"

Mia touched the dashboard and switched to driver mode and sped up. Neave leaned to the side, trying to look behind them.

"Get down!" Vin commanded, shoving her head onto the seat.

As soon as he turned away, she raised her arms above her head, hoping the officer could see she was handcuffed. Which brought Vin's wrath down upon her again in the form of a fist to her shoulder. She grunted in pain.

"There's two of them now!" Mia cried.

"Floor it!"

"I am! I am!"

Sirens blared behind them as they tried to outrun the police.

"Jesus!" Mia screeched and swerved hard, tossing Neave to the right side of the car. "We're surrounded!"

"Squeeze between 'em!"

The wail of sirens was deafening with cop cars now in front too.

"I can't!"

Then they were bumped from behind and Mia gasped. A voice on a loudspeaker ordered them to pull over. A few seconds later they were rammed from the front and the car came to a sudden stop, throwing Neave off the back seat and onto the floor.

"Get out of the car with your hands up!"

No one moved or said anything for a moment, then Vin whirled around and cut the restraints from Neave's wrists and ankles and ripped the tape from her mouth.

"She was holding a gun on us," he coached Mia. "She was the mastermind and she was holding a gun on us. She tossed the gun out somewhere – we don't know where it is. Got it?"

No reply.

"Capiche?"

"Yeah, I capiche. We're screwed."

They opened their doors as Neave struggled to pull herself off the floor, realizing as far as the cops were concerned, she was on Vin and Mia's team. She opened the door and stepped out, immediately overcome with dizziness. She leaned against the car, hoping the weakness and vertigo would pass.

"Hands up!"

She raised her arms slightly as cops converged on the three of them. Vin and Mia were quickly placed in handcuffs and led away. She thought an officer might speak with her, maybe ask her some questions, but no one said a word as she was brusquely whirled around and cuffed behind her back once again.

"We've got her," one of the officers said into his iCom. "We're heading for the jail."

"Officer," Neave said.

"Save it."

"But..."

"Huddleston, Camacho, take her in your car."

As she was led away, she noticed a black drone hovering directly above them.

Chapter 24

The holding cell was about six by eight feet, with white walls and a plasteel toilet. The only window was a small reinforced observation glass in the door. Neave sat on a narrow bed, studying the bare floor. She was arrested for unlawfully possessing a gun, which she knew was a lie; for endangering the lives of others by causing widespread panic, another lie; for disturbing the peace, yet another lie; and for trying to elude police, which she found utterly ridiculous. But the scariest charge was involuntary manslaughter for causing the deaths of three demonstrators, the biggest lie of all.

But how could she prove her innocence? If she told police to talk with Alexei, that might blow his cover. And Katya... well, there was no way police could interview her former bodyguard. Even though she was furious with Katya for betraying her, it hurt her deeply to think she'd died of an overdose, yet another of her father's victims. She needed help. Expert help. When she spoke with her mother after she was booked, she promised to hire an attorney. But she had no idea how long she might be stuck in jail.

Then she thought of the three demonstrators who lost their lives thanks to her father. They joined a peaceful protest to send a message. No one deserved to die. Will was right – her father was evil incarnate.

She kept hoping someone would come, but finally collapsed on the hard mattress when the lights went out.

~~~

After hungrily consuming a breakfast of bland oatmeal, two slices of bread, canned fruit and coffee, she sat once again on the cot and waited. Hours later a guard brought her a plate of chicken and rice, a slice of bread, an apple and a bottle of water. Once again, she waited. Then supper was served – two tacos on stale tortillas, beans and rice, overcooked carrots, a dry brownie and milk. Determined to regain her strength, she ate every crumb. Still, nobody came.

The second night in her tiny cell was more unnerving than the first. She lay on her back in near total darkness, afraid she might actually have to serve time behind bars. Surely, some-one would come the next day, which, unfortunately, didn't come soon enough.

A recurring nightmare tormented her. She was in a room with her father and couldn't get out. She would wake up with a start, sitting bolt upright in bed, finally drift off to sleep again, only to fall back into another variation of the dream. It was a different room each time and she was always facing her father with something sinister afoot as he uttered the word "cariño."

~~~

"I'm sorry I couldn't spring you any faster, but you're actually facing some pretty serious charges."

Renee Baker was the New York attorney her mother hired. She was a sharp dresser, bi-racial and reeked of big city savvy.

"Your mother put up a wad of cash for your bond," she continued. "She obviously believes in you. I won permission for you to return to Atlanta to continue your studies but you'll be required to wear a GPS device at all times until your case is adjudicated."

She stayed with Neave while the ankle bracelet was

attached and her iCom was returned. Then she escorted her from the jail to a waiting hub car.

"I'll need to interview you at length, but I haven't got time right now and I'm sure you're tired."

She handed Neave the address of the hotel where her mother had reserved a room for her and said she'd be in touch soon.

After programming her destination, Neave messaged Will first, telling him she was okay, that she loved him and would call him soon. Then she messaged her mother, thanking her, telling her she was all right and that she would call from the hotel. Then she messaged Alexei, asking where he was. He replied immediately. He was still in NY2 and needed to talk with her right away. They agreed to meet at the hotel in an hour, which would give her time to shower. When the car pulled up to the entrance, she flashed her iCom to pay the fare and sprinted into the hotel lobby.

As she was checking in, the desk clerk did a double take.

"The stampede," he said. "You're the one who..."

"No I'm not," Neave replied rather more forcefully than she intended.

She kept her head down as she hurried to the elevator, doing her best to hide her face until she was finally in her room on the sixteenth floor. First stop was the shower but she was taken aback by her reflection in the large bathroom mirror. Her arms were bruised and scratched, she had marks on her wrists from the restraints, she had an ugly scrape on one cheek and a nasty bruise on her forehead. On top of that, she was rail thin. Her appearance brought to mind an emaciated twentieth century fashion model. She even had the zombie stare.

Once she was cleaned up, she put on fresh clothes that her

mother had ordered. Then she messaged room service for pizza and two slices of their Decadent Chocolate Cake.

The normally businesslike Alexei was not at all businesslike when he arrived. He took one look and, without a word, wrapped his arms around her in a bear hug, holding her close and rocking back and forth. Which, for some reason, opened the floodgates on her tears. She had to admit, it felt good to have someone to lean on, someone who might have an inkling of what she'd been through.

"You're hurt," he said.

"I'm fine."

She pulled away to wipe her eyes and blow her nose.

"I'm ashamed and deeply sorry that one of my people betrayed you," he said, shaking his head.

"I have to admit I never suspected Katya would turn on me. She seemed so sweet. I'm so sorry she..." but she couldn't continue.

He waited patiently while she collected herself.

"The overdose," she whispered, reaching for another tissue.

"She didn't overdose," he replied.

"But I thought..."

"No, she's all right."

She wiped her eyes, trying to absorb the news.

That's when a message arrived saying the food was at the door. Alexei set the tray on the table, retrieved two waters from the micro fridge and they sat down across from each other.

"Katya is enroute to Moscow," he explained. "Her brief career with the government is over. She will face charges and punishment."

"They gave her Discretion. They got her hooked on it. Vin

said she'd be dead as soon as she…"

"She never took the drug but let them think she was addicted. Your father offered her a lot of money but apparently had no intention of paying, assuming she would overdose after she delivered you to his operatives. It's true – a fatal dose was in that packet."

She laced her fingers together and closed her eyes for a moment, a wave of thankfulness washing over her.

"I'm so glad she's alive," she whispered, then took a slice of pizza, gesturing for Alexei to help himself.

"She needed the money," he continued. "That's why she took the job as bodyguard. Her mother has a rare disease that will probably kill her in a few years if she doesn't get a lung transplant. But insurance in my country only pays for routine medications, not a transplant. So she was desperate for cash."

She shook her head, feeling sad for Katya and her mother.

"When she left you with the kidnappers," he went on, "she called me immediately and told me what happened. She said they assured her beforehand you would not be hurt, that no one would be hurt. But she came to her senses too late and was filled with remorse."

"So she called the police?"

"I called them. They were searching the city for you, thinking you were the one who sabotaged the demonstration. So I just told them where you were. It was the fastest way to save you. They dispatched a drone, which followed the car you were in until police arrived."

"And I'm guessing all this played out on the newswebs?"

"Yes. I watched live coverage as police surrounded the hub car. I cringed as they handcuffed you like you were a common criminal."

"So everyone thinks I'm guilty."

"True. The video from the protest shows a woman in a black and white striped sun hat with auburn hair and a green shirt pointing a gun into the crowd. And everyone believes you're that woman."

"Even Annie?"

"Annie's under a lot of pressure from her organization..."

"Damn. Even Annie. Well, Katya may be a decent person but she did a bang-up job of helping my father frame me."

"Which is why my superiors have given me permission to speak to police. Besides Katya, I'm the only one who can explain what happened. Katya would be better, but my government doesn't trust her."

She realized talking with police might jeopardize his work and, who knows, possibly trigger his recall to Russia. She knew he was in the US on a student visa.

He must've read her mind.

"You are more valuable to my government than I am," he said. "Don't worry, I agree with the decision."

"You sure?"

"I'm sure."

"Thank you, Alexei."

He nodded and took a bite of pizza, as if it was no big deal.

"Could you please call Annie and convince her I didn't do it? Tell her I'm holding a news conference this afternoon so we can explain what really happened. Can you can speak at the news conference?"

"Yes. But we must keep Katya's name out of it."

"I understand."

It was obvious he wasn't thrilled with the idea of a big press event. Neither was she.

"After you talk with her, I'll call her too," she said. "I'd like her to appear with us. And I'm hoping she'll send out a blast to the news media. She's got a huge distribution list."

She breathed a sigh of relief when Annie not only agreed to support her and notify the news organizations, she said she'd make a few remarks herself. She was also heartened when her activist friend said she never believed Neave was the culprit.

They gathered on the courthouse steps, which provided plenty of space for a horde of reporters and photographers jockeying for position like a pack of wolves scrambling to get a hunk of meat after a kill. She'd watched some news reports and understood she was Public Enemy Number One. Nowhere more so than among the environmental groups that organized the giant march.

The police were notified about the event as well, so officers were positioned around the perimeter. They were also attracting a growing crowd of onlookers.

Annie opened the proceedings in her usual self-assured, chatty style.

"Okay, news peeps, time to get going. My good friend, Neave Alvarez, wants to talk with you about what really happened at the demonstration the other day. But before she steps to the mic, I just wanna say that she did not seek the limelight. I had to practically browbeat her to speak out. Just wanted you to know that."

Then she stepped aside and Neave moved to the microphones.

"First," she began, "I'd like to express my deepest condolences to the families of the three demonstrators who died. I was extremely saddened to learn of their deaths as well as the dozens of injuries. And I was shocked that what started as a peaceful demonstration was subverted for political purposes. My heart goes out to those families. And the criminals who were responsible must be brought to justice. But I want to make it clear that I was framed by my father and his mercenaries."

A bystander in the back said: "yeah, right."

"My father hired agent provocateurs, plants, agitators," she continued. "He also hired a woman to steal my sun hat, wear a wig and clothing to look like me, and to point a squirt gun into the crowd and then disappear. The last thing I wanted was for the protest to be a failure. I stand with the UN Secretary-General and environmental groups in calling for the president to back off from this aerosol scheme."

Reporters shouted questions at her but she held up her hand.

"I have a friend and fellow student with me today who also wants to say a few words. Alexei?"

Alexei stepped forward and cleared his throat. His Russian accent was unmistakable, but he seemed to be trying to minimize it as much as possible.

"My name is Alexei Sokolof. I'm a graduate student at Georgia Geosciences University in Atlanta. I met Neave in one of my classes and traveled with her and Annie Roanhorse to New York for the big protest. As you know, Neave was scheduled to be one of the speakers. I was with her at the front of the crowd and we were moving towards the stage when agitators pulled their plastic squirt guns. I can vouch for her. She knew nothing about this sabotage. She ran for her life along with thousands of other people, not knowing those guns were not real, not knowing that another woman used her hat to impersonate her.

"I will be giving a statement to police. But I would urge the media outlets that were on hand during the demonstration to study their video for a woman who stole Neave's hat and then used it to implicate her. Thank you."

Neave stepped forward again.

"Police need to give lie detector tests to the two people who kidnapped me – they called each other Vin and Mia – and ask them who hired them. They bound my wrists and ankles," she said, holding her bruised wrists up for everyone to see, "and forced me to make a statement – which they dictated – after threatening to hurt my mother. I'd also suggest that President Cohen, herself, is partly responsible for what happened the other day because she let my father go to China where he's free to do as he wishes. Free, I believe, to continue advising the president on climate policy and to threaten and attack me and my loved ones."

She glared at the reporters, one by one.

"Why aren't you asking the president about this? And maybe the Chinese government too. You're supposed to be journalists. Do your job!"

~~~

"I hope you're heading home now," Will said.

She waited to call him until late that night, which was early morning in east Africa.

"Not yet," Neave answered. "I've got some network interviews scheduled for tomorrow."

"Neave…"

"I have to exonerate myself."

"I know, I know."

"And we're finally getting some traction. The Secretary-General says she's calling for a vote in the UN General Assembly."

"I saw you online," he said. "You look like a prison camp escapee."

"Thanks."

"I just mean you need more rest, more food, more TLC. Which is what I'm going to give you when I get home."

"Yeah?"

"Yeah, and lots of it. Oh, by the way, can we can trust Alexei anymore? Jesus!"

"It wasn't his fault."

"Right."

Chapter 25

"I'm so sorry, chica," Rosa said, hugging Neave close. "You've been through the wringer. And those poor souls who died. Dios mio. Muy triste."

She'd stopped by with a homemade Mexican casserole and brownies loaded with walnuts, insisting Neave eat six meals a day until she had more flesh on her bones. A part of her liked having Rosa fawn over her. But another part of her wanted to avoid thinking about the tragedy. So she asked how Isabel was doing.

"She's been talking non-stop about the outing to the Old Timey Game Pavilion," Rosa said. "But I told her we'll have to wait a little bit because you're not feeling well right now."

"Good idea," said Dr. Sullivan.

"No way," Neave said. "I'm fine. In fact, it would be a pleasant change of pace to do something just for fun. No stress, no pressure."

Because she was definitely feeling pressure. Annie was pushing her to do more interviews. She said Neave was a rock star now in the anti-aerosol campaign after being abducted by her father's goons and showing up on the news two days later looking like she'd been in a prize fight. And Alexei said they needed to call her father again, that the Russian IT people had tweaked his tracking device and he was anxious to give it a try. Will and Charlie were supposed to fly home after a successful sales trip that lasted a lot longer than anyone expected. And she wanted to make sure she had time to spend with Will. So she was feeling a little overwhelmed.

She didn't want to let Isabel down, or Will. After all, she'd promised him she'd take his baby sister somewhere. There was also the attraction of doing something as simple as going to a kiddie amusement park and not thinking about anything else for a little while.

"Let's go tomorrow," Neave said. "It'll be a relaxing outing."

~~~

She concealed her bruises and scrapes with makeup as best she could and wore her long-sleeved pale blue climate suit to cover the marks on her wrists and ankles.

Angela and Jaz didn't go with them. They had a couple of Skype sales appointments. It was Rosa, Isabel, Gib and their bodyguard, Dmitry, who stopped by in a rented hub van for Neave and Alexei that morning. Alexei was staying close to her until his government dispatched another female bodyguard.

"You can sit next to me," Isabel said, as Neave stepped in.

So she sat in the middle seat with Isabel while Alexei squeezed into the back with Rosa. Dimitry was in the driver's seat with Gib up front beside him.

"What's wrong with your face, Neave?" Isabel asked. "Did you fall down?"

"As a matter of fact, I did," she replied, glad the family had shielded her from the troubling news.

Rosa leaned forward and whispered in Neave's ear.

"You did good. I've been seeing more reports on the president's ties with Roberto."

Neave had seen them too, but this morning she was hoping for a little vacation from worrying about all that.

"What kind of games do they have there?" Isabel said,

squirming happily in her seat.

"Well, one of them is a game called hopscotch," Neave said. "It's a lot of fun."

"How do you play it?"

"You have to hop on one foot."

"Oh boy!"

Although it was a weekday, the pavilion was crowded and noisy, with kids' shrieking voices echoing off the high ceiling. It was a brick building, about twice the size of a school gym. A combination of AC and fans kept the temperature a comfortable eighty-five degrees. The walls were covered with viewscreens displaying a changing kaleidoscope of brightly colored children's art and neon balloons. The pavilion was divided into sections for different games. Isabel was keen to find out more about hopscotch, so that's where they headed first.

As they walked, Neave leaned over and whispered to Rosa.

"I want to take Gib on some kind of outing too. Any idea what he's into?"

"One thing I know for sure – he wants to be an actor."

Neave nodded, wondering if he'd enjoy seeing a play.

"Hop… scotch," Isabel said, sounding out the sign above the play area.

She was fascinated as they watched kids hopping this way and that on a dozen painted hopscotch grids. Then Neave took her hand and led her to an empty court.

"Okay," said Neave, "first, let's do some hopping before we actually play a game."

Neave took off hopping on one foot through three single blocks, then landed on both feet in two side-by-side squares, then hopped on one foot again till she got to the other end, where she turned around and hopped back.

"Now, your turn," she said.

Isabel imitated Neave's performance, although she was a little shaky and had to put her other foot down a couple of times.

"Yay!" Neave cried when she got back to the starting point.

"You're a natural," Rosa added, causing Isabel to beam with pride.

Gib gave it a try as well, obviously enjoying himself. Then Rosa attempted to hop on one foot but couldn't keep her balance.

"You just have to practice, Aunt Rosa," Isabel piped up.

Rosa laughed but Neave wondered if she was just faking it to make Isabel feel superior. That's definitely something Rosa would do.

After spending fifteen minutes at hopscotch, Isabel was ready to move on.

"What other games do they have?"

"Let's see," Neave said, scanning the signs, "there's jacks, hide and seek, jump rope, marbles, pickup sticks, tag, croquet and four square."

"Let's do jump rope!"

So they visited the jump rope area. Neave and Rosa held either end of a long rope, slowly swinging it from side to side to get Isabel used to jumping over it. Then Gib took Neave's end of the rope and he and Rosa swung it in a big arc, round and round, so Neave could jump over the rope each time it hit the floor. Rosa chanted an old jump rope rhyme as Neave bounced up and down.

"Not last night but the night before, twenty-four robbers came a knockin' at my door. As I ran out, they ran in, hit me over the head with a rolling pin."

"Rosa! That's so violent! You used to sing that?"

"My grandmother taught it to me. She said her grandmother taught it to her. That's what they used to sing when they played jump rope at school."

Everyone laughed, even Alexei and Dimitry.

Jump rope was a bit of a challenge for Isabel, though. So Neave guided them next to the hide and seek area, which had several smaller enclosures and two larger ones where lots of kids were playing together. Each one included artificial rocks and trees and various sized structures for hiding. Neave chose a smaller area that was being vacated by a birthday party group.

"Okay," she said. "Everyone hides except for one person, who has to find all the others. That person is called 'it.'"

"It?" Isabel asked, crinkling up her nose.

"That's right. So the person who's 'it' covers his eyes and counts to twenty-five while everyone else hides. This is home base," she said, touching a small fake tree behind her. "You have to run and touch home base without 'it' catching you."

She could see Isabel wasn't quite sure about the rules which were posted on an LED sign that Gib studied with interest.

"The easiest way to learn is to play the game," Neave said. "Okay, Gib, you're 'it.' Close your eyes and count out loud while the rest of us hide." She took Isabel's hand to help her find a spot.

Dimitry and Alexei stepped back and folded their arms across their chests, talking genially in Russian. Rosa scurried toward the right and Neave guided Isabel to the left side, behind one of the large artificial rocks near the fence.

"...thirteen, fourteen, fifteen," Gib counted, loud enough for everyone to hear.

Isabel giggled in her hiding place and Neave put her finger

to her lips to shush her, then rushed off to find a hiding place for herself.

"...twenty-two, twenty-three, twenty-four, twenty-five. Ready or not, here I come!" Gib turned around and rushed into the play area. "Where is everybody?" he said, prompting another giggle close on his left. He turned right and searched behind a green playhouse. "I found you!" he cried, pointing his finger at Rosa.

"Ay caramba!" Rosa said, playing along.

Then he charged around the play area until he spied Neave crouching behind a wooden gate.

"I found Neave!" he cried. "Now, where can Isabel be?" He took his time checking every possible hiding place except the one where he knew she was hiding. "Not here," he said, moving to another spot.

"Gib's a natural," Neave whispered to Rosa, as the two came together.

"It's like he's an experienced children's camp counselor," Rosa agreed, chuckling.

Then Gib suddenly took off running, full throttle, across the play area to the fence that divided it from a larger hide and seek enclosure. For a split second, Neave thought he was playing but he leaped over the fence without breaking stride, calling Isabel's name.

It took a moment for Neave and Rosa to realize what was going on as Alexei and Dimitry raced after him.

Neave caught a glimpse of two men wearing red and white striped shirts galloping through the theme park, weaving through the crowds, heading toward the exit. One of them was struggling to carry something. That something was Isabel.

"Stop them, stop them!" she called out, pointing at the

men, then joined in the chase.

Gib looked like a cheetah pursuing a couple of wildebeests, running full tilt. But he was one skinny teenager against two full-grown men used to doing bad things for money. And there was too much confusion, too much noise. The men were also dressed like pavilion staffers, so people stepped aside to let them pass. Alexei was not far behind but Neave could see the kidnappers approaching the exit and she feared a car was waiting just outside the door to whisk them away. Just as they were about to disappear through the doorway, Gib caught up with them, Alexei close behind. She couldn't see what happened next, racing as fast as her legs would carry her. When she reached the exit, she found Isabel and Gib sprawled on the floor, the men in the striped shirts gone and Alexei and Dimitry nowhere in sight.

Isabel was bawling as Gib crawled over to her and scooped her up in his arms. Neave collapsed beside them, out of breath, noticing blood trickling down Isabel's arm. She pulled her iCom from her pocket and called 911 as Rosa jogged toward them.

"Chiquita, are you all right?" Rosa cried, dropping to her knees beside Gib and Isabel.

But Isabel was crying and unable to answer, clinging to Gib's neck.

"I had to tackle the guy," Gib explained, gasping for breath. "So she landed on the floor pretty hard."

"You did the right thing," Neave said.

Dimitry and Alexei returned empty handed, red-faced and sweating profusely. Guilt hung over them like thick smog. Then Neave caught Rosa's eye and saw that Rosa, too, blamed herself for suggesting they come to the pavilion in the first place. But she knew that she, not Rosa, was the one to blame for the danger to Isabel and the rest of the Galloway family. Since they told no one outside the family about the outing, she could only assume they were followed. So much for bodyguards and encrypted iComs.

Neave briefed two police officers about what happened but they were not encouraging about finding the two men. Gib didn't have much of a description to offer. He only saw them from the back.

The paramedic said Isabel only suffered scrapes and bruises. Gib as well. But they were both shaken. Neave heard Isabel talking quietly to Gib as he continued holding her.

"I wanna live somewhere that has rainbows," she said. "And flowers. And I don't want anymore snakes or hurricanes or floods or dust storms or anymore mean outlaws."

"Me neither," Gib said, stroking her shiny black hair.

Rosa called Angela to explain what happened as they headed home. Better that she knew ahead of time than walk in and surprise her, Rosa said. Neave and Alexei dropped them off without going inside.

"We're all being watched," she said once they were alone.

"Let's go to the campus library," he said. "We'll stop by and pick up your old iCom."

It was two o'clock by the time they reached the study room. Neave dreaded speaking with her father again. But the attempted abduction, coming so close on the heels of events in NY2, made it perfectly clear how serious he was, if anyone had any doubt.

"You've got to trace his location. So crank up that tracking device."

She tapped her fingers impatiently, waiting for him to give her the go-ahead.

"God, what am I supposed to say?" she said.

"It doesn't matter."

She closed her eyes and steeled herself before clicking on his code.

"Cariño."

"Father."

"Thank you for calling me. I hope the little girl was not injured."

She took a deep breath, trying to calm herself.

"She's all right, no thanks to you."

"I saw news coverage of your latest charges against me."

"Father, you had me kidnapped!"

"I was just trying to bring us together…"

"Three people died!"

"Sweetheart, I warned you. You're responsible. Not me."

She couldn't think.

"I told you I was punishing you," he said. "You aren't paying attention. And it's not just a single lesson, sweetheart. When you repeatedly cross your own father by continuing to have relations with a subhuman clone and making all those nasty accusations… well, enough is enough. I need you to pack your suitcase for a flight to China. I have a beautiful home here to share with you. A pretty bedroom with a window overlooking a lovely garden. You always wanted a window."

"Father…"

She wanted to tell him that she would never live with him, no matter what, and that she would not help him with his work.

"Are you still there?" he said.

"Yes. I'm just tired."

"I'm sure you are. But once you're here with me, you won't have to worry about the Galloways anymore. I'll make sure you get plenty of rest."

"Your men scared Isabel to death. You can't drag an innocent child into this."

"You have only yourself to blame, cariño."

She ended the connection and slumped in her chair as Alexei tapped away on his laptop. He muttered something in Russian.

"The Galloways need to go into hiding," Alexei said. "We'll make arrangements immediately."

~~~

Will and Charlie returned the next day. She only found out because Rosa called her on the sly.

"Esta furioso," she said. "He won't even talk about it. But Charlie told Angela when they got to their meeting in Addis Ababa, they were told the meeting was cancelled because they found out Will is a clone."

"Oh no!"

"Charlie said at first that Will tried to reason with them, telling them Galloway Energy is a well-established company they could trust to get the job done at a reasonable price. But when the man refused to even talk with them, saying they only dealt with 'real people,' Charlie said Will got so angry he said some vulgar things. He wouldn't tell Angela exactly what Will said, so it must've been pretty bad."

"God."

"They tried to set up some other meetings but word spread very fast, so no one would meet with them. Charlie says Will wanted to head straight to Somalia to set up some sales calls there but he convinced him they needed to come home and lay the groundwork before showing up uninvited."

"Oh, Rosa, I need to see him, to talk with him."

"Well," she said, "better wait for him to contact you. I wouldn't come over here, that's for sure."

She waited all day. He finally called her that night.

"I've gotta make this quick," he said, his voice strained. "You know how much I love you, Neave. I dream about you every night. At least twice a night. Usually, three or four times a night. I wanted to come home and wrap my arms around you. But I can't. After what happened at the park, we've decided to take Alexei's advice and disappear for a while. So I have to keep my distance."

"Will, I'm so sorry."

"Not your fault. I know that, we all know that. But no more visits, calls or messages till further notice. I wish... well... when it's not necessary anymore, we'll..."

"Will..."

"I have to protect my family."

She found it hard to breathe.

"This is the way it's gotta be for the time being," he said, his voice so low, she could hardly hear him.

"Will, I heard what happened in Ethiopia."

"Can't talk about that right now. I've gotta go."

There was no way she could sleep. No way she could even sit still. So she grabbed her cooling cloak and slipped out the door into the muggy night air without saying a word to anyone. But Alexei caught up with her before she reached the corner.

"I need to be alone," she said.

"I'll keep my distance."

She took the subway downtown and looked for a shop where she could get a coffee or something. Alexei kept his promise, hanging far enough behind so she almost forgot he was there.

The revolving skyscrapers were bathed in blue light, their fluid outlines shifting ever so slowly, reminding Neave of unearthly ballerinas dancing to the sorrowful, dramatic strains of *Dance of the Swans* in *Swan Lake*. She remembered how she and her best friend J'Nai wiped tears from their eyes as the curtains closed when they were twelve years old. She had imagined her father as Rothbart, the evil knight.

Her iCom buzzed, and thinking it might be Will, she checked the screen and was surprised it was Charlie. He wanted to talk so she agreed to meet him at Coffee Casa.

He gave her a hug when he joined her at the table. He was wearing a camo safari hat, which, somehow, made him look like a totally different person – not the sophisticated, mild-mannered family peacemaker she'd come to know. He sipped on a mocha while she had a frap.

She resisted the urge to pepper him with questions, waiting for him to speak.

"It was your father," he said finally. "He had his people send out information to anti-clone groups all over the world about Will. Pictures, bio, info on our company – the works. Will suspects that not only does your dad hate clones, but that he also hates Will, in particular, because he's pushing clean energy products. And your dad's all about dirty energy, which helps sell his geo-engineering plan."

It was odd hearing her father referred to as "dad," something she'd never called him. She didn't call him "daddy" as a little girl either. Which her friend, J'nai, asked her about more than once. She always replied "he's not my daddy, he's my father." No wonder J'nai thought her family was weird.

She exhaled sharply as though that might release the pressure inside her.

"And Will's on the warpath," he continued. "When the Ethiopian energy secretary sent one of his minions out to tell us our meeting was cancelled, and then told us it was because

Will's a clone, I thought he was gonna collar the guy and strangle him right there in the lobby."

She couldn't even formulate a response.

"But I've gotta give it to him," he continued, "he's not taking it lying down. The Clone-Aid eJournal has been after him for a while to do an interview about our energy business. So, he's decided now's the time. He's totally coming out of the closet. He figures if your mother can do it, so can he. I get it, but I'm worried about possible repercussions. There's lots of anti-clone sentiment out there."

She looked up, focusing on the ceiling fan spinning around above them.

"He must wish he'd never laid eyes on me," she finally said. "And I don't blame him."

"That's not what he wishes," Charlie said.

"Mm-hm."

Chapter 26

Dragging herself out of bed the next morning was hell. What little sleep she'd gotten was more like dipping a toe into slumber lake rather than taking a swim. A tall coffee helped. But her day was a blur. She still felt like she was sleepwalking when she got home. And when she stepped through the door, she thought for a split second she might be in the wrong place. It smelled like an Italian restaurant, the tangy aroma of garlic and onions filling the air. She found her mother at the stove, stirring with one hand and holding a glass of red wine with the other.

"I decided to make you a home-cooked meal, dear."

Which meant first, that her mother had come home from work early, and second, that she thought Neave needed to gain weight.

"I didn't know you could cook. Besides that peanut butter sandwich, that is."

"Well, I'm living proof that you *can* teach an old dog new tricks." She laughed and took a sip of wine. "I looked up directions to make spaghetti online but I cheated with the garlic bread – bought a package of frozen pre-made bread sticks. Wonderful air freshener even if it doesn't pan out, don't you think?"

Neave chuckled and opened one of her wine chillers.

"Tell Alexei it's time for dinner," her mother said.

Neave found him out front talking on his iCom in Russian. She signaled him that supper was ready but he whispered he'd be in later. So it was just her and her mother at the table. Which suited her fine.

She was pleasantly surprised at how good the meal was.

"Reminds me of the spaghetti Will made when I first met him at..." But her voice cracked unexpectedly and she paused a moment.

"At Charleston?" Dr. Sullivan said.

She nodded.

"I feel like my life is on hold, Mother."

"I disagree, dear. You're working on your master's, you're helping Will find prospects for his energy business and, amazingly enough, you've become a de facto leader of the anti-geo-engineering movement. All this, while doing your best to prevent your father from..."

"From putting my life on hold! And screwing the planet! God, he makes me crazy!"

"I know it's hard, dear, but try not to..."

"I'm not a calm person like you are."

"But you're a good person, a caring person, and you don't give up. Now, eat some spaghetti. Please?"

She took another bite, but spoke again with her mouth full.

"And I'm mooching off of you! You're paying all my bills. I can only guess how much you had to fork over to that New York lawyer to get me out of jail! And I have to go back next week for a hearing."

"I have enough money. I'm also putting the house on the market. I decided you can have the proceeds. Sort of like an early inheritance."

"Mother!"

"Listen, I'm not a billionaire or anything, but I started out with some money and invested wisely, unlike some people we know. And, for the first time in my life, I'm happy. So, try to relax. At least about the money. I'm so proud of you."

Neave suddenly felt like a little girl again.

~~~

"I am visiting relatives in Korea." That was the caption for a picture of a nondescript high-rise apartment building – the latest post from Kwan.

All wrong, she thought. It was almost ten o'clock but she jumped up and headed out the door, Alexei jogging to catch up with her.

"Where are you going?" he asked.

"To Kwan's apartment."

She quickened her pace toward the transit station. She'd been to Kwan's a couple of times with Lena, but not recently. He had a new roommate and she hoped to find him at home.

"Who's Kwan?" Alexei asked.

So she filled him in as they rode the train, telling him how she became friends with Kwan after getting to know him in her climatology classes. She also told him about the mysterious trip to Korea.

"Gabe?" she said, when the door opened.

She looked up into the face of the handsomest man she'd ever laid eyes on. He was about six-two, multi-racial, and had the look of a guy who was happy to be alive. Which Neave envied.

"Do I know you?" he asked.

"I'm a friend of Kwan's. Neave Alvarez."

He nodded enthusiastically.

"Come in," he said, motioning for them to enter. "Kwan's right – you're even better looking in person. Of course, he made it clear when I met you to forget about it, because you're unavailable." His laugh was as attractive as he was.

"This is my friend, Alexei," she said.

Alexei nodded as they stepped into the apartment, which was a mix of colors and textures – not your typical manly décor of greys and tans.

"You do know Kwan's not here, right?"

"Yeah. But I was wondering if he might've told you where he was going and why."

"Ya know, it's kinda weird. You'd think he'd tell his roommate. But I didn't know anything about his trip until I got a message saying he was flying to Korea to take care of family business. That was *after* he left, though, not before. So I assumed maybe there was an emergency or something."

"So you don't know what kind of family matter it is?"

"No idea. And I can't tell anything from his weird posts."

"No kidding. And they don't even sound like Kwan."

"Exactly," he said. "It's like a robot writes them. But I figured – hey, he's posting in English and using the translator into Korean."

"So he hasn't contacted you directly?"

"Nope. And I don't have a clue how long he'll be gone. He's missing classes, though. Don't know if he worked something out with his professors or what."

"Do you know anything about his family in Korea?"

"He never mentioned them," he said. "I assumed he didn't have any family there, any more than I have relatives in Europe or Africa or South America. His dad's a college administrator in California. His mom's in advertising."

"Has he been having any problems recently?" Alexei asked.

Gabe thought for a moment before answering.

"Well, he's been kind of frustrated about working for Dr. Yong. He told me he thought it would be fun, but it hasn't turned out that way. He says they started out good buddies, but as soon as Yong began working at the university, he was all business, all the time. But, I think what really threw him for a loop was Lena's death. That really hit him hard. Did you know Kwan was in love with Lena?"

Neave shook her head. She'd always thought they were compadres, partners in crime. She was clueless about Kwan's true feelings.

"But Lena told him they should just be good friends," Gabe continued. "That way, no one would get hurt and they could be friends forever."

"And I thought I knew them," Neave said, disappointed in herself for not caring enough to know her friends better.

"You think something's wrong?" Gabe asked.

"I don't know."

Which was a lie. All of a sudden, she did think something was wrong.

She declined his offer of a drink and thanked him for his time. She and Alexei said their farewells and headed home.

She wished she could talk with Will but he told her not to call. And while she understood completely where he was coming from, it didn't make the silence between them any easier.

They sat side by side on the train, but she was lost in thought. She should've realized sooner that Kwan wasn't the one posting on his social media page. If he ever visited Korea, he would've made a big deal out of it even if there were some kind of family emergency, which she didn't believe. Gabe confirmed the impression she'd always had of Kwan – that he knew nothing about Korea and didn't have any connections. But apparently someone else didn't know that. Someone made the false assumption that if he was Korean American, his parents were immigrants. That person also had no clue how Kwan talked. His posts didn't have even the tiniest trace of his ever-present, politically incorrect, crude sense of humor.

It was subterfuge. Someone had Kwan's iCom and was trying to cover up... what? She didn't want to consider the possibilities. It had never crossed her mind that Kwan, of all people, might be at risk. She'd worried about Will and his family and her mother and Rosa. But she never considered that Kwan might be a target.

They were walking home from the transit station before either of them spoke again.

"It seemed like Gabe was flirting with you."

She cocked her head in thought.

"Yeah, what was it he said at the door?" she said.

"He said Kwan indicated he should not pursue you because you're unavailable."

"Exactly. Kwan told him I'm engaged."

Alexei was scrolling on his iCom as they walked and abruptly came to a halt.

"Something wrong?" she said.

"My government says the aerosol injections have already begun, that Chinese aircraft have been spraying sulfates into the atmosphere for several days. They have released this information to the media."

She pulled her iCom from her pocket and found the web exploding with the news. News organizations were clamoring for comment from the White House.

They stood on the sidewalk in the dark, watching reports, reading articles – both of them stunned. Then there was a live broadcast of a statement by Canadian Prime Minister Leo Habib. They both tuned in.

"The Canadian government has received confirmation

that the United States and China have been spraying sulfate aerosols into the atmosphere at least since last Thursday. I have calls in to President Rachel Cohen and President Guo Jianping, but have not heard back from either of them. I speak for Canada in denouncing the secret launch of these aerosols as an act of war by the US and China. Canada calls for the immediate suspension of these flights and a halt of what amounts to geo-engineering vigilantism."

Then he repeated his statement in French.

"I expect my president will be speaking out as well," Alexei said. "This is a grave development."

Chapter 27

She'd planned on getting to class early the next day to get a seat near the front and had already asked Alexei to give her some privacy after class so she could talk with Yong. But when she hurried into the kitchen to get a banana to eat on the train, her mother was on her iCom, eyes closed, shaking her head. Neave stalled, brewing herself a cup of coffee as Alexei wandered in, a quizzical expression on his face.

"You don't know the cause?" Dr. Sullivan said, then paused. "How long will the investigation take?" Another pause. "Do I need to file any forms?" She waited again. "Really?" She listened. "Yes. Certainly. Thank you."

"Mother?"

Dr. Sullivan nodded her head slightly, her eyes unfocused, as though processing an information overload.

"That was the fire department," her mother explained. "There was a major fire at my house last night."

Neave squinted in disbelief.

"Investigators don't know yet what caused the blaze," Dr. Sullivan continued, "but they say it spread so quickly, they believe it may have been intentionally set. And while the house is a total loss, thankfully, since it was vacant, no one was hurt."

"I'm very sorry," said Alexei.

"The 'for sale' sign had only been up a few days," Dr. Sullivan said. "But the realtor had already gotten several inquiries."

"Father," Neave said angrily.

"Maybe."

"No maybe about it!"

"Don't worry, dear. I have good insurance."

"That's not the point!"

"And the lieutenant told me they found something very interesting in the yard," Dr. Sullivan said. "Little spy bots. The size of a roach. That's how Robert was spying on the Galloways."

"Makes me wonder how long they've been there," said Neave. "And it also makes me wonder if he can deploy them anywhere he wants to without even going inside. Like maybe this condo."

She looked straight at Alexei who rubbed his beard thoughtfully.

"We'll scan the apartment," he said.

Neave detected a guilty look as though his people should've thought of this possibility already.

She stormed out of the house, forgetting her coffee and banana on the kitchen counter.

By the time they got to class, the seats in front were taken so they had to sit toward the back. As soon as Yong concluded his lecture, she was out the door. Lucky for her, another student delayed his departure for a couple of minutes, so she was waiting in the hallway when he hurried from the room.

"Li, can I walk you to your office?"

"I have a meeting I must attend."

"Just wanted to ask if you've heard from Kwan."

"I have not. But he has posted on social."

Which made the hairs on her arms prickle.

"Yeah, I've seen the posts. But I've messaged him and he doesn't reply."

"Maybe he is busy with his family matters."

"I guess so. By the way, I'm going to New DC again next week. I'm dreading the trip, it's so hot up there. I think it's the kind of heat you and I had to deal with when we flew up to stop the treaty signing."

"You must be careful then."

"Yeah, I'll wear a climate suit this time. I guess I could sit in the fountain to keep cool like we did last time."

He didn't reply.

"I think the fountain saved us that day," she said, chuckling. "But you're the one who made it possible for me to get away from the cops. You were wearing that yellow mini-dress and pink leggings, with a scarf on your head and lipstick. You told police Nat tried to kiss you. Remember that?"

She waited for him to object to her twisted version of events, but he only nodded and walked faster.

"You did look like an odd young woman," Neave added. "I think it confused Nat and those officers."

She watched him out of the corner of her eye as he nodded again.

"Oh, and I was hoping to buy another hat at that shop where you bought one for me after we got off the train," she lied, remembering only too well how Yong bought the hat from some random woman who was wearing it at the time. "I was really out of it. Do you remember the name of the shop?"

"No, I do not remember."

"Well, I'll probably recognize it. It was on the right side after we got off the subway."

They arrived at his office and he quickly unlocked the door, turning briefly and nodding at her.

"So sorry, I must go," he said.

"No problem. But please let me know if Kwan calls or messages you."

"Certainly."

She had to force herself to walk normally rather than run down the hallway and out the door. Hurrying through the entryway, she was about to call Alexei when she heard familiar voices and saw him and Annie engrossed in conversation at the bottom of the front steps.

"Have you heard the news?" Annie called.

"What?"

"The UN General Assembly has voted to condemn the United States and China for the aerosol plan!"

"The resolution was sponsored by my country," Alexei explained. "It calls the plan illegal, a direct violation of the UN charter and a violation of the sovereignty of other nations."

"Will there be any sanctions?"

"Only in the court of world opinion because the UN Security Council won't follow suit. The US and China are both members and would block any sanctions."

"Well, it's still humongous news," Annie said. "A real victory, if you ask me!"

Alexei raised his right hand toward her.

"Do Americans still do the high five?"

Annie slapped his hand hard and laughed.

"Gotta go," she chirped, prancing along the sidewalk. Then she turned around and called out to Alexei: "See you tonight!"

He nodded as his cheeks reddened.

If she hadn't been so preoccupied she might've asked him if he was dating Annie. But right now, it was irrelevant.

"I have some important news too," she said. "But we need to talk privately."

She'd never been to Alexei's apartment and didn't know he lived in micro housing.

"How many square feet?" she asked.

"Three hundred twenty."

"Cool."

"It's like a closet."

Which was true. But it was an attractive closet. Tan sofa, white lamp table, Oriental rug and touches of Russia. There was a framed picture of St. Basil's Cathedral in Red Square, a set of brightly painted Russian nesting dolls, and a small, rectangular plaque on the wall with Hebrew lettering and a Star of David carved on it.

"That's a replica of a mezuzah," he said, noticing what she was looking at. "It contains verses from the Torah."

"You're Jewish?"

"One of the few Russian Jews left. And while I don't have a Samovar, I do have some excellent black tea and Russian tea cakes."

He opened a cabinet door, revealing a stovetop, and fixed them both a cup of tea and spread a few cookies covered with powdered sugar on a plate, inviting her to sit with him at a small white table. Sunlight streamed through French doors that opened onto a small balcony.

He offered her a cookie, but she waved it away.

"So, tell me your news," he said, blowing into his steaming cup.

"I've been a fool, Alexei. I couldn't see the forest for the trees. I didn't realize the scope of his offensive."

"Your father?"

She nodded and sipped the strong, aromatic tea, trying to figure out where to start.

"When did I tell you Kwan left suddenly to go to Korea?" she said.

"Last night when we went to his apartment."

"You see? I didn't think it was significant enough to tell

you. How naïve I've been."

He tasted his tea and waited for her to continue.

"He didn't really go to Korea. I'm sure of it. He disappeared and someone has his iCom and is posting ridiculous, fake travel pictures on social media. Or, as Li says, 'on social.'"

She yanked out her iCom and searched until she found Kwan's original post, which she read out loud. "'I am on my way to Korea to take care of unexpected family affairs. I will post on social.' Who says that? Except maybe a non-native English speaker. And since when does Kwan sound like a robot, as Gabe put it? I'm an idiot!"

"When did he leave?"

"I'm not really sure. But there's more, much more. I think Yong has disappeared too."

"But..."

"Yeah, I know. He's been at the university teaching classes. He's been in New Washington, advising the president. He's appeared with her at two news conferences. But, you know what? I think the guy we've been watching these past few weeks is not Yong Li at all. He's an imposter."

"But..."

"It was hard for me to believe too. If I'd paid closer attention, I would've realized what was going on sooner. He asked me to go on a date with him. I was stunned. And when I reminded him that Will and I were engaged, he said Kwan told him we'd broken up. Except I never told Kwan that Will broke off our engagement when I was recovering from Dengue fever. I told my father, though. Which makes me think this imposter Yong Li is working for my father, acting as his surrogate, pushing the shade ring until the huge international backlash made the president shift tactics. Then the fake Yong – whatever his real name is – came out in support of aerosol spraying."

"Neave…"

"And ever since we got back from Florida," she continued, "I've noticed Yong speaking differently. Kwan said he'd been coaching him, helping him improve his English. And suddenly, he didn't have a sense of humor. Not even a tiny smidgen. And I happen to know the real Yong Li even knows how to tell a joke."

"But…"

"I'm not through yet. Listen to this. I gave him a test today after class."

"A test?"

"Yes. I told him I was going to DC again and I was recalling our trip to New Washington when he helped me stop the shade ring treaty signing. I intentionally lied to him about some details – about what he was wearing when we were in the fountain, about what he said to distract the police, and about where he bought a sun hat for me – and he didn't even know the difference. He's not the man who helped me get to the treaty signing! He's a fake!"

"But…"

"And, you know what?" she continued. "When he asked me out, he wanted to take me to a 'music play' – his words – which is exactly what my father encouraged Nat Patel to do, after pumping my old friend, J'nai, for information."

She could tell she lost him there but didn't care.

"I kept trying to figure out who told my father Will and I had reconciled," she said. "I thought it might've been Katya or one of the other bodyguards. I suspected Barry King. But it didn't dawn on me that it was Li, after we had lunch that day. I trusted him as my friend."

Alexei rose from the table and set their tea cups in the tiny sink. Without a word, he mixed two martinis, dropping an olive in each, setting one in front of Neave and sipping his as he paced around the cramped living room. Neave took a swig of hers as well.

"I heard rumors of a second clone of Dr. Zhang," he finally said. "But there was never any confirmation. They must have kept him well hidden."

"It crossed my mind that Yong might be under pressure to do as my father says because his mother might be killed if he doesn't."

"His mother?"

"Yes, he has a mother… a surrogate mother. She raised him till he was, like, eight years old. But if it was coercion, he'd still remember our trip to New Washington. So I dismissed that. Is there any chance some kind of brainwashing might be involved?"

"I suppose it's possible."

"But if I'm right and the guy who's been standing with the president is a fake, where's the real Yong Li? Is he still alive? And what about Kwan? How do we find them?"

He downed his drink and fixed himself another.

"Alexei, we've got to locate my father. He's the one pulling the strings."

"I know."

"If your government isn't serious about this, I have to find another way."

"My government is serious. I received a message today that President Kupchenko will make a statement this evening calling on China and the US to back down. I'm told her address will be aggressive, maybe even bordering on bellicose."

"Good God."

She finished her martini and stood to leave.

"Please don't do anything... rash," he said. "I'll be in touch very soon. I need to talk with my superiors."

"You tell your superiors that Kwan is missing, possibly dead; Yong Li isn't Yong Li; and the real Yong Li might also be dead or in some prison in China; Will's six year old baby sister was nearly kidnapped despite having two bodyguards with us at the time; his family has gone into hiding and I can't even communicate with him anymore; Will's sister Toni is dead and my cousin Lena and Dr. Osley were both murdered because of my father; and you say your Russian operative was killed as well; one of your own bodyguards was bribed into helping my father cause the deaths of three innocent people and nearly succeeded in having me hauled off to China. And now, your president is about to threaten war with my country over this aerosol spraying program! I'm beginning to think your government is just stringing me along. I don't have time to screw around any longer!"

"Neave..."

"Enough's enough! I'm not sitting around waiting anymore for you to trace my father's location. I'm tired of being used as bait. The big fish is too smart for your Russian anglers. I'm done!"

"You can't do this by yourself."

"Sometimes, Alexei, I wonder if your superiors never had any intention of really tracking down my father's location at all. Maybe you and your bosses were manipulating me, using me as a Russian mouthpiece to further your country's political agenda."

"That's not..."

"I'm beginning to wonder if Russia actually prefers higher sea levels."

"Neave…

"Because it opens up more Arctic shipping and maybe more usable land in Siberia."

"We…"

"Regardless, I'm terminating our partnership."

"You can't do it alone!"

"Well, maybe I'll find a new partner."

And she stalked out, slamming the door behind her.

The walk from his apartment to the transit station took longer than she expected and she was broiling in the ruthless sun, despite her climate suit and umbrella. She was relieved when she descended the stairs into the station. But she wanted more than just relief from the sun.

If Alexei and the Russian government couldn't track her father's whereabouts, maybe she should turn elsewhere for help. She thought of Barry King. Had she burned her bridges with him? And what about appealing to the president, herself? What could she offer them in exchange for their assistance in bringing her father to justice? Or at least, reining him in. It might be a long shot, but a long shot was better than no shot at all.

~~~

"Barry, thanks for calling me back," she said, forcing herself to use his first name.

"Always a pleasure, Neave."

"I wondered if we could meet in the next day or two to talk about something."

"I'll have to check my schedule. What's on your mind?"

"It's about my father. Actually, it's about stopping my father. I really need your assistance."

"What kind of assistance?"

"I'm hoping you can help me set up a meeting with

President Cohen."

"You're kind of on her shit list right now."

"But I think she'd be interested in what I have to say."

"So you want me to convince her to give you a few minutes of face time."

"Precisely."

"And what's in it for me? You gonna tip the media that you're taking me out to an expensive restaurant so they can take our picture together? Help me further my political career? I mean, you've become tabloid fodder now, as famous as a movie star and just as beautiful."

She paused for a moment to steel herself, absent-mindedly adjusting the ankle bracelet that monitored her every movement.

"What would you like to be in it for you?" she said.

He chuckled softly.

The End

Review it

Thank you for reading *Albedo Effect*. If you enjoyed it, please tell your friends or post a short customer review on Amazon, Barnes & Noble or Goodreads. Thank you!

Book 3 of *The Shade Ring Trilogy* coming 2017. If you want to be notified, sign up on my website: www.connielacy.com

About the author

Connie Lacy writes science fiction, magical realism and historical fiction, all with a dollop of romance. She worked for many years in radio news as a reporter and news anchor. She's also the author of *The Shade Ring, Book 1 of The Shade Ring Trilogy, The Time Telephone* and *VisionSight: a Novel*. She lives in Atlanta with her husband.

I'd love to hear from you

Email: connielacy@connielacy.com
Website: www.ConnieLacy.com
Facebook: www.Facebook.com/ConnieLacyBooks
Twitter: https://twitter.com/cdlacy
Goodreads: www.Goodreads.com/ConnieLacy
Amazon page: www.Amazon.com/author/connie.lacy

Sign up for occasional updates

connielacy@connielacy.com

Acknowledgements

Special thanks to Renee Jacobs, Jennifer Perry and Doug Lacy for their valuable suggestions and feedback.

If you liked *Albedo Effect* you might enjoy *VisionSight: a Novel*, also by Connie Lacy...

Jenna Stevens' life is turned upside down when her mother dies and she inherits the gift of "vision-sight." She has no control over it – when she looks into her loved ones' eyes, she sees their future. Unfortunately, the future is full of heartache and misery that she cannot prevent.

So she pushes everyone away – her best friend, the guy she's falling in love with and her family. She turns instead to her acting career, a director she's not too sure of and a newly acquired taste for whiskey sours.

VisionSight is the story of a young woman's search for courage as she tries to help the people she cares about. What she doesn't realize is that she must save herself as well. A heartfelt novel of secrets and unexpected love.

Magical realism and contemporary women's fiction.

Available on Amazon and Barnes & Noble